NEVER
FORSAKEN

NEVER
FORSAKEN

Kathleen L. Jacobs

CROSSWAY BOOKS • WHEATON, ILLINOIS
A DIVISION OF GOOD NEWS PUBLISHERS

Cover design: DesignPoint Inc.

Cover photos: Ellis Island photo: © Black Box
                Tornado photo: © Everett Collection

First printing 1999

Printed in the United States of America

Library of Congress Cataloging-in-Publication Data
Jacobs, Kathleen L., 1969–
   Never forsaken / Kathleen L. Jacobs.
     p.   cm.
   ISBN 1-58134-110-5 (alk. paper)
    1. German Americans—Missouri—Saint Louis—History—
19th century Fiction.. I. Title.
PS3560.A2544N48 1999
813'.54—dc21
                                        99-20906
                                          CIP

15	14	13	12	11	10	09	08	07	06	05	04	03	02	01	00	99
15	14	13	12	11	10	9	8	7	6	5	4	3	2	1		

To Garrett, my husband,
for many loving reminders that God
does not forsake His own.

The LORD is a refuge for the oppressed, a stronghold in times of trouble. Those who know your name will trust in you, for you, LORD, have never forsaken those who seek you.
                              —*Psalm 9:9-10, New International Version*

For explanations of many German words and phrases, see German Glossary at the end of the book.

Contents

PART THREE

The Schuhmacher Family Tree — 1894

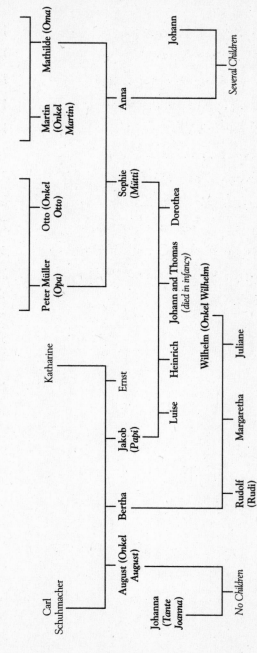

Notes:

- The characters who are mentioned in this story are printed in **bold** lettering.
- If a character's title in the book is different from the given name, the title appears in parenthesis. German titles are as follows:

Mütti:	Mommy	*Papi:*	Daddy
Oma:	Grandma	*Opa:*	Grandpa
		Tante:	Aunt
		Onkel:	Uncle

- The German pronunciation of the name *Luise* is similar to the English pronunciation of *Louisa*.

PART ONE

CHAPTER ONE

The Letter

May 1894

Luise plunged a timeworn trowel deep into the earth and carefully lifted a tender seedling from the ground. Raising her shovel to eye-level, she examined the roots for damage. Satisfied with the undisturbed tangle of white threads, she rose to carry the plant to its new home.

As she walked to the far side of the garden, sunlight pierced the clouds that had shaded the land for most of the afternoon. Luise raised her face to greet the warm rays and witnessed the delightful emerald sparkle of the lush ridge that stood before her. The Bramwald hills encircled her small German village, marking the boundary of her world. In her seventeen years, Luise had never strayed far from her valley. In fact, she had spent most of her time either tending the garden with her brother Heinrich or completing housework inside her family's cottage.

Since early morning, Heinrich had been preparing a plot of ground destined to be the summer home of the seedlings Luise was transplanting. When Luise approached, he pointed toward several evenly spaced holes that he had recently dug. Luise knelt beside the nearest one and gently placed her plant in its center. As she pressed dirt around the base, their mother's voice diverted her attention.

"Luise! Heinrich! Come quickly!" called *Mütti*. Luise immediately raised her eyes toward the spot where she expected to see the speaker. At first she could discern little more than the shape of the

family's cottage, but soon her adjusting eyes noted her mother waiting in the doorway.

Mütti was the only family member who had not been born in
the cottage that Luise's Great-grandfather Schuhmacher had built.
Mütti began her life there not as a baby, but as the beloved bride of
Jakob Schuhmacher. To Luise, who had been born two years after
her parents' marriage, *Mütti* was as essential to the stability of their
home as the wooden beams that had supported the walls for so
many decades. This young woman's perseverance as a wife and
mother brought order and love to her family.

Mütti held a letter high in the air for her children to see. Joy
glistened in her brown eyes as she beckoned to Luise and Heinrich.
Such news this envelope contained! Rarely did such an evident
reason for rejoicing present itself to Sophie Schuhmacher. Yet,
despite the many hardships *Mütti* had known, her hopeful smile
and her graceful carriage at that moment were not uncharacteristic of this young woman. They were as much a part of her as the
home where each of her three children had been born.

Luise, discerning her mother's enthusiasm, was elated at the
sight of the letter. "Look, Heinrich!" she cried. "The letter *Mütti's*
waving must be from *Papi*!" She pushed her light frame from the
ground and raced toward the cottage. A moment later Heinrich
joined her, and for a few paces they ran together. An onlooker
might have mistaken them for twins, so alike were they in appearance—hair the color of wheat in the moonlight and eyes as blue as
the lake that lapped the shore near their home. In truth Heinrich
was Luise's junior by two years; yet in customary fashion he surged
ahead of his older sister as they neared the cottage.

After Luise finished the last few strides to her brother's side, she
questioned impatiently, "Is it from *Papi*? What does he say, *Mütti*?"
Coming to a stop, she passed a roughened hand across her forehead
to lift the long bangs that tickled her eyelids. The wayward strands
slid limply back into place with defiance unknown to the obedient
braid that hung straight down her back. Luise clasped *Mütti's* arm.
"Has he sent for us? Has he made enough money for tickets to
America?"

"You ask too many questions, Luise," accused Heinrich. "If you would just let *Mütti* talk, we might actually find out what the letter says."

"Come inside and sit down," said *Mütti*, resting her hands on her children's shoulders to hasten them through the doorway. Once inside the kitchen, the two joined their six-year-old sister, Dorothea, at the table, and *Mütti* began to explain the contents of the letter. "*Papi* sends all of us his love. He especially wants to assure Dorothea that he has not forgotten her."

The little girl beamed but pressed *Mütti* for more reassurance. "Maybe he's forgotten what I look like. He left *two years ago!* Now my hair is longer!"

"You still have big ears though," Heinrich teased. "They haven't shrunk at all!"

Dorothea's countenance fell at the mention of her ears that, due to the cruelty of a neighboring boy, she had grown to detest. Observing her silent despair, Luise rebuked Heinrich. "You always have to spoil all the fun of getting a letter from *Papi*, don't you?"

With a piercing glance, *Mütti* quietly intervened. "If you children decide to argue, the good news will have to wait until later." She paused for a moment until Luise and Heinrich made the expected apologies and voiced twin pleas to continue.

"The most exciting part is that, yes, *Papi* finally has saved enough money to buy our tickets for the voyage to America! Even though the times have remained difficult since last year's bank panic, he has not lost his job, and he has a home waiting for us in St. Louis," *Mütti* announced triumphantly.

"Oh, how wonderful!" gasped Luise as she clasped her hands together. "I can hardly wait to see *Papi* again!"

"When do we have to leave, *Mütti?*" asked Heinrich in a tone more subdued than his sister's. His eyes dimly betrayed an underlying sulkiness at the thought of departure.

"Well, *Papi* let me know several months ago that he had nearly saved enough money. I began at that time to get the necessary exit papers; so now that *Papi* has purchased tickets, everything is in order. Since we can take any ocean liner owned by the shipping company that *Papi* chose, we will board whichever one is in port when we get to Bremerhaven. The sooner we leave home, the sooner we will set sail! I don't want to linger here any longer than necessary. We have already waited long enough to see *Papi* again!"

"How will we get to Bremerhaven?" Heinrich asked.

"We will find someone from the village to take us to Hannoversch Münden. There we will board a small cargo boat that will carry us to Bremen. Do you remember my *Onkel* Martin who moved to Hameln when I was a little girl? *Oma* wrote him several months ago, and your grandmother tells me he has agreed to let us travel on a cargo ship that he now owns. This is a marvelous provision because we won't have to pay to ride a train, and we need to save as much money as possible. Once we reach Bremen, we will take a ferry to Bremerhaven. According to *Papi's* letters, just getting to the ship can be quite a challenge!"

"Why, *Mütti?*" questioned Luise.

"Well, dear, not everyone in Germany is as kind and honest as the people we know in our little village. *Papi* ran into some real scoundrels on his journey to Bremerhaven. Even though we're taking my *Onkel* Martin's boat, he will not be traveling with us, and I don't know what the crewmen will be like. Besides that, even I have never left the area surrounding our village. It will be an adventure, that's certain!"

"Sounds exciting to me!" interjected Heinrich, his enthusiasm ignited at last. "I'll protect you, *Mütti.* Don't you worry one bit. Why, Luise, I might even defend *you* if a robber comes your way. That is, if I'm feeling especially kind and heroic," he added with a sly wink.

"One thing we all must understand," *Mütti* reminded, "is that the only way we can hope to reach America is for each of us to look out for all the others. We must care for and love one another. Your father has been working very hard so we can join him. When he emigrated, he endured all the hardships alone. I could tell from his letters that the loneliness made every step even more difficult for him than it might have been if his family had been with him. We must never forget the sacrifice he has made to enable us to go to America."

"*Mütti*, will we be safe once we get to the ship?" Luise wondered aloud, still contemplating *Mütti's* warning about scoundrels in Germany.

"First of all, I want you to know that sea travel is much safer now than it used to be. My mother and father nearly went to America when I was Dorothea's age. They decided to stay here after they read my *Onkel* Otto's letters about his voyage. On his ship fourteen children died from cholera, and most of the adults were also sick before the journey's end. It took nearly three weeks to reach America. Now some ships cross in seven or eight days. *Onkel* Otto had brought food along with him, but some of the other passengers stole what little he had. So he had to eat the ship's food that was rancid and moldy! Even the water was polluted. *Onkel* Otto wrote that just smelling the contaminated water was enough to make him horribly sick. Can you imagine? Apparently the crew stored the water in old, dirty casks that had held oil or vinegar on previous voyages.

"Thankfully, some things have improved. Your father wrote that although the food still tastes terrible, it is at least edible. Another advantage these days is that doctors check every emigrant for disease before departure. Ships will not transport sick people because the unhealthy are not allowed to enter America. Any immigrants whom the officials in New York deem unfit are sent back to Europe on the same boat that brought them. Since the ship's owners must pay for their transport, the shipping companies save money by keeping such unfortunate people off their boats."

"That's cruel," Luise protested.

"I used to think so," *Mütti* replied, "until recently. Now I think it is kindness to turn people away at a European port rather than allow them to spend all they have on tickets when it's probable they will be deported back in a penniless state. Besides that, it is safer for the healthy passengers. The Lord willing, we will make our trip in good health, free from the sickness and death that surrounded *Onkel* Otto during his voyage."

Luise shivered. "I hope our trip will not be so terrible. If *Papi* were not in America, I think I might rather stay home."

"America will be a wonderful place, Luise," *Mütti* reassured her. "You've heard news from the letters that people in our village have received from relatives in America. Nearly everyone loves their new country, and *Papi* writes that we will like St. Louis. Remember also that *Tante* Johanna and *Onkel* August live in St. Louis. How good it will be to see them again!"

"But they left thirteen years ago," Heinrich commented, his mood swinging once again. "I was only two then. I'd rather stay here where there are people I know!"

"Heinrich, you know we must leave. Your father is a good furniture maker, but in recent years the farmers have not made enough money from their crops to allow them to buy new furniture. And the shoes I make only bring us an occasional basket of berries or bag of flour. You yourself have grumbled countless times about wanting more meat for dinner. Your father and I just couldn't sit by and allow you to go hungry. And beyond that, we had to think about your future. We didn't want to risk the possibility that you might one day be required to enter the army. Moving to America is best for our family. We prayed about it for several years, and two years ago we made our choice—clearly the best choice. Now we must join *Papi*; it has not been good to be apart."

"I know, I know," said Heinrich resignedly. "I just wish we had more time to say good-bye."

"Heinrich, I cannot give you more time. I'm afraid the next few weeks will be sad for each of us."

Heinrich nodded and, with *Mütti's* permission, left the room.

"I'm going to *Oma's* right now," said Luise. "I want to spend every minute I can with her before I have to leave."

"I'm sure *Oma* will be happy to see you, and she'll want to hear the news," *Mütti* affirmed. "Be back for dinner," she called as Luise reached the door.

The two weeks of preparation passed quickly. The family spent long, heart-wrenching hours sorting through all their belongings. Furniture had to be sold or tearfully passed on to relatives. A young couple gratefully carried away the baby crib that *Mütti's* father had so lovingly made for his first daughter. *Mütti* emptied the cupboard that had stood in the corner of the cottage since *Papi's* father had been a young boy. They would leave it behind for

the new owners. With the exception of a few cherished possessions, the Schuhmachers parted with all items that were not necessary for survival. Of course, since the family was poor, this did
not require that they relinquish too much. Even so, Luise was
tempted several times to beg, "*Mütti*, can't we fit in one more
book, please?"

The one time she did ask, *Mütti* gave a frustrated reply. "There's
no room, Luise. We must be able to carry everything. There are so
many things we must take just to survive—eating utensils, blankets, extra food, and clothing. There is just no more room!"

Luise knew the truth, but this did not soften the sadness she
felt as she carried two books and a small painted box to a friend's
house.

All too soon the final day at home came. Luise rushed to *Oma's*
house as soon as breakfast ended. There an unfinished task waited.

Oma staunchly believed that all girls should learn to sew.
Nearly everyone in the village agreed with her to an extent, but
Oma's passion went beyond the typical assertion that sewing was a
practical means of providing cheap clothing for a family. To *Oma*,
sewing was an art. True skill could only be attained through careful instruction and practice. She had set about teaching Luise, and
during the past ten years the young student had produced ornamented tablecloths, pillowcases, and blankets. Now one final project awaited completion—an embroidered wall hanging.

Just before lunch Luise completed the last few stitches and
secured the loose ends on the backside of the fabric. "I am finished
at last, *Oma*!" she exclaimed, holding the fabric high for the old
lady to see. Red letters proclaiming *Wilkommen* curved elegantly
across the smooth, white muslin. A creeping green vine encircled
the script, and a pink rose graced the right corner. Even a master
artist would have been proud of producing with a brush the exact-
ness that Luise had achieved with a needle.

"A treasure, *mein Kindlein*!" cried *Oma*. "I will frame it tonight.
May it still hang on your wall when you are old! I trust that my
granddaughter will never forget to welcome into her home stranger
and guest alike."

"No, *Oma*, I will not forget. I will remember forever the things you have taught me."

"I don't know what I'm going to do without my dear grand-children," gasped *Oma*. She turned tearful eyes toward the window. The wetness on her cheeks glistened in the soft sunlight that brightened the corner where she sat rocking. "I know I must let you go. I have always known this day would come. Your father, mind you, is an honest man. When he asked your *Opa* for your mother's hand, he said, 'One day I hope to go to America.' He did not want us to be surprised when they sailed far away. To tell the truth, I thought this day would come sooner. Every year I have thought that I would soon have to let my dear ones travel to the uttermost part of the earth."

"That's what America is, isn't it, *Oma?*" groaned Luise with tears in her eyes.

"*Ja, mein Kind*, but soon it will be home for you."

"No! It will never be!" Luise retorted, wiping her tears. "How could I love any place the way I love this village? You love it too, *Oma*. Remember the prayer you taught me when I was very lit-tle? I have not forgotten: 'Thank You, Lord, for our little home at the foot of the hills, on the banks of the lake, and in the palm of God's hand.' How can you say I could ever call another place home?"

"But you will, dear, although you do not believe me now. This is not the only place on earth where God will be with you. Wherever you go, the Lord will already be there. What is more, it is right for you to go to America where your family will be. You belong with them. And don't forget that *Tante* Johanna and *Onkel* August will live very near you. Won't you enjoy seeing them again? It has been many years since they left."

"I hardly remember them," moaned Luise. "You're the one who belongs with us, and you won't be there."

"It is true that I have been with you until now, *mein Kind*. The Lord has granted me the blessing of being near your precious fam-ily." The old woman paused a moment. "But now you must go, and I must stay behind. Your *Oma* is too old to travel so far." Luise looked at her grandmother and knew in her heart that her words were true. The old woman's hair was pure white and as thinly spread as October frost. She kept it pulled back into a strict and proper bun, claiming that stretching her skin tautly kept the wrinkles at bay. This method had not been overly successful, however, and the furrows of eighty-five years had been plowed deeply across her forehead.

Luise went forward to *Oma*, bending to gently kiss one wrinkled cheek. The old woman smiled and lifted her hands to embrace her granddaughter's face. Then, dropping one hand, she began to sort through the folds of her apron and skirt. Luise watched the gnarled fingers fumble and grope. How little remained of their former strength and dexterity! At last *Oma* located her pocket. Then, with a smile of triumph, she retrieved a small roll of fabric.

"I suspect you can find room among your baggage for this small gift!" *Oma* declared with a smile. "With this I give you a part of me." As she began untying the two ribbons that bound the fabric into a roll, Luise realized with a thrill that this was *Oma's* seed bag. When unrolled, its full beauty was evident, a testimony to the skill the old woman's hands had possessed in earlier years. Across every inch of the smooth, white fabric wound a marvelous maze of embroidered leafy vines and colorful flowers. Luise stood silently with the awed respect of one who after long laboring to learn the humble skills of a beginning artisan beholds with new appreciation a master's work. *Oma* rested the pouch on her lap and folded back the ornamented cover to reveal the many small pockets that lined the inside. Each one bore a carefully stitched flower or vegetable name. Within each, wrapped in paper, were *Oma's* precious seeds.

"I made this when I was a young girl," *Oma* explained as she had many times before. "I loved gardens so very much and felt that I must make my seed pouch reflect their beauty. I collected these seeds last fall, knowing it might be the last opportunity I would have before your father sent for you. When you take these to America and plant them in good soil, they will grow. I want you to enjoy their beauty and to think of me. But I also want you to learn from these seeds."

"What can I learn from seeds, *Oma?*"

"You must discover that you can grow and flourish no matter

where you are planted. A flower can bloom just as splendidly in America as it does in Germany, and you will do so as well. What matters is *whose* you are, not *where* you are. You will always be a child of God no matter where you live. The Lord has been faithful to our family through many generations; He will not forget you, Luise. Remember your Savior, He will care for you forever. As it is written in Isaiah, 'Behold, God is my salvation, I will trust and not be afraid.'" She paused for a moment. "Luise, know that I love you, and never doubt that God's love is far more precious than mine." The tears shone in her eyes.

Luise flung her arms around the one who had been such a store-house of wisdom and strength for her.

"Now you must hurry home, dear," *Oma* said quietly. "It is get-ting late, and you will leave early in the morning."

Luise pulled away. Running her hand under her nose in a vain attempt to stifle a sniffle, she tried to smile. "Good-bye, *Oma*."

"Good-bye, dear," answered the old lady, pressing the seed pouch into her beloved granddaughter's hand.

CHAPTER TWO

Farewell

May 26, 1894

Before dawn the next morning, *Mütti* brushed a gentle hand across her sleeping daughter's face and brought it to rest on Luise's shoulder. She prodded her child from sleep with a persistent tenderness. "Wake up, dear. It will soon be time to leave."

Those words cleared Luise's mind. She jumped out of bed into the cool morning air and quickly pulled on several layers of clothing as *Mütti* left the room. Luise had no doubt she would be hot before the day was over, but *Mütti* had instructed the children the night before, "The more you wear, the less you'll have to carry!"

From the neighboring room, *Mütti* called to someone outside. Curious, Luise walked to her window and, pulling aside the coarse curtains, noticed a figure carrying a lantern toward the barn where the family's horse slept. She decided it must be *Herr* Handelmann. The neighboring farmer had joyfully purchased the Schuhmachers' horse and wagon a few days earlier at a price greatly below their value. He had offered as much as he could afford, and *Mütti*, unable to find any other buyer, had accepted his bid. The kind man, realizing that *Mütti* had been hoping to get more money, had offered to drive the family to the river town of Hannoversch Münden, where they would begin their boat trip to Bremen. He had arrived that morning to prepare the horse and wagon for an early departure.

Herr Handelmann truly was generous because the trip to town would take all day, and that meant he would lose two days of work

on his farm. Besides that, he would have to pay for a night's lodging before returning home. His sacrifice went quite a way toward
making up the amount *Mütti* had lost on the sale of the horse.
"How blessed we have been to have such honest neighbors," *Mütti*
had said when he made the offer.

At the time Heinrich had muttered, "Then why are we leaving?" As Luise stood at the window on the morning of their departure, she was thankful *Mütti* had not heard his grumbling.

Luise turned from the window. There was no time for idle musings. The family had packed the wagon the night before. Now only
a few items remained for Luise to bundle up—the blanket she had
used during the night, her down pillow, and a blank journal *Mütti*
had given her. These she placed in the middle of a shawl.
Gathering its worn edges together, she twisted them into a tight
knot to secure the contents.

As Luise finished the preparations, her six-year-old cousin
Margaretha slipped into the room. The little girl went straight to
the rocker in the corner and enthusiastically set the chair in
motion. "My *Papi* said I could take this home today!" she said
triumphantly.

"*Guten Morgen*, Margaretha," grunted Luise, her eyes narrowed
and teeth clenched.

"I've wanted a chair so much!" babbled Margaretha. "*Papi* said
Onkel Jakob would have made me one, but he left too soon."

"Yes, Margaretha," replied Luise tersely, "I'm sure my *Papi*
would have made you one. Now you'll get the one he made for me."
She wished her cousin would go away. The little girl's comments
made leaving her things behind even more difficult! Luise could
hardly bear to part with the beautiful chair her father had made for
her seventh birthday. She had cherished that chair since the day
of *Papi's* departure.

Margaretha rose and began scanning the room. "Where's the
doll that I get?" she asked, not suspecting the boiling pot she was
stirring.

"Margaretha, leave me alone!" Luise demanded. "Can't you see
I don't want to talk to you?" She grabbed her bundle and rushed
out, leaving her bewildered cousin in tears. Upon entering the

kitchen she nearly marched into Margaretha's eight-year-old brother Rudi. He looked distraught, and this immediately put Luise in a more tender frame of mind. "Rudi, what is the matter?"

"So you are really leaving?" he questioned.

"Of course, Rudi, you know that," she answered as she lowered herself into a chair.

"I know," he sighed. "I just wish you'd take me with you. You're more fun than Margaretha, and Juliane is just a baby. She cries all the time!"

"You'll just have to get to know some more of the boys in the village," Luise consoled with a smile. She did not have a chance to wait for his response because *Mütti* called to her from the kitchen.

Luise obediently rose. Once she had joined her mother, *Mütti* shut the door and indicated that they would sit at the table. "Luise, can you explain to me why Margaretha is in tears?" she asked, lowering herself into a chair beside her daughter.

Luise moaned. "It's probably because I snapped at her," she admitted with an annoyed shake of her head. "But she was bothering me, *Mütti*! She kept talking about all of my things that she was going to take, and I don't want her to have them! *Papi* made that rocking chair especially for me!" Tears punctuated her lament.

"I know the rocking chair is special to you, Luise. You need to remember, though, that you are too big for it now anyway. *Papi* made it for a little girl. But what is more important, you cannot blame Margaretha for your anger. She may have been saying things that hurt you, but that does not give you a right to strike back." *Mütti* paused a moment to let her words sink in. "This may be the last time you ever see Margaretha. She is a very little girl. Do you want her to remember you as a greedy, angry person?"

"I'm not a greedy and angry person," Luise countered.

"I know that," replied *Mütti*, "but right now Margaretha does not. You need to apologize to her. By apologizing you are not stating that what she did was right; you are, however, admitting that what you did was wrong." *Mütti* gave Luise a moment to consider her words. "Do you agree that you treated her harshly?"

Luise nodded humbly.

"Are you ready to apologize?"

"*Ja, Mütti.* I just wish we didn't have to leave. I wish *Papi* could come home instead."

"I know it's hard to leave, dear, but God will be with us. Just think—it will be an adventure! You will get to see places you would never visit if you lived your entire life in Germany. And now," *Mütti* counseled, "I think it's about time that you found Margaretha. You wouldn't want to forget your important duty."

"*Ja, Mütti.* I will go now." Although Luise submitted with reluctant enthusiasm, *Mütti* nodded her approval as she nudged a stray lock of hair back beneath the pale pink scarf she always wore neatly tied around her head.

The time for departure soon arrived, and a loud summons by *Onkel* Wilhelm and his son Rudi drew the Schuhmachers and their assembled family and friends to the loaded wagon. The dawn wore a cape of cool, gray mist as Luise approached the gathering with Margaretha, who was joyfully hugging her new doll. Noting a satisfied nod from *Mütti*, the repentant daughter guessed that her mother saw ample evidence that the expected apology had occurred.

Once everyone had gathered, an awkward silence ensued. At last *Oma* stepped forward carrying a large basket stuffed with fruit, sausages, and bread. "There now, that should see you through a few days," *Oma* said as she handed the basket to *Mütti*. "Good-bye, dear," she murmured, biting her lower lip in an evident struggle against tears as she held her daughter in her arms for the last time.

Onkel Wilhelm helped *Mütti* climb into the wagon seat and lifted Dorothea up beside her. He then walked to the back of the wagon, shooed Heinrich into the area that had been left open behind their belongings, and turned toward Luise. However, before he could grasp her hand to steady her ascent, she bolted to where *Oma* stood and threw herself into the old woman's arms. Luise's evident grief prompted little Margaretha to rush to her cousin's side and clasp her around the waist with a wail. In the presence of such emotion, *Oma* also succumbed to tears. Her hand tenderly brushed Luise's cheek and then guided her granddaughter's chin upward so she could gaze into Luise's eyes. "I love you, dear child. Never forget that your *Oma* loves you," she whispered, clasping Luise close once more. Then she resolutely pushed Luise toward the wagon. "You must go now. It is right that you go."

Onkel Wilhelm grasped Luise's hand firmly and guided her up beside Heinrich. He pushed the wagon's back wall upward into place and secured it with a rope before signaling to *Herr* Handelmann that all was ready.

With a jolt the horse pulled the wagon from its rest and Luise's family from their home. Looking back upon those who remained behind, Luise saw her own anguish mirrored in the faces of the people who had filled her world—relatives and neighbors who had provided love and security. The familiar faces grew small and blurred until finally the wagon rounded a corner and those loved ones slipped out of view and into memory.

As the wagon passed beyond the outskirts of the village, Luise continued to survey the only home she had ever known. Tears streamed from Luise's eyes. "I don't even care what Heinrich thinks of me," she muttered to herself, although she carefully turned her face away from him. She was surprised when a loud sniffle mingled with the wagon's clatter. Luise cautiously peeked toward Heinrich and saw his tear-filled eyes. He looked back at her without embarrassment and then slipped his arm around her shoulders. With weary thankfulness for this tender gesture on his part, Luise rested her head against his shoulder. They remained thus, drawn together by the double bonds of kinship and hardship, until the valley was long out of sight and both had drifted into peace-bearing sleep.

CHAPTER THREE

Encounters After Dusk

At dusk they approached the town of Hannoversch Münden where the Werra and Fulda Rivers join to form the Weser. There, in the morning, they would meet the boat that would take them to Bremen; meanwhile, they needed to locate lodging. The family had never seen such a large gathering of buildings as that which stood before them. The falling darkness made the place appear even more foreign and foreboding to Luise than it might have had they arrived at midday.

"*Mütti!*" Heinrich hollered, casting his voice over the heap of belongings that lay between them. "Is St. Louis as big as this city?"

"Actually, it's bigger," *Mütti* called back. "It's probably as large as several towns like this one." *Mütti's* answer produced a sinking feeling within Luise. Such a huge place would swallow them up! Heinrich, however, could hardly contain his excitement. He forced his way to the front of the wagon, stepping over the largest box and then tumbling onto the cloth-wrapped bundles when the wagon's lurch upset his balance. When he finally reached the seat, he peered around *Mütti* to get a view of all that lay before them.

In light of Heinrich's fall, Luise decided it would be safer to stay in the back, even if that did mean being alone.

Soon *Mütti's* voice drifted back across the baggage. "Turn right once we reach the end of the bridge over the Werra River." Her words came from one of *Papi's* old letters in which he had written down the directions to a reliable and honest inn. Now his family followed the path he had carefully chosen for them. They began by crossing an old stone bridge. The faint remaining light allowed Luise to view the riverbank where a solid row of buildings seemed to keep the rest of the town from spilling down into the water. Even in the twilight many of the stores and houses displayed a delightful design of brown timbers upon white walls.

Soon the horse stepped off the bridge. Luise strained her eyes. She could just make out a street, right where *Papi* had indicated it would be. Luise smiled to herself as they began to travel between parallel rows of half-timbered buildings. *Papi* had taken care of them even though he was very far away. How she longed to see him! A few weeks seemed too long to wait.

The next instructions soon followed. *Mütti* directed *Herr* Handelmann to turn down a street just before the town square. As the horse pulled the wagon around the corner, *Mütti* explained, "We need to watch for a cobbler's shop on our right and a blacksmith across the street."

"There's the smithy!" Heinrich exclaimed a moment later. The enthusiasm in his voice trailed off, however, as he added, "But there's no cobbler in sight." The farmer slowly brought the horse to a stop so *Mütti* could evaluate the surroundings. The shop across from the blacksmith obviously belonged to a cooper, for a row of buckets, awaiting a potential customer's inspection, lined the ledge of the window. Inside, a lantern burned brightly near a chair where the cooper himself sat fitting an iron ring around the wooden slats he had fashioned into a bucket.

"Do you think this is the right place?" *Herr* Handelmann questioned as the horse pawed with hungry impatience.

Luise twisted to hear her mother's answer. When *Mütti* briefly turned her eyes toward the back of the wagon to scan the street behind them, Luise noted the concern in her expression. "I'm sure Jakob didn't make a mistake," *Mütti* stated. "We haven't come far on this road; maybe there's another blacksmith down the road a little farther."

Convinced that they would drive on, Luise turned back toward the rear of the wagon, only to immediately encounter a pair of cold, piercing eyes. A darkly clad figure stood before her, his gnarled hands gripping the wagon's wall only inches away from her. Luise shrank back against the baggage that formed a barrier behind her. A scream fought to break forth from within her, but her tightening throat trapped her voice. The man evidently recognized her fright, and a delighted, sinister grin slowly spread across his face. As Luise watched with terror, one hand began to loosen its grip on the wood before her. The man leaned toward the wagon until he was close enough for Luise to detect the noise of his grinding teeth. At last a whimpering cry loosed its way from her constricted throat, and her eyes shut on their own accord to block out the image before her.

When she opened her eyes a moment later, a friend had replaced her tormentor. "Where has he gone?" she asked with a voice that had not entirely thrown off its trembling.

"He is gone. That is enough," *Herr* Handelmann replied. As though she were no bigger than Dorothea, he plucked Luise from her spot among the baggage and set her on the ground. "No one is going to hurt you, Luise. I will promise you that," he comforted with a strange mix of determination and softness. "You must be courageous. Will you promise me that?" Luise nodded as the kind man led her up to where Heinrich sat. "You look after her," *Herr* Handelmann commanded as he handed Luise up. For the second time that long and weary day, Heinrich put a comforting arm around his sister.

As the farmer walked around the horse on the way back to his seat, an elderly gentleman approached.

"Is that the man who frightened you?" Heinrich asked eagerly.

"Of course not. If *he* had come to the back of the wagon, I certainly wouldn't have been scared," whispered Luise. Her brother nodded. There could be no argument; this gentleman possessed a kind countenance. As he glanced at the family, a smile lit on his face, and its fire spread through every wrinkle until his entire face radiated joy.

"*Guten Abend!*" he greeted cheerfully. "Can I help you in any way?"

Herr Handelmann quickly explained the confusion they were experiencing regarding the directions.

"Oh, that is explained simply enough! I am the cobbler who used to own that shop," he declared, motioning toward the cooper's building. "Earlier this year I finally admitted that my old hands were getting too tired for such regular work. You see, I still make shoes, but I like to do it at my own pace these days. And I must admit it's a rather slow pace," he observed, chuckling. "My son now works in the shop as a cooper; and in fact I am just bringing him his dinner." He raised a small parcel. "This is indeed the street you are looking for. And I might add," he stated, nodding to *Mütti*, "I know the inn that your good husband mentioned. After you turn down this street, it will be on your left. It is as safe and good a place as any weary traveler could wish to find."

Mütti smiled her thanks.

"*Guten Nacht!*" the children cried as the farmer urged the horse to resume his journey.

A few minutes later they reached the inn. As soon as the horse stopped, Heinrich propelled himself over the wagon's edge and ran up to an inn window.

"Heinrich, come back beside the wagon!" *Mütti* commanded.

"Why don't you go in to make arrangements while I stay here with the children?" *Herr* Handelmann suggested gently. *Mütti* nodded and stepped up to the door with an expression of grim determination.

"*Mütti* has acted strangely today," Heinrich noted after she had entered.

"Hasn't it occurred to you," *Herr* Handelmann asked, "that all of this is new to your mother? She has lived in the village ever since her birth, and I doubt she's ever been very far from the valley. Now she has to speak with strangers, and soon she will be left alone with all of you children. That's a heavy load to carry, even for a person with your mother's strength. See that you children don't make things any more difficult for her," the farmer commanded.

The inn door opened again, emitting a hazy, warm glow as *Mütti* returned to the street. "This place will be wonderful!" she announced to the farmer. "Jakob knew I would feel at home here. I also found out where you can spend the night, *Herr* Handelmann. The lady inside told me that if you go around the corner at the end of this row of buildings, there will be an alley on your left immediately after the corner building. It will lead to a nice barn where you may sleep. Are you sure you will be all right there?"

"*Jawohl*, that will suit me fine," *Herr* Handelmann replied.

Mütti instructed each of the children to grab their smallest bundles; then she led them inside. Once they had all gathered within, a smiling woman greeted them. "Come right this way," she called out as she turned and briskly started up a stairway. At the top she swung open a door on her left and sang out, "Here we are!" The children cautiously stepped through the doorway and silently waited just inside until *Mütti* had thanked the woman and shut the door behind her. The door had a bolt that *Mütti* quickly drew into place.

"Now, children," she said, surveying their questioning faces, "we must get a good rest tonight, for tomorrow will be a long day. We will need to share space on the beds, but that should be no problem. How wonderfully *Papi* has planned for us! The woman who showed us to our room told me that even though *Papi* was here such a long time ago, she remembers him clearly because he spoke so highly of us all and with such love. He carefully described us to her and asked that she treat us kindly when we came."

"Where is *Herr* Handelmann going to stay?" asked Heinrich.

"He will stay in the barn with the wagon. He is such a good man. Have I told you that he and your father were best friends as children?"

"Yes, *Mütti*, many times," answered Heinrich before impatiently continuing. "Don't you think it would be a good idea for me to stay with him? That would certainly give all of you more space."

"No, Heinrich. He will have enough to look after with all of our things. I cannot ask him to watch you as well." Heinrich began to protest, but *Mütti* continued, "I don't want to hear any argument. We will eat some of what *Oma* packed, and then it's time for bed."

CHAPTER FOUR

A Path to Bremen

May 27-28, 1894

The next morning *Mütti* awoke the children before sunrise. They took only a few minutes to collect their baggage and then headed downstairs to a sunlit room where breakfast awaited them. The children stowed their odd assortment of parcels beneath the table before eagerly dividing the crusty rolls among themselves.

Before Luise had fully satisfied her appetite, Heinrich announced, "Look, there's *Herr* Handelmann!" They all turned toward the window and saw the farmer bringing the old, familiar horse to a halt outside. *Mütti* rose instantly and bade her brood follow her out the door. She carefully climbed up to her seat while the children launched their bags over the wagon's side. Heinrich and Luise scrambled in after their baggage, joining Dorothea, whom the farmer had assisted. All was ready for departure.

The horse pulled the wagon toward the place where *Onkel* Martin's boat reportedly docked. Soon Luise saw the river and spotted a small cargo boat docked along the shore. "That's the one," *Herr* Handelmann indicated. "Your mother made arrangements with her brother, correct?"

Mütti nodded.

The farmer brought the horse to a stop and jumped down. He looked back up at *Mütti*. "I'll just go confirm things for you," he said. "No, don't protest," he added when *Mütti* began to object. "I'm not overly trusting of these boatmen even if your great-uncle does own the boat. I'll just make sure they understand the agreement you have with your uncle. I would rather deal with such men myself than throw you in among them." *Mütti* nodded in evident relief, and *Herr* Handelmann strode confidently toward the boat. Luise soon lost sight of him amidst the flurry of activity on deck. She began to understand why *Mütti* had hurried that morning. It seemed that the boat was nearly ready to depart.

In five minutes *Herr* Handelmann returned and remarked grimly, "They shouldn't give you any trouble." Luise would have been more reassured if the farmer had delivered this report with a smile. As it was, the distrustful glance he threw toward the boat produced unwelcome apprehension. However, this was not the time to succumb to fear. They must embark; *Papi* was waiting!

Herr Handelmann and one of the crewmen led the way. Together they hefted the large trunk that *Mütti* had tightly packed. After they had stowed all the baggage in a small supply room, the farmer tested the trunk's locks. "Good! All's secure," he declared. "I'd suggest you get some men in Bremen to carry that straight to the ferry you will take to Bremerhaven. You'll just have to take your chances, I suppose, and hope no one steals it."

Mütti looked grim at these words. "I will follow your advice about the trunk. We will also pray for God's protection for both our possessions and ourselves. I do not expect this journey to be without trials."

It was time for the farmer to leave. He wanted to be home with his family before nightfall. "*Auf Wiedersehen*, Sophie," he said, raising his hat.

"*Auf Wiedersehen*, Sebastian, *und vielen Dank*," replied *Mütti*.

How strange it was to hear them call one another by their first names! Luise often forgot that years before, they had played childhood games together.

Herr Handelmann laid a hand on Heinrich's shoulder, then addressed all three children. "It will be a long journey; I know you will help your mother." This was a command; each child felt the intensity of the gaze he maintained a moment longer in silent emphasis. Then a smile spread across his face as he proclaimed, "May God keep you and grant you speed to America!" He quickly turned and walked down the gangway.

Luise dropped her eyes to the deck in sadness. That man's departure cut the last thread that bound her to her Bramwald home. She heard his firm command to the horse. Raising her eyes, she witnessed the departure of the dear old beast as he plodded toward the village that was no longer her home. With a lump in her throat, she turned her gaze to the river and surveyed the beginning of the watery path that would lead to America.

Soon the boat began to move down the Weser River. *Mütti* warned the children, "The trip will take several days, and we will make many stops. You all need to keep away from the crewmen. They have work to do and will show little kindness to troublesome children."

Luise decided that such instructions would be easy enough to follow. Even before her mother's warning she had determined that she wished to avoid the crewmen. She shuddered as she glanced toward a rough-looking man sauntering into the cabin.

Luise grabbed one of her bundles and hunted for a good place to settle down. Near the boat's prow she found the perfect spot on a platform where the quarter-moon curve of the outer wall provided a cradle for her back. To her great joy, this raised position allowed her to view the shore over the opposite wall. She contentedly stretched her legs before her, jamming her feet against a metal stump surrounded by a tangle of rope.

After fumbling a moment with the knot at the top of her bundle, she succeeded in loosening its grip. The shawl dropped limply to the ground, exposing the contents. On top sat the journal *Mütti* had given her. What better time to start writing than now! There was already much to record. Luise lifted the pencil *Mütti* had given her and began.

den 27. Mai 1894

How awful to watch Herr Handelmann drive away with our horse today. Before we walked to the boat, I stopped to touch the dear creature's mane one last time. I could see in his eyes that he still trusted us and little guessed that we were leaving him forever. Will he look for me in the morning? Will he miss me when I don't bring him breakfast tomorrow? I hope that Herr Handelmann is nice to him. Certainly he was nice to us, but sometimes you can't tell how

*a person will act toward animals. I am so tired of saying good-bye.
Giving away the rocker that Papi built for me was so hard. Saying
good-bye to the people was even worse! I don't know how I will
manage without Oma. Oh dear, I am crying and getting my paper
wet! I hope Heinrich doesn't make an appearance any time soon;
he will only make fun of me. Sometimes I wish I could say good-bye
to him. No! I don't really mean that. I have lost too many dear people to wish for the removal of my own brother! But he can certainly
be a burden! I can't believe that he actually cried yesterday when we
left. He was so kind, I was actually thankful for him.*

    *We stayed in a wonderful inn last night. We were able to find
it because Papi had written down the directions for us. Mütti says
he is precious, and I agree with her. I have missed him so much!
How can I wait any longer to see him! We don't even know how
long the voyage will take. Mütti says it depends on the weather. I
hope there isn't a storm because I would surely get sick!*

Glancing up, Luise spotted Heinrich approaching. Quickly,
she closed her journal and tied it safely within her bundle before
he reached the bow. He silently slid down beside her, his gaze fix-
ing upon the scenery lazily slipping past.

Thankful that he came in silence, Luise turned her attention
toward a town that sprawled along the bank, soaking up the pros-
perity brought by the river trade. She remained in that spot, contentedly gazing at the ever-changing shore until dusk blurred her
view and the boat docked at a city. Heinrich departed then, but
Luise remained, her eyes drawn to the picture before her. Although
most buildings had lost their distinct features in the darkness, the
churches were still discernible, their steeples adding artistry to the
town's rooftop silhouette. How still and silent all appeared at that
hour when the sun had nearly slipped below the horizon. Luise
sighed deeply as she surveyed the thousands of lights before her. In
countless windows the gleam of twinkling fires and lanterns bore
testimony to the life harbored behind the panes. Yet the cheerful
lights brought pain to Luise's heart. *She* was far from the peace and
comfort of a Schuhmacher home fire.

A warm hand on Luise's shoulder drew her from her chilling
musings. *Mütti* knelt beside her. "It's time to go inside," she murmured. "I have dinner unpacked." Luise nodded and followed

Mütti to the closet where they had left their belongings. Dorothea and Heinrich already sat near the door.

After a meal of fruit, cheese, and bread, *Mütti* announced, "The captain said we could sleep here. All we need do is roll out our blankets!"

"On the floor?" queried Heinrich.

"On the floor," repeated *Mütti*, mustering a smile. "You can pick your spot first."

"No . . . you choose first," Heinrich replied with forced courtesy. *Mütti* nodded and began unrolling Dorothea's blanket on the dusty floor. The older children silently followed her example, and within half an hour they were all asleep.

The family awakened early the next morning to the noise of cargo bumping across the deck. Luise moaned as she stretched her aching body. "I feel like someone beat me last night!"

"It's this hard floor!" muttered Heinrich. "I wish we were home."

"Heinrich," *Mütti* cautioned, "there are to be no more complaints about our journey."

Although Heinrich obediently avoided making additional comments, Luise knew he was still groaning inwardly. Heinrich's attitude did not radically change until late in the afternoon when a tremendous noise drew all three children to the boat's bow. On a bridge that crossed the river, they caught sight of a most amazing invention they'd never seen before.

"*Mütti*, it's a train, isn't it?" Heinrich cried, whirling to face his mother as she stepped up behind them. "It is even more wonderful than *Papi's* description in his letter! I wish we could ride on a train instead of this old boat!"

"We will, remember?" *Mütti* replied. "When we get to America."

"Will we get to ride one as soon as we get there?" he pressed.

"Of course. That is how we'll get to St. Louis."

Heinrich's smile widened his eyes. With enthusiasm, he turned back to the slow-moving train. "Look, there's writing on several of the cars. They say, '*Russische Auswanderer*.' That's strange."

A crewman who was passing at that moment eagerly offered his input. "That train's full of immigrants. The people in those cars left their homes in Russia, and now they're traveling through our country to get to a boat that will take them to America. The officials keep all those foreigners locked up in those cars."

"Don't they ever let them out?" questioned Luise.

"I certainly hope not!" the man grunted. "I don't want any dirty emigrants bringing disease and crime into my homeland!"

"Well, they must be miserable," Luise persisted. The sailor shook his head in disbelief at her sympathy and went about his work.

"Can't you be quiet?" questioned Heinrich in embarrassment. "They don't belong here. Why shouldn't they be kept in the cars?"

Mütti stepped beside her son as he made his proclamation. "You're right, Heinrich," she observed. "They don't belong here. But then again, we will be no different. We will not belong in America. Do you want the Americans to lock us up when we get there?" Heinrich turned to *Mütti* with a subdued countenance. "I do not want to hear you speak unkindly of any people," *Mütti* commanded. "Every person who is locked up within those cars has cried tears just as you did when we pulled away from our home. And each lonely heart imprisoned in that train shares our fear of what awaits us across the ocean. In more ways than one, Heinrich, they are our kin."

CHAPTER FIVE

No Room in the Inns

May 30—June 4, 1894

As they approached Bremen two days later, Luise noticed a gradual increase in the number of houses and stores gathered along the river. A blue evening sky, decorated with bold strokes of white and soft hues of pink, spread out behind the stark, shadowed buildings. "The city looks like a child built it with giant blocks!" Luise exclaimed to *Mütti* and Dorothea who sat nearby.

"And a master painter supplied the sunset," *Mütti* murmured.

"Everything is so much bigger than I ever imagined possible," Luise observed.

"Yes, dear, I know how you feel," *Mütti* quietly agreed as she stroked Dorothea's hair and drew the small girl's head near to her own to kiss the wispy curls in silent contemplation.

Rousing herself, *Mütti* stood and led her two girls to their pile of belongings so they could prepare for disembarkment. Heinrich ambled into view just as *Mütti* began to fret about how they would manage their large trunk. "Don't you remember, *Mütti*? *Herr* Handelmann told you to have some men carry it to the ship," Luise offered.

"I know, but I didn't expect to arrive at night. We have to take a ferry to Bremerhaven, and that will be impossible this evening. We'll have to find an inn here. The captain did suggest one, but I forgot to ask him whether we could leave the trunk here during the night. I wish I knew if I could trust this boat's crew!"

A crewman walked by at that moment, and *Mütti* asked

whether the trunk could remain on board until morning. He flatly refused to allow this, for the crew evidently desired a complete removal of all human cargo and baggage. *Mütti* received an equally unsympathetic reply when she asked two crewmen whether they would consider carrying the trunk to an inn. One carelessly pointed to some men lounging near the edge of the docks. "You might ask them for help," he suggested before sauntering back to work.

Mütti glanced suspiciously toward the ragged men who leaned lazily against the back of a wagon. Then, setting her jaw, she strode to the trunk and unlocked it. Rummaging through the contents, she pulled out several items—an old clock that had been her grandfather's, a pair of wedding candlesticks, several photographs, and a few other small items. These she shoved into other bundles.

"I'm not going to risk losing these things," she muttered. "I've had to part with enough already."

Realizing that her mother feared they might lose the trunk, Luise cried out, "*Mütti*, get my sewing! Please!" *Mütti* returned to the trunk, retrieved the stitchery bearing the word *Wilkommen*, and passed it to Luise without a word.

Mütti straightened herself with resolve. She left the children with the baggage and marched down to negotiate with the men. After a short conversation, *Mütti* led the way back to the spot where the trunk sat. Pulling a piece of paper from a pouch, she read the inn's address to the men. "The trunk must get there as quickly as possible," she insisted. "We will be staying at this place tonight. You do know how to get there, don't you?"

"To be sure," said one of the men with a smile that made Luise shiver as though tiny insects were dancing across her skin. *Mütti* counted out payment to the two men, and Heinrich called out, "*Mütti*, that's—" But the men glared at him, and *Mütti* indicated sternly that he should be silent. Luise overheard him mutter, "That's practically robbery! She should never give them that much. They'll probably get lost anyway."

Mütti watched the men hoist the trunk and carry it to their wagon. Considering the beaten expression in her eyes, Luise suspected that *Mütti* would have agreed with Heinrich had she heard his pessimistic sentiments.

"Can't we ride on the wagon with the trunk?" Heinrich pressed.

"No," Mütti said. "They would not agree to that. I have done all I can." The resignation in her tone silenced Heinrich.

When they reached the inn fifteen minutes later, the trunk was not in the main hallway. Mütti went up to the innkeeper to inquire about it, but he merely shrugged and said he had not seen a trunk of that sort all day. Her next question concerning lodging brought equally grim news. "I'm sorry, but we have no empty rooms."

Mütti's eyes closed for a moment as though weighed down with weariness. "Now don't be too distressed," the innkeeper cheered. "I am sure there is another inn that can give you lodging for the night. It is not too late yet."

"I must wait for my trunk though," Mütti said wearily. "I hired some men at the dock to bring it here. Who knows how long it will be before they come?"

The innkeeper looked at her curiously and shook his head. "I'll be honest with you—I doubt you'll ever see that trunk again. Most of the men who haunt the docks are thieves. Most likely they are now selling your goods to another crook or spending your money on a fine meal. They prey on unsuspecting folk like yourself who come down the river from small, safe villages."

Mütti sank into a nearby chair, and the innkeeper awkwardly moved back to his business at the desk near the stairs.

Heinrich blurted out, "I knew this would happen!"

Luise jabbed him before rushing to her mother's side. "Mütti, it will be all right," she cried. "You kept the most important things with us. They're still safe."

"But my dishes and all of my cobbler's tools," she wailed. Then, remembering the loss of immediate import, she added, "And what will we do on the boat without our eating utensils?"

Heinrich, still smarting from Luise's smack, finally offered some encouragement. "I am sure we can buy some more in this big city. And we can share plates and forks if we have to."

Mütti, uplifted by her children's kind words, managed a weak smile. "Yes, dears . . . of course . . . you're right." She smiled at Dorothea who stood wide-eyed with concern in a corner near the door. The sight of *Mütti's* tears was foreign and obviously unsettling to her. When *Mütti* stretched out her arms to the small girl, Dorothea rushed forward for comfort.

With partially restored courage, *Mütti* approached the innkeeper once again to inquire about nearby inns. There were several possibilities, so the family gathered their bags and returned to the street.

"I will come back tomorrow," *Mütti* remarked before shutting the door, "just in case my trunk shows up." The innkeeper nodded, but his eyes held no promise.

When the four suggested inns contained no available rooms, *Mütti* displayed obvious concern. Observing her distress, the last innkeeper mentioned, "There is one place where I'm certain you can find a room." *Mütti* listened carefully to the directions, and the Schuhmachers swung their burdens across weary shoulders and left the warmth and security of yet another inn.

The streets had grown dark, contrasting sharply with *Mütti's* pale face. Luise moved next to her. "Now I know how Mary and Joseph felt when there was no room for them in the inn," she stated mournfully. "I don't like it one bit!" *Mütti* smiled weakly and nodded her agreement.

Fear gripped Luise as they trudged along the street. Her mind conjured up images of men lurking in every dark alley they passed. Each phantom resembled the stranger who had crept up to the wagon in Hannoversch Münden. And now there was no farmer to protect her. "I wish *Papi* were here," Luise moaned quietly.

"Hush, Luise," hissed *Mütti*. "Please don't make things worse by saying things like that."

"But it's true. I'm frightened."

"I know, dear, we all are," *Mütti* replied tersely. Luise waited for Heinrich to protest that he had courage, but no such boasting came. When she glanced back at him, she saw a face alert with fear and suspicion.

"We won't have to sleep in the streets, will we?" asked

Heinrich tremulously. Before *Mütti* could reassure him, Dorothea began to cry.

"We will be cared for," *Mütti* insisted. Luise felt, though, that her mother was struggling to convince herself of this.

"Heinrich, please don't bring up horrible thoughts anymore," *Mütti* commanded. "You're scaring Dorothea." She rearranged the bundles she was bearing and bent down to hug her youngest child.

"I think we should pray," suggested Luise.

"Yes, we will stop for one moment," answered *Mütti*. Everyone froze in instant obedience. *Mütti* bowed her head and began, "*Unser Vater im Himmel*, please guide us. Do not forsake Your children in their hour of need. Amen." Luise, afraid evil men might have appeared while her eyes were off-duty, cautiously raised her eyelids. To her relief, the street remained empty.

The small group continued forward and finally reached their destination. The door of this inn stood in an alley, and the entrance did not appear nearly as pleasant as the others had. No one commented on this, however. By this point their standard for evaluating lodgings had shrunk to one imperative desire—protection from the dark streets. They knocked on the door, and a woman's voice yelled, "What do you want?"

"We need a place to stay for the night," *Mütti* stated hoarsely.

An unseen hand from within cracked the door, and a hard, cold eye examined them suspiciously. When the door finally opened fully, an unkempt young woman who continued to regard the family with silent mistrust admitted the weary travelers. *Mütti* quickly explained their need of shelter. The woman grunted a price in reply and eagerly grabbed the money that *Mütti* presented. The Schuhmachers then followed the stranger to a room at the top of a stairway.

Flinging open the door, the woman marched to the middle of the room and held her candle high above her head so that its flickering flame cast an eerie light upon every wall. "This is the room," the woman curtly stated. A small bed in one corner was the sole adornment, and Luise's quick eye noticed that the covers were rumpled. With haste that denied time for comments, the woman turned and disappeared down the dark staircase. With her went the light.

On this clouded night, the trembling family did not even have moonlight for illumination. During the few seconds it took for the numbing shock of their circumstances to lessen at least a little, *Mütti* and her children stood in silent darkness, chilled by the cold draft that the open door funneled toward them.

At last *Mütti* pushed the door shut. A moment later she exclaimed, "There's no bolt! Very well, I shall sleep against the door myself. Just let anyone try to sneak in!" These words were small comfort to the children who stood shivering only a few feet away.

Luise heard a light thump before her—*Mütti* had leaned back against the door. "Children, do you still have our things?"

"*Ja, Mütti*," Luise and Heinrich answered.

"Good. Where is Dorothea?"

"She is with me," stated Luise who stood with Dorothea's head clasped against her side. The little girl gripped Luise's legs with her arms, her face buried in her older sister's skirt.

"Bring her to me . . . carefully," *Mütti* instructed. "Then go back and get the bags. Heinrich, bring what you have to me." The children shuffled forward and soon accomplished what she had directed. *Mütti* placed all their belongings against the wall near the door so they would be able to find them. Then, with Heinrich sitting protectively against the door, *Mütti* and Luise searched the baggage for their remaining food supply. Relying completely on her sense of touch, Luise detected through a cloth bag the round smoothness of the fruit they had bought in a village along the river. After fidgeting with the tie for a moment, she unfastened the bag and gradually removed the contents. Each piece of fruit was passed safely into Heinrich's hands before another one was sought. Luise knew she must not let even one fall and roll into the darkness.

Mütti located the food in *Oma's* basket rather quickly. Soon she made her way back to the door and slid down beside Heinrich. When everyone had received a portion of food, and Dorothea had settled on her mother's lap, *Mütti* led the children in prayer. "We praise You, Father, for Your protection. Thank You for this food and for this place to stay. Please protect us tonight and during the remainder of this journey. Enable us to be kind to one another. Be with *Papi* and take us to him with speed. To You be all praise and honor. Amen."

As the family ate their meager fare, they heard the tread of footsteps on the creaking stairs. In frozen stillness, each person's ears traced the noise as the steps drew nearer. Soon Luise felt that if there had not been a wall to separate them, the mysterious walker could have reached out to touch her. Suddenly there was silence. The stranger had stopped just outside their door! A moment later Luise heard a rattle and the sound of their doorknob turning. An uncontrollable scream shot from her mouth. Heinrich lunged toward her and placed a firm but trembling hand over her mouth, quieting her. All other noises had also been silenced, and the Schuhmachers huddled in breathless fear, waiting to learn what the intruder would do next.

To Luise's surprise, a muffled and garbled voice mumbled, "*Es tut mir leid*," and retreating footsteps sounded in the hall. Soon the sound of a nearby door closing signaled the end of the disturbance.

Mütti sighed with relief, "A drunk no doubt who couldn't find his room in the darkness." Luise, who was still shaking, failed to see how *Mütti* could find much comfort in that explanation.

"Did he try to push open the door?" she asked tremulously.

"No," answered Heinrich softly.

"Now we must try to sleep," insisted *Mütti*. "There's a bed, but I don't want any of you sleeping on it. Who knows when the sheets were last washed in this horrible place. Here, snuggle close."

Their weariness proved stronger than their fear, and within minutes the entire family slept soundly.

When the family awoke the next morning, welcome sunlight streamed through the window. The warm rays transformed their surroundings from frightening to merely distasteful. In the shafts of light, flecks of dust shimmered like tiny insects swarming in the brightness. Many of the particles had settled on the floor like a layer of frost, disturbed only in the small area where they had shuffled about the night before.

Mütti handed out the bread that remained from their evening meal. It had been stale at dinner, and now its dryness parched Luise's mouth. Neither she nor the other children complained, however; they were learning to be thankful when their basic needs were met even in unpleasant ways.

As soon as they finished the meal, *Mütti* stood up, straightened her clothes, and urged the still groggy children to their feet. "We're leaving this place!" she declared. "We will catch the first ferry to Bremerhaven. Then, even if it takes the rest of the day, I will find better lodgings. I will not rest my head in such a place again!" She helped position the bags and pouches on her children's shoulders and led them from the room. They exited the building in silence. No one stood in the hallway to mark their departure, and Luise was secretly relieved that she did not have to look again into the eyes of the frightening proprietress.

By the time the Bremerhaven church chimes struck 4, the Schuhmachers had arrived in the port city and located a suitable inn. *Mütti* settled the children inside their room, then announced she was going out to buy food, book passage on a ship, and make sure their exit papers were in order for admittance to America.

"Luise, bolt the door after me," she instructed. "You are not to let anyone convince you to open the door. Try to get some sleep while I'm away." Heinrich begged to go with her so he could see the city, but *Mütti* insisted there would be plenty of time for that later. After her departure he sat by the window sulkily, complaining that there was nothing to do.

Luise smugly decided that her behavior would not mirror her brother's. She pulled a loose sheet of paper from a bundle and began to compose a letter to *Oma*.

Bremerhaven, *den* 31. *Mai* 1894

Liebe Oma!

Mütti says it will be a few days before we leave for America. I am beginning to think that day will never come! I don't think I could stand another night like the one we endured last night in a horrible, scary place. Our room didn't have a lock, and someone nearly attacked us!

I am a little frightened about the boat trip. What if we sink in the middle of the ocean? Mütti tells me not to worry, God will watch over us, but I have heard stories about ships collapsing at sea. My friend's uncle and his wife sailed to America several years ago, and every passenger on board that ship died. How dreadful! Oma, I do not want to die. I know I would go to heaven, but there are too many exciting things I want to do in life. Most of all, I must see Papi again!

I can't write any more. Mütti has finally returned with food for lunch. Remember me always!

Deine,
Luise

Luise put down her pen and carefully folded her letter. Remembering that Oma always insisted that things be done neatly and exactly, the granddaughter made sure the creases were sharply pressed. Finally she stashed the letter in an envelope that bore the address of the well-loved village.

Luise delivered the letter to a post office the next day when all the Schuhmachers went out together. They also visited several stores, finally locating an establishment some distance from the docks that would sell them eating utensils and dinner pails. Even in that less expensive part of town, the goods were not cheap. As the Schuhmachers exited with their new purchases, Mütti commented resignedly, "Well, maybe it's best that we lost the dishes I had packed in the trunk. Papi said these dinner pails would be better anyway."

"Why?" Dorothea questioned.

"Soup is often served on the ships. Since passengers must eat while sitting in their berths, any disturbance can result in a soup-soaked mattress and soiled clothes. From what Papi writes, there is no way to wash any clothes or sheets. With the pails, we won't spill as much." Mütti grimaced as she finished her explanation.

A few nights later, on the eve of their departure for America, Mütti retold the tale of "The Musicians of Bremen" before blowing out the candle. Dorothea loved the tale and smiled with delight as her mother told of a group of animals that came to a town to form a band. The story sobered Luise, however, in spite of its lighthearted telling. The donkey her mother described reminded her of the dear creature she had left behind only days earlier. Besides that, a cynical side of her warned her that to enjoy a story about a German city would stoke the flames of her love for the land of her birth. She could not bear to part with anything else that she cherished, and she would not willingly grow fond of any part of Germany that she did not already hold dear.

CHAPTER SIX

*

The Voyage

June 5-14, 1894

The next morning the Schuhmachers rode a streetcar to the docks. *Mütti* agreed to this novel luxury since they were loaded down with baggage. Throughout their lives the family had traveled in wagons and boats, nothing more. What a thrill to board a streetcar! Even *Mütti* stood in awe during most of the ride.

As they passed through the city, Luise carefully observed the scenery. Ornamented buildings and steepled churches that had stood for hundreds of years surrounded her. She wanted to store as many images in her mind as possible. This was farewell to Germany; in all likelihood she would never return.

All too soon they reached the docks where the oceangoing vessels anchored. The activity along the waterfront rivaled the bustle the Schuhmachers had encountered in the streets. Every person seemed driven by an urgent mission. *Mütti's* pace matched that of those who surrounded her, and Luise noticed that Dorothea had to run several times to remain only a few steps behind her.

At last they approached a building that was nearly ten times the size of the family's forsaken cottage home. *Mütti* stopped outside the door to explain what the next few hours held for them.

"Just beyond this building is the ship that we will take to America. Each of you must do exactly what I tell you and obey any instructions the officials give you. Even if someone asks you to do something strange or uncomfortable, do not protest. We must be allowed to board the boat; it is our first step toward being with

51

Papi." She surveyed her children with expectant eyes. "Do you all understand?"

"*Ja, Mütti,*" the children chorused. *Mütti* scrutinized each child's appearance, straightened Dorothea's head-scarf, and nodded in satisfaction. "We're as ready as we can be." She sighed and led the children through the front door.

They entered a room larger than any Luise had ever seen. A crowd of people stood in disorderly lines in front of a counter that spanned the length of the room. Brass lamps with white shades stood at even intervals atop the counter; and to the left of each lamp sat a uniformed official.

"Do we have to talk to those men?" whispered Luise. "They look so stern!"

Mütti spun around. "Luise, please, now is not the time to worry me with such questions." After a pause her face softened. Placing her hands on Luise's shoulders, she admonished, "You must be brave, Luise. We don't have to talk with these men. They are selling tickets for passage, and *Papi* already paid our way. It is very likely, however, that soon we will have to talk to officials just like these. Each of us must have courage. Can I depend on you for that?"

Luise bit her lip and nodded.

They walked into the next room, a twin of the first. Two long lines wound toward neighboring doorways. *Mütti* explained that they would wait in one line so the doctors could examine them. A half hour later they reached the door, and an official directed them down a hall and into a small room. Inside stood two doctors dressed in long white jackets. The doctors checked *Mütti* and Dorothea first. As Luise watched their rough evaluation, she developed a distinct dislike for these men.

All too soon Luise's turn came. She shuffled forward, resisting her longing to turn and run. As the doctor checked her scalp and poked her stomach, she could feel redness creeping across her face. Never had she allowed a stranger so near! Her submission to the examination resulted only from the knowledge that this man had the authority to destroy her hopes of sailing to America. At last the exam was complete. After enduring a routine vaccination, Luise eagerly exited out a door opposite the one she had entered.

The family then passed out of the building and onto the dock. There, in front of a large steamship, a long line of emigrants stretched along the dock to the gangway entrance. *Mütti* positioned her family at the end of the line. "We may have to wait awhile," she explained. "At the foot of the gangway the officials are asking each family a series of questions. If we can get through that, we will be able to sail for America."

If all went well, they would never stand on German land again! That thought struck Luise as she surveyed the steamer that would carry her to a new land and a new life. How unstable everything seemed to her as she teetered on the edge of change in more ways than one. No longer truly a dutiful citizen of Germany but not yet an American, she also hung precariously between a youth's carefree world and the heavy concerns of adulthood. *Papi's* departure had introduced her to sadness, and now her own journey was burdening her with responsibility and worry. Even so, Luise knew *Mütti* expected her to keep a cheerful disposition. Remaining joyful had proved difficult since she keenly understood the challenges their emigration presented. How she envied Dorothea who now sat calmly on the edge of the dock. The little girl seemed able to adapt easily as long as *Mütti* stood near.

Luise nearly began to pity herself as she stood on that dock, but a promise that *Papi* had given her the night before his departure kept her from becoming despondent. When her father kissed her good night for the last time, he had spoken words of comfort to his eldest child. "Luise, I know it is hard for you to let me go, even for this short time. The next months, maybe even years, will be frightening for all of us. It is very difficult for me to let my precious ones out from under my care and protection even for a little while. In fact, there is only one way I will be able to endure and allow this separation—I will tell myself over and over, every day, that you are in God's hands, just as you have always been. You will be as safe and cared for in my absence as you would be if I remained, for God will never forsake you." Papi had then pulled out his Bible and turned to *Deuteronomium* 31:8. There he had read, "*Der Herr selbst wird vor dir herziehen* . . . The Lord himself goes before you and will be with you; he will never leave you nor forsake you. Do not be afraid; do not be discouraged."

"Do you understand, Luise, why this verse is so important to us?" *Papi* had asked. "When you cry or when you miss me, I want you to remember to be courageous and to do so because you know that God has not forsaken you. And always remember that I have not forsaken you either. I will send for you and *Mütti* and the others. I love you all so much!" Luise remembered the tears that had been in *Papi's* eyes. How often over the past two years the memory of those tears had convinced her that *Papi* really did love them!

She found it difficult to wait patiently on the dock since thoughts of *Papi* intensified her eagerness to sail. The line moved so slowly! After a half hour of edging forward, the Schuhmachers finally stood directly in front of a desk where a uniformed official questioned a husband and wife. Soon the official allowed the couple to board, and *Mütti* resolutely stepped forward to the desk. The official repeated the questions he had asked the others, and he recorded *Mütti's* answers on the ship's manifest. When the man finally motioned for the Schuhmachers to board, Luise sighed with relief.

As they started up the gangway, Dorothea dropped one of her bundles. "It's too heavy!" she cried in frustration.

"Keep moving," Luise urged. "I'll pick it up." She cautiously bent down to grasp the stray bundle, taking care not to send any of her own baggage tumbling to the ground. By the time they reached the deck, the pressure from the drawstrings of several weighty bags had caused numbness to spread through Luise's left hand Although the family had brought little, their few precious belongings were hard to manage.

On the deck *Mütti* hugged all three children. "We've made it!" she exclaimed. "Now let's find our berths!"

A crewman directed the family down steep, slippery stairs to an area just below the deck containing sleeping berths designated for women and children. One hundred berths, two feet by six feet, were crowded into the compartment. Narrow aisles that barely provided enough room for a person to walk separated the bunks. *Mütti* put her baggage down on a bunk and indicated that the children should do likewise.

Heinrich pointed to his mattress. "It's just a burlap bag with straw sticking through the holes! Do I have to sleep on that? It's all rough and prickly," he grumbled.

Luise, wincing at the rancid and unclean stench that pervaded the air, added, "How can it smell this bad at the *beginning* of the voyage?"

"Children, please stop complaining!" *Mütti* insisted. "We cannot afford to sleep in better quarters. If we had waited until we could travel in style, we would have spent many more years apart from your father. It is important that we are reunited with *Papi* as soon as possible." *Mütti* looked at them intently and then continued, "Heinrich, Luise, Dorothea, there are some things we need to discuss. Listen carefully." The children nodded, and she continued, "After a few days you may begin to feel more comfortable and safe here, but I want you to remember that these ships can be dangerous places. I have heard of—" She cut herself short. "No, there is no need to frighten you with those tales. It is enough for you to know that we must always stay with one another and our belongings. If you ever leave me, you must go together. Heinrich, will you promise me that you will never leave either of your sisters alone?"

"*Ja, Mütti,*" Heinrich agreed soberly.

"Very good," *Mütti* replied as she sat down on her mattress and pulled her knitting from a bag. "Now we must wait while the others board."

With the help of a few dim lights, Luise studied their dirty surroundings and the people who were claiming spots in the room. *Mütti* had chosen berths near the stairs, which allowed them to benefit from gusts of fresh air that occasionally blew down from above. Such pleasurable wind certainly never reached the berths that were further back. As other passengers carried their belongings to the far corners of the room, some glanced jealously in the Schuhmachers' direction.

The people themselves were fascinating. Luise found she could only understand the conversations of two other families since several different languages were being spoken in that one room. The

varied display of regional attire equally impressed her. Some passengers wore long sheepskin coats, and some had fur hats. How
amazing that a common quest had drawn so many nationalities
together!

Once all the passengers had boarded, the Schuhmachers learned
that each day they would be allowed to go up to the deck during
the second half of the morning and of the afternoon. Since steerage passengers paid the lowest fare for their crossing, they were
only allowed to occupy a specified section of the ship's deck;
therefore, time in the coveted fresh air had to be enjoyed in shifts.
Luise overheard a German mother nearby repeatedly assuring her
children that they would be allowed on deck at the same time as
their *Papi* who was staying in a compartment that was designated
for men.

During the Schuhmachers' first night on board, the ship
remained at the dock. Getting ready for sleep was simple. Since
everyone slept in their clothes, only the beds had to be prepared.
Within two minutes the Schuhmachers had untied and unrolled
their quilts. Then *Mütti* wrapped shawls around their life pre-
servers to create pillows, while the children stowed all of their
belongings on their berths along the wall. *Mütti* muttered that no
one would be likely to steal belongings that the owner had snuggled beside.

Soon Luise curled beneath her blanket, relishing the warmth
it provided. As she gazed across the colorful surface, drowsiness
numbed her senses, and she could almost ignore the stench of
unclean humans and the sharp poke of hay from the mattress. Even
her makeshift pillow provided a degree of comfort. *Mütti* leaned
down to kiss her, and Luise imagined herself at home. As she closed
her eyes and whispered a prayer, she remembered *Papi's* words.
Even in the hold of a ship, she was not forsaken. She quickly fell
into a contented slumber.

When Luise awoke in the morning, the stuffiness and stench of the
steerage hold instantly confronted her. Oh, that she could have
remained asleep for the duration of the voyage! A desperate desire

for sunlight and air welled within her, propelling her toward the
stairs. *Mütti* put out a hand to stop her daughter.

"We must wait our turn," she gently reminded.

A half hour later the noise of the ship's engines announced to
steerage passengers that their departure from Germany had begun.
Since the Schuhmachers were below deck, they were not granted
a final glimpse of Bremerhaven. Perhaps that was just as well, Luise
thought, for she was certain she would have cried.

When their turn above deck came, the Schuhmachers had
been ready for two hours. They had rolled up their blankets and
gathered their belongings into bundles so they could carry everything with them. After losing her trunk to thieves, *Mütti* was determined not to let anything out of her sight. The Schuhmachers were
not alone in their untrusting attitude, and soon only the mattresses
and the seasick remained behind to wallow in the eternal dusk of
the compartment.

The Schuhmachers quickly located a spot on deck near a wall
that provided shelter from the wind. After they had settled amidst
their baggage, *Mütti* craned her neck and scanned the shoreline
with tears in her eyes.

"What's wrong, *Mütti*?" Luise asked.

Mütti wiped her eyes. "We are in the North Sea, and this is our
last view of *Deutschland*. I will never see my homeland again."

As they steamed forward, a misty rain drove dampness into the
Schuhmachers' clothing; yet even this did not tempt them to consider seeking shelter below. All their fellow passengers remained on
deck, a vast and sprawling human quilt that even Luise's blanket
did not rival in color and variety. Despite their individual distinc-
tiveness, however, common uncertainties and hopes had stitched
these strangers together.

The next morning as the ship traveled through the English
Channel, *Mütti* reminded her children to enjoy this final opportunity to view land since the ship would soon slip out into the vast
expanse of the ocean. The grayness of the day hid England; but distant France, appearing like mounded moss on the banks of a lake,
lined the southern horizon. Luise sincerely hoped America would
not look so gray and dismal.

On the third day of the voyage the ship encountered rough waters, and seasickness confined Mütti to her berth. Frau Weiss, a young German mother who noticed Mütti's illness, offered to accompany the children to the deck and watch over them. Mütti agreed, admitting that the steerage compartment conditions were unhealthy.

Thus began two relationships—one that brightened the dullness of the voyage for Dorothea, and another that provided a tolerable distraction for Luise. Frau Weiss had a six-year-old daughter named Amalie and a fifteen-year-old named Elsa. Amalie was the perfect companion for the youngest Schuhmacher. The girls spent hours above deck playing games with pieces of string and telling each other about their German homes. Luise, however, found less joy in her friendship. Elsa prattled endlessly about all that she would do and buy in America—how perfectly wonderful everything would be! Luise knew life would not be so carefree, and the younger girl's naïve sense of reality strained her patience.

During the times when they were in their berths, Luise was happily left to her own musings. Little aboard the ship escaped her observation, and everything she saw refused to rest quietly in her mind. There was too much to think about for mere spectatorship. On the fifth day she opened her journal to record her impressions of the sea crossing.

den 10. Juni 1894

There is a large bell in the middle of the deck. It rings to announce meals (which are disgusting), and I suppose they would clang it furiously if we ever began to sink. That's what Heinrich said—but I'm not sure I should believe him. He's probably just trying to tease me. Anyway, I don't want to think about such a tragic ending.

The ship is unlike anyplace I have ever been. I feel like the real world has disappeared! On this ship there must be people from at least half the countries in Europe! I can't understand what most people say, and many women have dresses I would never dream of wearing! Of course, there are some Germans. There is one family that gathers around an old bearded man whenever we're on deck. He plays a violin and reminds me of Papi. How I hope Papi still plays his horn! The violin player has a niece who is Dorothea's friend. Sometimes they join hands and whirl around in a crazy dance until they're nearly exhausted. Mütti lets her do this because she knows we're cramped and crowded on this old boat. (There is not even enough room for everyone on the deck at one time!) How I wish I could go for a long walk through the woods near our old village. I would climb the highest hill and see unending green, beautiful land. How I yearn to see land again!

There are two people on board that I wish I could meet. One is an old Rumanian woman, and the other is a girl who must be her granddaughter. For the first part of the voyage, they were both in bunks near us, and they worked all day to make beautiful lace. Yesterday the little girl got sick and was taken to the ship hospital. Now the grandmother is very sad. Just looking at her makes me sad because I know Oma must be lonely now that we're gone!

Mütti was sick, but now—thankfully—she is better.

The food is terrible! Today Heinrich found a beetle in his breakfast oatmeal! We've had lukewarm soup, boiled potatoes, and chewy stuff that faintly resembled meat. The cooks haul in big pots, and we must stand in a long line to get the food. I'm tired of being squashed between smelly people! After the food is sloshed into our pails, we must eat crouched over in our bunks. The only place to wash the dishes is in a bucket of salty water that is the same bucket people wash their faces and hands in! It is disgusting! People have even gotten skin infections from it, so we don't wash our hands or faces anymore. Mütti also refuses to wash our dishes in that water. We wipe them clean as best we can. Unfortunately, the cloth we use is becoming filthy, and the dishes are covered with grease. Sometimes I dream of Oma's hot rolls, and I want to cry!

While the Schuhmachers sat on the deck during the afternoon of the ninth day of their voyage, the ship came to a stop and the engines quieted. The immigrants looked at each other in confusion. Was the ship in trouble?

An experienced German traveler restored Luise's peace by pointing out a smaller ship steaming toward them. "It's the pilot ship!" he announced. "It's bringing the man who will steer us to land. We must be very close!"

The passengers who understood his German turned westward despite the fact that most could not see over the heads of the people standing in front of them. Nevertheless, exuberant shouts soon

arose from those on the railing. "Land! America!" Soon every passenger knew land was in sight.

Heinrich scrambled atop a nearby box and pulled Luise up after
him. "It's true!" they shouted down to *Mütti* and Dorothea.

"Finally!" *Mütti* breathed. "Tonight we shall sleep on
American soil!

Luise remained on the box, unwilling to remove her gaze from
the faint gray line of land that rose from the sea. Never mind that
this sight held nothing to distinguish it from the French shoreline
that had bored her little more than a week earlier, for now her
young and water-weary eyes looked upon the fulfillment of a
dream!

After the pilot came on board, the ship resumed its advance,
and the Schuhmachers returned to their berths for dinner. Soon
they received news that the ship had reached Lower New York Bay.
The passengers eagerly began packing their belongings in preparation for landing. An atmosphere both festive and tense permeated
the crowded compartment as the immigrants anticipated the joy of
entering America, though also fearing the possibility of rejection
and deportation.

A moment later a crewman brought news that inflamed some
and saddened others—the ship had arrived too late in the day, and
the harbor had closed. They would anchor for the night and continue toward land in the morning.

Before Luise had an opportunity to voice her own disappointment, *Mütti* crumpled onto her bunk in despair. Propelled by confusion and love, Luise jumped down from her bed and rushed to
Mütti's side. Heinrich and Dorothea joined her. An ill wind had
come against these tender shoots, and the sturdy stake to which
they had lashed themselves was faltering. The children attempted
to comfort *Mütti*, sliding their hands along her shoulders and
around her neck, whispering, "We love you. We will reach land
tomorrow." Despite their efforts, she continued to hide her face in
her pillow.

Amidst the confusion of the throng that surrounded them, the
Schuhmacher family formed an inconspicuous, forlorn pile. Yet the
eyes of a little friend noted their plight.

"Dorothea, what's wrong?" a young voice chirped from across the crowded room. A mild commotion followed, and Luise noticed passengers moving aside to let someone pass. A moment later Amalie burst through her final barrier, a family that daily gathered in the passageway that ran along the Schuhmachers' bunks. She ran toward Dorothea, followed closely by *Frau* Weiss who made repeated grasps toward her escaped daughter. When the chase ended, however, Amalie's mother did not scold. Instead, she dropped to her knees beside *Mütti's* bed, motioning to the children to step back. They immediately obeyed. Back on her own bunk, Luise listened carefully to the conversation that followed.

"Now, Sophie," *Frau* Weiss began, "we're all upset about the wait, but we'll be able to land in the morning. Don't waste your tears."

"We're so close," *Mütti* choked. "To be held back at this point . . . I want to be with Jakob so much. I am tired of doing everything by myself. It has been so hard. I have no more strength."

"*Ja.* I think most of the people in this room would agree with you. But look, they haven't given up hope. You must have courage." Luise surveyed the room and observed several others who wore expressions of extreme disappointment. She glanced back at *Mütti*, hoping she would not notice the despair that surrounded her. To Luise's relief, when *Mütti* raised her head, she looked straight into *Frau* Weiss's face. Apparently she found encouragement there, for soon her own countenance brightened, and the Schuhmachers' storm cleared.

Elsa walked up to investigate the situation. Finding the excitement calmed, she sat beside Luise. "Guess what?" she began. "Well, of course, you'll never guess. It's just too wonderful. You will be so excited when I tell you!"

"Well, go ahead and tell me then," urged Luise with amusement.

"We're going to live in St. Louis! *Papi* finally made his decision! A man he met on board told him there's no better place to do business than in that town. Why, we'll be neighbors! What fun it will be! Don't you agree?"

"Of course," replied Luise indifferently. "St. Louis is a big place though. We may not exactly be neighbors."

"But you'll come see me, won't you?" Elsa pleaded. "Even if we do live far apart, we'll always be friends, Luise."

Frau Weiss interrupted at that moment and spared Luise from the temptation to make any insincere commitments. "We must be getting back to our things," she remarked.

As they rose, *Mütti* pressed the Schuhmachers' St. Louis address into *Frau* Weiss's hand. "Thank you so much," she whispered. "I will never forget your kindness. Please come to see us in St. Louis."

When they were gone, *Mütti* whispered to her children, "I'm sorry I scared you. We all need a good sleep tonight. Tomorrow we face our greatest challenge yet!"

CHAPTER SEVEN

Ellis Island

June 15, 1894

Even the most commonplace details of the day on which they reached Ellis Island would be forever etched in Luise's mind. She was so excited about the arrival in America that it was hard to remember *Papi* would not be there to meet them on the dock in New York City.

Early that morning a crewman entered the compartment to announce that all passengers should make sure their immigration papers were in order. Luise saw *Mütti* pass a hand across her waist where her apron band concealed a secret pocket in which all their documents were safely stowed.

A few minutes later several uniformed men began to circulate through the compartment, distributing one white tag to every immigrant. The Schuhmachers were among the first to receive their tags. *Mütti* quickly attached one to her own dress and to Dorothea's before checking to make sure Heinrich and Luise had adequately secured theirs. Luise fingered hers, examining the large number and various words printed on the front.

"What is this for?" she asked.

"It's a code that will help the officials at Ellis Island identify us," *Mütti* explained quickly. "They will match this number with one in the ship's book. Don't ask any more questions now," she continued. "Let's go up on deck quickly. Most people aren't ready yet, and I think we'll be able to get a good spot for seeing the shore!"

Soon the family located a place near the rail where they had a full view over the water. Within minutes a wall of people gathered behind them. Since the crew had made no attempt that morning to keep any of the eager immigrants below, no room remained on deck for anyone to sit down. Even the sick now stood on deck, attempting to feign health and slip into America with their ailments unnoticed. Only those who had been taken to the ship's hospital were missing.

The crowd stood eerily silent and still. Fiddles had been packed away and unfinished lace put aside for another day. Although land finally surrounded them, these last few hours of the journey were more solemn and weighty than all the long days at sea. Luise attempted to remain calm amidst the pervasive tension, but this proved difficult when strong men looked pale and Mütti's hands were trembling. Questions rose in Luise's mind. Would this day bring admittance or cruel rejection? Would America be kind to her family? Would she ever learn to call this land *home*?

Luise leaned against Mütti's shoulder. "Remember the whale we saw yesterday?" she asked.

"Yes. It was a marvelous creature!"

"It frightened me," Luise remarked. She looked out over the water and then continued, "What is the ocean like under the waves? We've been sailing for days and days, but I don't know what I would see if I were a whale."

Mütti chuckled. "I have no idea, Luise. I have never wondered."

"But you wonder what America is like, don't you?"

"Of course, but we have some idea from Papi's letters."

"Yes," murmured Luise, "but not enough. Mütti, I used to be afraid of the ocean and of the ship, but now that I'm about to land, I'm more afraid of America!"

"Luise," Mütti sighed, "I wish I could tell you what to expect. The truth is, I can no more describe America to you than I can tell you about a whale's life. We've all dreamed of this moment when we would reach America. Now that we're here, even I'm scared to see what our new life will hold."

Their conversation was interrupted by the arrival of a small cutter that anchored alongside the ocean liner. Several uniformed officials raised a ladder against the ship and began boarding. This development panicked some of the passengers who apparently feared these newcomers would bar them from continuing to Ellis Island.

Frightened by the confusion surrounding her, Luise grasped *Mütti's* arm. "What is it, *Mütti*? Are we in trouble? What's happening?" Before her mother could reply, Dorothea began crying. *Mütti* managed to nudge the people nearby aside until she had enough space to kneel on the floor beside her youngest. She pulled Luise and Heinrich down beside her.

"*Papi* wrote about this," *Mütti* explained. "The men who have boarded the ship will examine the people who paid for cabin-class tickets. Those passengers do not have to go to Ellis Island. Instead, their inspection is done on the ship."

"But why don't they have to go to Ellis Island?" Luise pressed.

"They paid more money for their tickets."

"But, *Mütti*—"

"Luise, don't protest. There is nothing we can do to change this situation. We have enough before us as it is; we can't waste energy complaining."

Luise silently bristled at the injustice of the system. During the voyage she had observed the cabin-class voyagers from a distance. They had spent their days lounging on an uncrowded upper deck that was visible but inaccessible to steerage passengers such as the Schuhmachers. At times ladies in fine dresses and men in dapper coats had moved to the railing to peer down upon the steerage deck. They had seemed amused by the scene and sometimes taunted the passengers below with their laughter and haughty observations.

Heinrich, who apparently shared his sister's frustration, leaned over to Luise and muttered, "It probably didn't stink where they slept!"

The majority of the steerage passengers did not see the immigration officials after the initial boarding. They did observe, however, one result of the visit. Before the inspectors left, another small vessel pulled away from the ship's side. Passengers from the ship's hospital lined its decks. At the sight, an old woman near Luise wailed, holding her arms out toward the boat as it pulled away. Tears formed in Luise's eyes as she recognized the Rumanian grand-mother who had reminded her of *Oma*. Luise turned to look at the barge. Near the front railing stood the young lace maker. Tears streamed down the girl's face as she leaned back against her mother. A woman nearby murmured in German, "*Wie Schade!* Her grand-daughter has been taken. So sad that the little girl ended up in the hospital. If the little one is sent home, her mother will have to return as well. I wonder if her husband is already in America."

Luise trembled as she considered those words, and *Mütti* slipped an arm around her shoulders. "Don't be frightened," she said, sensing the root of her daughter's concern. "I believe we will see *Papi* very soon. But whatever happens, the Lord will be with us. He never forsakes those who seek Him. Remember this truth, and find comfort in your God's promised faithfulness!"

At last the ship began to sail northward through a slim passage of water called the Narrows. Luise looked toward the rural shore. "*Mütti*, none of the roofs are orange!" she exclaimed. "How differ-ent from home!"

"Luise," *Mütti* reminded her quietly, "*this* is your home now. I guess people use different materials here to build their houses."

Luise did not respond, for beside her an old man had lifted his long, bony finger to point out another ship. "Look, Heinrich!" Luise shouted in excitement. "It's a boat just like ours! Look at all the people."

"I wonder if we look as bad as they do," muttered Heinrich as he surveyed the mass of people assembled on the deck of the other ship.

"Yes," sighed *Mütti*, "we're just as tired and in need of baths as they are. I'm sure that each of them has been through many trials to get this far, just like the people on our boat."

"Look!" Luise squealed as she looked in a different direction. "There she is! The lady that *Papi* wrote about. He said we would know we were really in America when we saw the Statue of

Liberty!" Others on board had also spotted the stately figure that rose from the harbor.

"*Was ist das?*" asked a German near them.

"Maybe it's somebody's tomb," another man answered.

Heinrich rolled his eyes and declared, "I can't believe they don't even recognize the Statue of Liberty!"

"Silence, Heinrich," *Mütti* warned. "We would not know either if *Papi* had not written. It is not your place to mock others."

As more passengers sighted the statue, those who knew her proper name began shouting, "The Statue of Liberty! The Statue of Liberty!"

"It's strange," murmured *Mütti*, "those are some of the only English words that most of us know. How are we going to fare when we reach land and everyone speaks a language that is foreign to us?" She sighed deeply, and the weight of her concern once again settled on Luise's young shoulders. Strangely, the teenager had never considered the fact that people would speak differently in America. After all, *Papi's* letters from America had been written in German!

The ocean liner's journey finally ended at a pier just beyond the mouth of the Hudson River. The cabin-class passengers, their journey complete, began disembarking down a gangway toward friends and relatives who waited on land to whisk them away. Luise watched with envy as the clean, well-dressed crowd entered America ahead of her.

Soon loud shouts from the ship's crew diverted her attention. These typically sullen men had begun a lively performance. From positions interspersed throughout the crowd, they yelled while flaying their arms like conductors of a wild symphony. Their spoken commands were at first unintelligible to Luise and many others, but their emphatic prodding and pushing quickly communicated that the passengers were to exit down a nearby gangway. As the Schuhmachers began to move forward with the press of the nervous crowd, they at last heard a command in German: "*Mach schnell!*" Then the sailor who had spoken immediately switched to yet another language.

It was a rough welcome to America, to be sure; but it successfully ushered the immigrants into a roped enclosure at the far end of the dock. Then the same voices immediately began herding the front part of the crowd onto an Ellis Island ferry. Luise felt the cruel irony of her situation. Though the immigrants stood a few yards from the New York shore, this longed-for land was not yet theirs.

As she stepped toward the ferry, the crowd surged, pitching her forward into Heinrich. "Sorry!" Luise muttered as she blew her brother's hair out of her face.

"Nothing to be sorry for," observed Heinrich. "I'm being hit from all sides! Can you see anything at all?"

"No—only the floor of this dock!" moaned Luise who, like a small boat in a dark storm, could never see when the next swell would come. Helpless, she could only await its impact.

At last stillness came. Remarkably the Schuhmachers were among those who had been able to crowd aboard the barge. As the boat began inching toward Ellis Island, Luise looked back at the dock and saw the remainder of their fellow passengers waiting impatiently for the next ferry. The silence that pervaded the scene on shore seemed eerie for such a large gathering, and the people on the ferry were equally as solemn. Pale faces surrounded Luise, convincing her that the nervous anticipation that had infected her own heart was epidemic. "I've heard it called the *Tränen Insel*," a women nearby remarked. "May it not be an 'island of tears' for us."

Mütti pointed out their destination. Even from a distance Luise could make out a prominent window-bedecked building on Ellis Island. At each corner of the sandy brown structure, pointed towers rose above the blue slate roof. This building bore some resemblance to Germany's ancient castles, but it lacked their charm. Besides, it had an ominous purpose. This was the immigration depot—the final barrier that stood between the Schuhmachers and America.

"What did *Papi* write about Ellis Island?" Luise asked.

"Nothing," *Mütti* answered. "He passed through a place called Castle Garden. Some new immigrants told him last year that Ellis Island is now being used instead of Castle Garden. He didn't know what to tell us to expect, though he did hear that the inspections are stricter now than they used to be."

That news was unsettling! As the boat slowed to approach the dock, Luise turned her eyes back toward the island and spotted a grassy area. The green lawn tempted her with its freshness, bringing memories of the fields that surrounded her home village. She could almost smell the sweet scent of dew-drenched hay that had crept through her window on cool mornings. Oh, to know the pleasure of such a fragrance once again!

Of course, memories of *Oma* followed. Happily, however, this contemplation of the one she had left behind reminded her of the dear father toward whom she was traveling. She resolved to think of nothing but overcoming the obstacle looming ahead. Before she could see *Papi*, she must gain admittance to America through the gates of Ellis Island!

A man standing beside Luise began softly reciting answers for the expected inspection questions. Most likely a friend or relative had provided written coaching through a letter. Luise wondered if he would answer honestly.

Other immigrants counted their money beneath the protective shield of a hat or an apron. "Otto, should we show it all to them or keep some hidden away?" one young man whispered anxiously to his brother. "Keep some hidden," the other answered in annoyance. "We don't want them to take everything from us, do we? Remember, Gustav told us that the officials tried to swindle him." His brother nodded and stuffed a portion of the money into a hidden pocket in his coat.

Other uncertainties plagued some of the immigrants as the ferry floated near Ellis Island. Some were going to cities where they had no acquaintances. Many had only vague ideas about where they would settle.

Luise rejoiced that she had a home waiting for her in St. Louis. How wonderful that *Papi* had gone ahead of them to prepare that home! Certainly not everything would be perfect—*Mütti* had cautioned the children not to expect a cottage, at least not at first. But Luise was confident that she would love her new home because her entire family would be living together again. Certainly *Oma* must have been right about that!

When the boat drew nearer to the dock, *Mütti* lowered herself to the floor, keeping the railing at her back. She indicated that the children should do the same. They all willingly dropped the baggage that had weighed so heavily upon them and wiggled downward until the skirts and trousers of fellow passengers surrounded them on three sides.

"I want us to take a moment together before we go ashore. This day has already been too full," *Mütti* began. Unconsciously she stroked Dorothea's soft hair. "We must not forget to pray, giving thanks to the Lord for having brought us this far. Many passengers fell seriously ill during the voyage across the Atlantic." Three anxious faces bowed without hesitation, signaling their agreement, and *Mütti* began, "*Unser Vater im Himmel,* we thank You for keeping us from all harm. We pray that You will now bring us safely to *Papi.* Amen." The children echoed her prayer's closing in soft whispers.

"I have been praying the whole day," Heinrich admitted. Luise cast a look of amazement in his direction. It was not like her brother to admit that he needed help from anyone, even God.

During *Mütti's* prayer the barge had reached the dock at Ellis Island. *Mütti* quickly passed a comb to Luise and Heinrich, commanding them to smooth their hair and straighten their clothes. "We must look our best for the inspectors," she admonished. Then, as the immigrants began to push toward the exit, *Mütti* rose with a smile and said, "Let's go!"

The children stood and gathered their belongings. To Luise's surprise, her brother helped place her largest bag on her back. "Thank you, Heinrich! That's easier," she said with gratitude. Heinrich silently shrugged off her thanks and led the way forward.

From the moment Luise stepped onto Ellis Island, she began to fear that she would never feel at home on American land. Even among others who had come from across the ocean, she felt isolated and was sure all the others felt the same way. It seemed to her that the nervous uncertainty shared by the crowd of immigrants standing on the dock did little to unify them. Their backgrounds were so varied and their ways so foreign to one another that each person regarded strangers with suspicious fear. Luise was thankful they did not loiter in that spot for long.

Another ferry reached the dock just as the last of the

Schuhmachers' fellow travelers stepped onto land. In response the barge attendants, guided by the manifest numbers printed on the immigrants' tags, hastily organized the crowd on the dock into groups of thirty. This accomplished, the officials herded the Schuhmachers' group into the main building.

Inside, an official directed them up a large flight of stairs to the second level. Everyone, even a tiny child, had to walk unaided. Luise noticed that several uniformed men stood at the top of the stairs. From that vantage point they closely observed the immigrants' ascent. One official walked over to a limping man and chalked an *L* on his coat lapel.

"*Wie Schade!*" a nearby woman hissed. "He should have hidden that limp. Those doctors are watching our every move!"

Luise trembled and stiffened with fear as she walked past the official a minute later. She certainly did not want to receive a chalk mark that might keep her from America and *Papi*. To her relief, her family ascended without receiving undesired attention.

The stairs led to an immense room that was filled with people. Although Luise's anxious eyes again focused on the uniformed officials who stood scattered around the room, the vast majority of the occupants were immigrants. Despite the huge number of people, the interpreters and officials maintained order, directing the manifest groups into lines that led to both of the immigrant checkpoints—first the health examination and then the legal inspection.

Luise, who stood first in line among the Schuhmachers, soon found herself face to face with a doctor. Her exam began with a search for scalp disease. The doctor removed her scarf and rapidly yanked sections of her hair to expose her scalp. She gritted her teeth, determined to appear unmindful of any pain. Meanwhile, an interpreter shot questions at her. "*Was ist deine Name?*"

"Luise Schuhmacher."

The doctor shifted his examination to her hands, neck, and face. This close examination by an American stranger froze Luise's limbs and muddled her mind. She had to force herself to concentrate on the interpreter's next question: "*Wie alt bist du?*"

"*Vierzehn,*" she replied, gritting her teeth as the doctor picked up a buttonhook, placed the hook just below her eyebrow, and rolled back her eyelid to check for trachoma. Although the action took only a few seconds, a painful sting remained after he removed the odd instrument. Luise felt it was cruel for him to use a tool for lacing shoes to examine her eyes.

She strained her ears for the next question and braced for the doctor's next move, but nothing followed. Her health had stood the three-minute test!

She stepped forward, continuing in the line that now led to the legal inspection desks. As she waited, she anxiously turned back to watch the rest of her family undergo the doctor's examination. Luise was relieved when, one by one, each family member joined her. All was well! There was not a chalk mark among them! Even Dorothea had surmounted her shyness and loudly told the interpreter her name.

The Schuhmachers readied themselves for a long wait. Already several families from their manifest group were waiting ahead of them. To Luise's surprise, however, this line moved rather quickly. In less than fifteen minutes, they stood before an inspector who sat behind a large desk. He peered at *Mütti's* identification tag and matched her number with one in the large manifest ledger on his desk. This took only a moment because the book stood opened to the right page. Everyone listed in that section shared the same manifest number and had been placed in the same inspection line. With the help of an interpreter, the inspector began a rapid questioning process that covered the family members' names, nationality, former residence, and United States destination among other things. *Mütti* quickly and honestly answered each of the man's questions. When the official asked to see *Mütti's* money, she nervously pulled it from her pocket. The official merely glanced at it, grunted, and handed *Mütti* an admittance card. The whole interaction had taken little more than a minute.

Mütti turned away from the desk with a smile. As she bent down to pick up her luggage, she came face to face with her children who had patiently gathered around her. "We've made it, children! We can enter America!" she whispered. "Our God has watched over us!"

Luise sank to the floor in relief.

"Come," her mother said, "we will find a place to rest for a minute."

As *Mütti* led the children away from the inspection area, Luise glanced toward several large wire enclosures that held detained immigrants. Chalk marks on their shoulders announced the ailments or questionable circumstances the officials had detected. Some showed symptoms of heart problems, others lacked money; all were suspect in the eyes of the officials, and all awaited further examinations to determine whether they would be admitted to America or sent back across the ocean. The drawn expressions of the people within those confines contrasted sharply with the smiles on the Schuhmachers' faces! Luise could not bear to look long in that direction and was relieved when *Mütti* led them to a spot where the enclosures were out of sight.

"Well," *Mütti* exclaimed, "I'm glad that's over!" Her children nodded wearily. "I am so proud of all of you. You did so well! Now I have a bit of funny news for you! You all have new names now. New names for a new country!"

"What are you saying?" Heinrich asked with concern.

"Not completely new," *Mütti* assured them. "We will just use the American spellings of your German names. *Papi* thought this would make your transition easier. You will probably meet many people your age who are not German. Our last name will be spelled differently too because the official spelled it incorrectly when *Papi* came into the country." *Mütti* pulled from her pocket a slip of paper that she had earlier shown to the inspector. Written across the paper in *Papi's* handwriting were their new names: Louisa Shumaker, Henry Shumaker, and Dorothy Shumaker.

"What if we sometimes forget to use the right name?" Louisa asked.

"That's okay. It will take all of us a while to get used to many new things about America. Now we must go buy train tickets and get some lunch."

Louisa suddenly realized that she was hungry. Nearly two hours had passed since they had landed on the island at ten o'clock.

The railroad ticket counters were easy to locate; the Shumakers did not even have to go downstairs. *Mütti* purchased four tickets on the Pennsylvania Railroad and sent *Papi* a telegraph. Her message relayed the happy news of their admittance to America and provided details concerning their planned arrival in St. Louis on Sunday morning. Along with the tickets, *Mütti* received tags that were similar to the ones the ship's officials had given them that morning.

"We can take off the old tags," *Mütti* explained. "We must wear these now. They will help the railroad conductors make sure we get to the right train and on to St. Louis. We won't get lost just because we can't understand English."

As soon as the tags were securely fastened to their clothes, *Mütti* said, "I know everyone's hungry, but I think we'd better first find out where we can clean up. It's been over a week since any of us have washed our hands! Does that sound like a good idea?" The children chorused their approval of that plan.

Once again, without complaint, the children hefted high their belongings and set their steps in the direction *Mütti* led. An interpreter pointed them in the right direction, and they quickly located a water closet. Here, as everywhere on Ellis Island, the signs near the doors were printed in several different languages. Since there were separate rooms for men and women, *Mütti* reluctantly allowed Henry to go off by himself.

Louisa was amazed by what she found inside the doors of the women's bathroom. It was almost too good to be true! "Look, *Mütti*! The water is running from the walls. No one is pumping it!" she exclaimed.

There were towels hanging on the walls and huge bath tubs where some women were frantically rubbing the grime of the boat from their children. This sight did not tempt *Mütti*, however. These community tubs were scarcely more attractive to her than the washbasins on the ship. She did, however, carefully wash her girls' hair and instructed them to clean their hands and faces. "We must look good for *Papi* when we meet him!" she declared.

Although Louisa longed for a complete bath, she was content. How delightful it felt to be clean, if only in the exposed spots! The only drawback was that now the rest of her body felt so horribly grimy. Just one more reason to want to reach St. Louis as quickly as possible!

When they left the bathroom, they did not find Henry where they had expected him to join them. *Mütti* grew frantic with worry and began pacing near the spot where she had instructed him to wait. Five minutes later he sauntered out of the men's water closet, grinning from ear to ear. Louisa noted with envy that he had obviously enjoyed a total bath and was now as clean (and as damp) as a boy of fifteen could make himself!

Mütti led her family to the lunch counter where she purchased sandwiches. They then located a spot for the family's first meal on American soil. Louisa watched the people who milled around the area. There was so much to see—women with bundles balanced on their heads, Scotsmen in short white kilts, Cossack soldiers with dramatic mustaches and swords! Although Louisa could not identify all their nationalities, the native costumes both fascinated and frightened her. How would she ever feel at home in a place so filled with the unfamiliar?

Reunion

June 15-17, 1894

A few hours later a Pennsylvania Railroad official began rounding up the passengers who had purchased tickets on the 7:30 westbound train. Under his direction, the Shumakers took a ferry from Ellis Island to the railroad station. Soon *Mütti* and her three children boarded a train bound for St. Louis.

None of the four travelers had ever seen a train until their river trip in Germany. They found the thrill of beginning a journey down the tracks exhilarating! For the first hour Louisa and Henry stared out the window at the ever-changing scenery. Soon, however, the wonder began to fade. After eating a box dinner that *Mütti* had purchased on Ellis Island, Louisa pulled out her journal. Despite the jostling of the train, she managed to record a few impressions.

> *den 15. Juni 1894*
> *What a tremendous noise the train made as it pulled out of the station! I am amazed at how fast it moves. I'm almost frightened!*
> *How beautiful America is! (Of course, any land would look good after days and days of the ocean!) I still can hardly make myself believe this is my new country. I know so little about America. I wonder if I will ever really be able to call this place my home.*

As the train moved, the wheels thumped in steady rhythm. Had it not been for the constant jarring and the hard seats, the train's music might have lulled Louisa to sleep. As it was, she remained wakeful despite her longing for rest.

Soon Dorothy pulled her legs onto her seat, laid her head contentedly on *Mütti's* lap, and closed her eyes. Louisa grumbled, "If I had a soft cushion for my head, I'd be able to fall asleep too."

"Hush, Louisa," *Mütti* commanded. "She is so little and very tired. The rest of us are more able to endure the journey."

Louisa turned toward the window in silent sulkiness. Her eyes began to burn with tears that she refused to release. *Mütti's* rebuke and the fact that even Henry had voiced no complaint caused her to wish she had remained silent.

Gradually the scenery before Louisa's eyes began to fade into darkness. A dim reflection of her own worn face soon replaced the view of rural beauty that had previously been visible beyond the windowpane. Weak, unreliable lamps lit the car, causing the glass to mirror a blurred portrait. Perhaps that distortion intensified the weariness in her face, for Louisa barely recognized the girl in the window. She looked older than she had in Germany!

Somewhere between Jersey City and Philadelphia, Louisa finally fell asleep, but the train refused to allow her peaceful slumber. She awakened at every stop. The first time the car stood still, she moaned as she looked out the window into the pitch-black night. She saw no town, no station, no apparent reason for the halt. Fifteen minutes later an eastbound train came charging down the tracks beside them. The Shumakers' car began to sway uneasily in the wind created by the passing train. Above the rattle of the windows, Louisa heard a nearby German man explaining to his son, "We had to wait because that train was using some tracks up ahead that we will need to use. If we hadn't stopped, the two trains might have crashed." Louisa shuddered and inwardly resolved to accept future delays without ill humor.

In the early light of the next morning, the train pulled into the Pittsburgh station. The platform bustled with activity. Runners, seeking the travelers' dollars, paced in front of the depot, ready to greet passengers and direct them to nearby hotels and restaurants. Enterprising locals boarded the cars to hawk food and drink to the passengers. The prices were high, but *Mütti* bought a loaf of bread and some fruit. This made the best breakfast they had tasted since

their last day in Bremerhaven. By the time they finished, the train
was well on its way toward the next destination.

Now that morning had come, Louisa enjoyed the ride despite
the discomfort. "Traveling in a train across land is definitely better
than floating along on a boat in the middle of the ocean," Louisa
wrote early that morning. "There is so much to see! Forests and
fields, rivers and ponds." She rarely pulled her eyes away from the
windows. This new land was a place of endless variety, as different
in landscape as the origins of its citizens.

The Shumakers spent one more night on the train. Soon after
they awoke the next morning, a passenger called out, "There she
is, the fine old town of St. Louis!" Although the city name was all
that Louisa understood, that word alone spurred her to glance up
from her sewing for a sight of the city that she would call home.

As the train drew nearer, she had a good side view of the city.
How proud it looked with its chimneys and steeples! The entire
city stood upon the banks of the Mississippi River, and a large
white, domed courthouse rose above many of the surrounding
buildings.

Soon the train rattled onto Eads Bridge, giving Louisa a sight
of the river. Glorious paddle-wheel steamboats floated like serene,
white swans among a clutter of barges and workmen's boats.
Wagons and cargo crowded the wharf, awaiting transfer to various
vessels.

With gleaming eyes, Louisa turned to her mother. "It almost
looks like Bremen, *Mütti*! I'm so glad there's a river!" *Mütti* forced
a smile, but her daughter noted the despair that lurked in her
mother's eyes. When Louisa turned back to the city, she perceived
for the first time the faint gray cloud of smoke that hovered over
the city's brick buildings and the murky, tea-brown shade of the
muddy Mississippi.

Blackness suddenly cut short her observation. The train had
cleared the bridge and plunged into a tunnel. Here the passengers
received a rough welcome to Missouri as they were immersed in a
bath of choking smoke that penetrated even small cracks in the
car's doors and windows. Just when Louisa thought she could
breathe no longer, the train emerged from the tunnel. Despite the

smoky haze that Louisa had noticed from the bridge, the open air seemed bright and clear in comparison to the oppressive night of the tunnel.

The engine slowly chugged its way amidst the maze of tracks that threaded through the Mill Creek Valley and led to Union Depot. At last the Shumaker family's long journey to join *Papi* was near its end. As the train pulled into the station, Louisa's chest tightened, and her face tingled. "Will *Papi* be waiting for us?" she whispered hoarsely, forcing her throat to cooperate with her efforts at speech.

Mütti laid a comforting hand on Louisa's shoulder. "Yes, dear. Remember, I sent a telegram to him to say we would be coming today."

Louisa's eyes scanned the crowded platform. The people waiting for the Shumakers' train mixed with a crowd that had just emptied from another train. "How will we ever find *Papi?*" she wailed.

"He won't leave until he finds us," *Mütti* replied. "Don't worry."

Despite *Mütti's* reassurance, Louisa grew increasingly uneasy as immigrant women throughout the train wept for joy as they spotted their husbands.

"I don't see him," Henry said pensively, voicing the concern in Louisa's heart.

"He's here," *Mütti* insisted quietly. "He said he'd come. The platform is just so very crowded. Gather your things so we can get off."

The train squealed to a halt, and the Shumakers stumbled from the train. Once they reached the platform, Louisa held her head high, searching the crowd for *Papi*.

Mütti spotted him first.

"Jakob!" she cried, dropping all of her baggage as she flew to meet him. Louisa could see tears of joy in *Papi's* eyes as he reached for *Mütti* with eagerness and tenderly enfolded her in his arms. The children watched in silent relief as their parents stood close for several minutes, *Mütti's* face buried against *Papi's* strong shoulder, and *Papi's* eyes closed as though to fully relish the joy of the moment.

When their parents stepped apart, Henry and Louisa rushed forward to join in the reunion celebration. They snuggled into

Papi's arms as he reached forward to receive them. Laughter, squeals of delight, and emphatic declarations of "Oh, *Papi*, I am so glad to see you at last!" punctuated the air. Then a sudden gasp from *Mütti* drew *Papi*'s attention from Henry and Louisa and silenced the joyous reverie.

In an instant all eyes turned to a spot amidst the family's baggage where Dorothy stood alone and bewildered. She had observed the past moments in wide-eyed silence. Now she stared at *Papi* with an expression of mixed curiosity and fear.

"Dorothy, come to *Papi*," urged her father from where he had crouched. He held out his arms to her, but the little girl shook her head as she continued to regard him with a slanted gaze.

Mütti slipped her hand through *Papi*'s arm and drew him upward. "It is just as I feared," she whispered. "She was so young when you left, she doesn't know how to act."

Papi nodded. Together Dorothy's parents approached her and knelt to speak with her. After a few minutes of whispered conversation, Dorothy reluctantly allowed *Papi* to draw her to his side and kiss her smooth forehead. It would take longer for him to regain his smallest daughter's adoration. But thankfully, there was now plenty of time for that!

Papi suddenly shouted, "I almost forgot!" He glanced around until his eyes rested on a round box that sat on a nearby bench. "Just a minute!" he instructed, striding toward the spot. *Papi* grasped the box and returned to *Mütti*. "A gift for you," he announced.

"Oh, Jakob!" *Mütti* exclaimed. "You didn't have to bring anything but yourself!"

"All the same, I thought you'd like something to usher you into your new life," *Papi* replied. He beamed as *Mütti* undid the box ties and pulled out a simple but pleasing hat.

"Oh, it's beautiful! I've never had anything like it," *Mütti* exclaimed with a shy smile.

"This is the fashion in America," *Papi* declared. "I was sure you'd like it. Try it on."

Mütti hesitated and peered searchingly into her husband's eyes. "Right now?" she whispered.

"*Ja, ja,* of course," encouraged *Papi.*

The children stood in awkward silence as *Mütti* slowly untied her scarf, glancing around to be sure no one was observing her too closely. Louisa realized with surprise that she could not remember a time when *Mütti* had not worn a scarf tied about her head. Even now she scarcely saw the top of her mother's head, for with one motion *Mütti* pulled off her scarf and slipped on the hat. She slowly raised her eyes to meet her husband's gaze.

"You look lovely, Sophie," *Papi* said tenderly. "Don't you agree, children?"

"*Ja!*" exclaimed Louisa. "Just like the rich women on the ship!"

Mütti blushed, awkwardly fingering the rim of the hat. "It just feels a little odd, that's all," she laughed. "I've worn a scarf since I was Dorothy's age. This will take some getting used to."

"*Ja,*" remarked *Papi,* "all of America takes some getting used to!"

CHAPTER NINE

An Introduction to Home

Summer 1894

Papi loaded the heaviest burdens onto his shoulders and led his family out of Union Depot to Popular Street. They did not have to walk far to reach a pair of silver streetcar rails that traced a path through the center of the dusty street. At a nearby corner, the Shumakers joined a group that had gathered at one of the stops. "We'll wait here for the next car," *Papi* explained.

When the streetcar arrived, the reunited family managed to crowd on board along with everyone else. There were no seats left, so the Shumakers were forced to stand as the car bumped, swayed, and clattered down the street. If Louisa had not been crammed against other people, she felt certain she would have toppled to the floor.

It took longer than Louisa had expected to reach that special address they had written on so many letters during the past two years. After they had switched streetcars twice in order to travel down different streets, *Papi* finally announced they were nearly home. At the next stop the family followed *Papi* down the streetcar steps and along a dirt and gravel street. Just to the right of their path lay a gutter that had been fashioned from gray cobblestones.

As Louisa detoured around a pile of trash, she wrinkled her nose and peered suspiciously at the brick flats that rose two stories tall on either side of the street. She vainly searched for trees and plants. In near despair she wondered how *Oma's* flowers would ever bloom where hundreds of hooves and shoes had solidly packed the only visible earth! Even Bremen had been better.

Louisa had never dreamed she would live on a street that looked so miserable. Why would *Mütti* and *Papi* want their home to be in such a place? The entire town smelled sour. Even the breeze had a foul breath of coal smoke and rotting sewage, and each gust of wind stirred dust from the streets. The sooty air soiled everything with its filthy fingers, leaving both buildings and hanging laundry darkened. Louisa began to wonder if St. Louis would be a place of perpetual misery. Turning to look into *Mütti's* eyes, she realized that similar misgivings haunted her mother.

Only Henry seemed to be enjoying himself. "Look at all those wires!" he exclaimed, staring up at the web of streetcar electrical lines that were strung in the air. "I bet if you dropped a hanky from the roof of a building, it would get caught somewhere and never reach the ground!"

Louisa grimaced, grimly fearing she would never again see an open sky.

Papi stopped after walking halfway down the block. "Here we are!" he sang out. Louisa watched his smile fade as he looked at the sullen faces that surrounded him. Without another word he led them through the door of a two-story building. Inside they walked down a dark hallway past two doors.

"Where do those doors lead?" Henry ventured.

"There are four separate flats in this building," *Papi* answered. "A different family lives behind each door."

"Oh," replied Henry, his tone dull with disbelief.

A water faucet and basin jutted out from the wall near the bottom of the stairs. "That's where we get our water from," *Papi* explained as they walked up the steps. "The entire building shares the faucet."

On the second-story landing, two closed doors stood on opposite walls. Papi opened the one on the left, and the reunited Shumaker family stepped into their new home. Louisa was shocked to see that the first room resembled a wide hallway rather than a room! Beneath the one tiny window, a bed covered half of the floor space. Only a narrow path remained for walking. "I made all the furniture," *Papi* explained. "I had to make this bed a bit shorter than usual so it would fit between the two walls. It will suit you well, Henry. You will sleep here."

He led the way into a more spacious room. On one wall there was a window that, though larger than the one over Henry's bed, still provided inadequate lighting. *Papi* lit a kerosene lamp. A tin plate attached behind the small flame magnified the glow and lessened the room's gloomy dimness. An odd assortment of furniture lined the walls. On one side stood a dresser, a double bed, and a fireplace. "Louisa and Dorothy will sleep in this room," *Papi* explained. The opposite side had been fashioned into a kitchen complete with an ornate iron stove, cabinets with glass panes, and an icebox. Five chairs surrounded a large table, and two extra chairs stood nearby.

The final room lay in the front of the building. There the sunlight streamed through two windows in the far wall. The glints of light played against a rocker that stood by the window. The sparkle of this one corner warmed Louisa's heart. At last she beheld a sight that made her feel she was home! *Papi* had evidently taken extra care in the room he would share with his beloved wife. A bed, decorated with one of *Oma's* quilts, stood centered against the left wall. On the right side a mirror hung above a walnut dresser. A small alarm clock, positioned on a lace doily, sat on top of the dresser. "There aren't any roosters in this part of town," laughed *Papi*, "and the boss doesn't stand for lateness."

"Oh, Jakob," whispered *Mütti*. "The furniture is all beautiful. Thank you for working so hard to make everything."

"I worked every evening. I had nothing else to do since my family was not with me," he explained. "But now, how about some breakfast? I'm sure you didn't eat on the train this morning. After that, we'll spend the whole day together. How wonderful that you arrived on a Sunday—I don't have to work!"

The hungry children greeted *Papi's* mention of food with applause. He quickly produced a cold meal that Louisa rated as the most delicious she had ever tasted. She knew that since this favorable judgment resulted primarily from a comparison with the rations they had endured on their journey, her high praise may have been a bit unmerited, but she put that thought aside quickly. In truth, the taste of the food was largely unimportant to Louisa;

the reunion of her family would have turned the poorest fare into a feast! *Oma* had been right—nothing could have brought her more joy than being with *Papi* and having the family together again! No matter how bleak and dingy the strange world outside might appear, the space inside these walls bore *Papi's* familiar touch.

Later that night *Tante* Joanna and *Onkel* August visited the Shumakers. Louisa had only vague memories of her father's older brother and sister-in-law and felt shy when they arrived. *Mütti* had always said she liked *Tante* Joanna, and that night Louisa understood why. After greeting *Papi*, the kind lady immediately rushed to *Mütti's* side. "You must be so tired from your journey," she observed. "I don't know how you made it with all the children to watch and no one to care for you. I truly admire you. Thanks be to God that you were brought safely to us. Tell me, how is your mother doing?"

Mütti happily launched into a discussion about *Oma*. She apparently missed *Oma* more than Louisa had realized. Soon *Mütti* began relating the entire story of their journey. Louisa noticed *Papi* eavesdropping to catch parts of the story he had not yet heard.

Meanwhile, *Onkel* August addressed the children. "I like your new American names. I've kept my German name, but your aunt became Joanna the week we settled in St. Louis. We've been in this city so many years that it would seem strange to call her Johanna now!"

"Tell us about St. Louis," Henry suggested eagerly.

As *Onkel* August began to speak of fur traders and riverboat captains, Henry and Dorothy drew nearer. Louisa, however, was not impressed. *Mütti's* conversation about *Oma* had stirred up memories of her old home, and she quietly withdrew to her bed in the corner. Pulling her knees to her chest, she pensively watched the others.

Toward the end of the evening *Tante* Joanna rose and walked to where Louisa sat. "May I sit down?" she asked.

Louisa nodded indifferently.

"I remember well the day you were born, Louisa," *Tante* Joanna began as she seated herself. "It was such an exciting day. You were an absolutely beautiful baby, and everyone was so pleased. I don't think anyone, though, was quite as proud as your *Oma*. You were her first grandchild, you know."

"*Ja*. She often reminded me of that," replied Louisa, warming to both the topic and the speaker.

"I was excited too. Your uncle and I had wanted children for so long, but the Lord never chose to bless us in that way. Your mother often let me walk with you. How I treasured those times! I viewed those walks as the beginning of a relationship I would enjoy throughout my life. One of my regrets in leaving Germany was that I had to leave you, Louisa. I realize that you were too young to remember the moments we had together, but I am thrilled that I will have the opportunity to become reacquainted with you." *Tante* Joanna leaned forward and kissed Louisa on the forehead before rising and returning to the table. Louisa was relieved that her aunt expected no response, for she did not how to answer such sentiments.

By the time the visitors left, Louisa had decided that she hoped *Onkel* August and *Tante* Joanna would visit often. Rarely did adults allow children such an opportunity to talk as the Shumaker siblings had enjoyed that night.

At breakfast the morning after their arrival, Louisa said, "*Papi*, I'm so glad we found you yesterday. What if we hadn't recognized you?"

Papi laughed. "Have I changed that much?"

"No, but your beard is shorter," Louisa retorted.

"I would have found you, even if you had not seen me so quickly," *Papi* assured her with an amused twinkle in his eyes. "I could have used my nose to track you down!" he teased.

"What do you mean?" Henry asked with a curious wince.

"You all smell like the ship!" *Papi* exclaimed playfully. "When people live on a ship for over a week, they start to smell as rancid as the ship." *Mütti* shuddered as *Papi* continued, "It takes a lot of soap and scrubbing to get rid of the stench. Americans like to joke that they can pick out new immigrants because of that lingering odor."

Papi glanced at the clock as he finished speaking. "Well, I must be on my way," he declared. "Sophie, Joanna will be over later this morning to tell you all about washing the clothes. Keep the fire going in the stove so you can heat the water when she gets here. Henry, get the bucket in the corner and carry up enough water to fill both of the large washtubs. I warn you, it will take many trips, so the less you spill, the better!"

"*Ja, Papi*," replied Henry, grabbing the bucket and heading downstairs to the hall faucet.

"I should think doing a washing would be pretty much the same here as in Germany," *Mütti* observed. "That is, if you have all the necessary equipment," she added with a coy smile.

"Of course I do," *Papi* assured her. "But I think Joanna will be able to show you a few tricks that weren't necessary in our little village in Germany." *Mütti* raised her eyebrows at that statement but let the matter rest. *Papi* kissed her farewell and strode toward the door.

Louisa watched intently as he stopped, his hand still on the doorknob, and looked with surprise at the framed embroidery that adorned the wall. Early that morning Louisa had hung her prized work in a spot just opposite the threshold. "How beautiful!" he exclaimed. "Now where did this fine work of art come from?"

"I made it, *Papi*! *Oma* taught me," Louisa explained, her face flushed with joy at his praise.

"What a pleasant welcome that will be for me each evening when I come home!"

"*Ja!*" Louisa agreed. "And for everyone else who comes to visit."

"Of course," *Papi* affirmed with a smile. "I am sure we will have more visitors now that you are all here!" He turned the knob and swung wide the door. Calling "*Auf Wiedersehen!*" over his shoulder, he walked from the flat.

An hour later *Tante* Joanna arrived just as *Papi* had predicted. She had several bags with her from which she pulled an assortment of worn clothes. "You can all change into these so we can wash the clothes you're wearing," she explained. "I borrowed most of the clothes from our neighbors. I hope they fit!"

Before changing, *Mütti* walked over to Joanna with a distressed expression. "Surely, Joanna," she whispered, pointing to the washtubs Henry had filled an hour earlier, "this is not the water we must use?" Louisa knew why *Mütti* was concerned. The brown liquid hardly resembled the unclouded water they had drawn from the stream in Germany.

"I'm afraid it's the best St. Louis has to offer," Joanna insisted. "On the bright side, it's clearer today than it will be after a hard rain. A pelting downpour washes extra mud into the rivers, and then the water comes out of the faucet dirtier than ever."

"And this is what I am supposed to use for cooking and cleaning?" *Mütti* persisted. "If I wash the clothes in that, they will come out dirtier than when I began!" *Mütti* sank into a chair and brought her hands to her face.

"Sophie," comforted *Tante* Joanna as she strode to *Mütti's* side, "come, look at the water now. It is not as bad as it was when Henry first carried it in." She walked to one tub and scooped out a glassful of water. Only a little murkiness remained. "Jakob had Henry fetch the water an hour ago so the silt would have time to settle to the bottom. Now we'll just take the water from the top and leave the mud behind. Then we'll use a filter that Jakob bought last year, and it will clear the water even more. Now you go change clothes."

Mütti obeyed, walking to her room with an expression that remained fretful.

A few minutes later the family returned to *Tante* Joanna's side in their borrowed outfits. Although Henry had needed to roll up the ends of his trousers and Dorothy had to leave two of the buttons at her waist unfastened, they were adequately clothed for a day of indoor work. They added the clothes they had been wearing to a formidable laundry pile *Mütti* had begun building earlier that morning. Even the items that had been stored deep within their baggage needed cleaning!

Tante Joanna quickly assigned jobs. Louisa and Dorothy sorted the clothes, sheets, and blankets into whites and darks, while Henry and *Tante* Joanna poured the clarified water from one of the tubs into a copper boiler pan that sat on top the stove. Although the huge pan nearly covered the entire stovetop, it did not take long for all the water to begin boiling. *Mütti* then shaved lye soap into the dancing water and threw in the white clothes. She stirred them with a large wooden stick until they were completely wet.

Meanwhile, Louisa and Henry hauled the mud-lined tub downstairs to clean it in the back alley. By the time they returned, *Mütti* and *Tante* Joanna had transferred the water from the second tub Henry had filled to a third tub they had designated for rinsing. *Tante* Joanna instructed the children to set the clean tub by the stove. Using the wooden stick, she lifted the white clothes from the boiling water. As she hoisted the wet garments over the stove and dropped them into the tub, drops of water sprinkled onto the hot stove, causing bellows of steam. *Mütti* then poured an equal amount of hot and cold water in with the clothes and began to scrub each item across a washboard. As she finished, *Tante* Joanna took the clean items, plunged them into the rinsing water, wrung out the water, and piled them in a basket she had set on the floor.

When they completed the whites, it was time for the midday meal. After lunch, they began work on the dark clothes, which did not require boiling. "That's why we got the whites done first," *Tante* Joanna explained. "We'll want to stay as far away from the stove as possible now that the day's getting hotter!"

The flat was indeed getting stuffy! Louisa happily obeyed when *Tante* Joanna instructed her to help Henry clean the mud from the second tub. Dorothy joined them outside and cleaned the sludge from the water filter. What a relief to get outside! When they returned, *Tante* Joanna and *Mütti* had washed and rinsed all the dark clothes. Since they no longer needed the water, Henry and Louisa scooped it from the tubs, bucketful by bucketful, and dumped it out the side window.

It was nearly three o'clock when *Mütti* and *Tante* Joanna carried the clothes downstairs to the back alley where several clotheslines stretched between the buildings. They hung the clothes and undergarments on an inner line and shielded them from sight by draping the sheets and blankets on either side.

At last the washing was done! As they climbed the stairs, *Tante*

Joanne sighed. "I must be getting home. I've got supper to prepare and sewing to do." She glanced at *Mütti*. "Now, you'll be wanting work, won't you, Sophie?"

Mütti nodded wearily. "*Ja.* Jakob spent precious money on a sewing machine so I can do work at home. He said you would show me how to use it."

"Of course," *Tante* Joanna agreed, "although you'll still sew a lot by hand. I'll see if I can't find someone who needs an extra seamstress. Times are tough, but I know you are very skilled. I should think it will be no problem to find work for you, and Louisa will be able to help you as well."

"*Danke*," replied *Mütti*. "I would be grateful. It would be wonderful if there would be enough work for us both. I don't want Louisa working in a factory." Louisa listened carefully to this conversation. She knew that both she and Henry would have to work so the family would have an income sufficient to meet even their basic needs. How she hoped she would be able to stay with *Mütti*; the prospect of working among strangers was terrifying!

Louisa's face plainly displayed these emotions, and before *Tante* Joanna departed, she put an arm around Louisa. "Now don't you worry," she insisted. "The Lord knows your fears, and He will provide the right kind of work for you." Then, donning a smile, she turned to the others and quipped, "Now that you know how to unmuddy the water, you can fill a tub to clean yourselves!" With a wink, she whisked out the door.

"Baths tomorrow," *Mütti* declared after the door closed. "I've seen enough water for one day!"

That evening, after the family had gathered for dinner, there was an unexpected knock at the door. *Papi* answered the door but did not immediately admit the visitors. However, when the children recognized *Frau* Weiss's voice, they rushed to the door to greet their friends from the ship. How wonderful it was to see familiar faces in the doorway of their new home!

In the hour that followed, the Shumakers learned that the Weiss family had moved into a tenement house only a few blocks away. Their most exciting news was that *Herr* Weiss had already found work as a harness maker. Elsa and her mother planned to begin searching for employment later in the week.

The visit ended all too soon. Especially for Dorothy and Amalie, who had revived all their old games. At the door Elsa pulled a piece of paper from her pocket. "I've drawn a map for you!" she explained. "Now you and Dorothy can come visit us. There are no street signs on the roads in this city, but a woman who lives downstairs helped me out. She's been here so long that she knows all the street names even without signs!"

Louisa smiled her thanks. As Elsa and her parents started down the stairs, Dorothy called out, "We'll come to see you soon!"

Tante Joanna quickly found a seamstress eager to hire *Mütti*. From the day the first bundle of fabric arrived at the Shumaker flat, Louisa began to spend many hours sewing at *Mütti's* side. She was to be an apprentice of sorts, starting with simple work and advancing until she could match *Mütti's* skill in creating a dress without a pattern. "The skills that *Oma* taught you will be helpful," *Mütti* explained, "but you have a lot to learn about turning fabric into fine clothing."

The other part of Louisa's job was taking fabric and clothes to and from the shop. When *Mütti* had completed the first load of work, she tied up everything in a large sheet so delivery would be easier. Even so, Louisa could barely get her arms around the heavy bundle. As she walked out the front door, she grumbled to herself, "Why do I have to be the one to do this? Henry's stronger than I am!" This logic was flimsy, however, since Henry was busily engaged as an apprentice at *Onkel* August's watch shop.

When Louisa finally reached the seamstress's shop on that first day, her bundle bumped against a load carried by a little boy who was coming out the door. He braced himself with a step backwards and managed to maintain his footing. For a moment his drooping eyes solemnly regarded Louisa across the expanse of their bundles. Neither reproach nor warmth stirred in those eyes. Then, without a word, the boy stepped into the street, following what must have been a familiar route for him. No doubt his mother worked hard. How else could she sew enough garments to make such a load?

Louisa glanced down at her bundle; how small it looked compared to the boy's! The somber lad had silenced her inner grumbling.

During those sultry summer days, at least there was some time for play. One afternoon Louisa, urged by Dorothy's pleas, pulled out Elsa's map, and they went in search of their friends' home. The sisters found the building without difficulty. They only had to travel to the end of their block, turn left, walk to the end of that block, and turn right.

The Weisses' building stood five stories high. Narrow alleys ran along either side, separating the structure from the buildings that rose on the left and right. How different from Louisa's block where the two-story flats connected in one long, continuous row!

Louisa and Dorothy entered the building and climbed up the tall staircase they found just inside the door. The Weiss family lived on the third floor. When Louisa knocked at the correct entrance, her friend opened the door with flour-covered hands. "Oh, Louisa! I'm so glad you came!" Elsa exclaimed. "Amalie, guess who's here to see you!"

In instant response to that summons, the younger sister eagerly raced into the room and threw her arms around Dorothy. "Come here! You must see! It is so much fun!" she exclaimed breathlessly as she pulled Dorothy into a back room.

Louisa followed and screamed when Amalie, still leading Dorothy, stuck one foot out of an open window.

"Stop!" she cried, running forward. "You'll fall!"

"No, silly," corrected Elsa who had entered behind Louisa. "She won't fall because there's a fire escape there. Come on, I'll show you." Louisa and Elsa stepped through the window and crowded onto a platform with the younger girls. Above them, a gray blanket stretched across the steps overhead.

"So how do you like it?" Elsa asked.

"What is it?" Louisa asked.

"It's a tent. Look!" Elsa pointed down to an open lot behind the building. "Amalie likes to pretend this is her own house, but I like it because I can see everyone who walks by. A group of boys sometimes plays baseball down below, and it's fun to watch. Some days they argue more than they play," she remarked, rolling her eyes and shaking her head with knowing superiority. "You should come sometime when the little boys are playing blindman's buff. That's a really funny sight! I call out sometimes, and that really confuses the boy who is blindfolded because he has no idea that I'm not in the game! When my voice comes from the sky, he doesn't know which way to turn. Then I just laugh and laugh!"

Louisa and Dorothy were not able to stay long. Since it was late in the afternoon, they had to return home to help *Mütti* prepare dinner. As Louisa stepped out the door, Elsa suddenly exclaimed, "Oh, I almost forgot to tell you! I'm going to be taking an English class in the evenings. *Papi* says it's important for me to learn this country's language. Would you like to go along?"

This question marked the first time Louisa was genuinely interested in what Elsa had to say. She certainly did want to learn English, and she knew Henry would share her eagerness. They had both already realized that although the older generation was largely content to remain immersed in their German community, most immigrant youths wanted to quickly become part of American society.

An hour later as Louisa peeled potatoes, she mentioned the class to *Mütti*. "It would be helpful if I could speak English," she observed. "Someday I may have to work among people who don't know German."

"Of course you are right," *Mütti* readily agreed. "*Papi* and I have already discussed this. You and Henry must start as soon as possible." A week later the brother and sister attended their first class.

One special evening *Mütti* and Louisa prepared a picnic dinner. Just before mealtime *Mütti* and the children traveled on the streetcar to a local *Biergarten* where *Papi* was scheduled to play his horn with a band. Louisa could hardly contain her excitement when they reached their destination. There were magnificent trees everywhere, and even a fountain! This was the first green, peaceful place she had entered since her arrival in St. Louis. A crowd had gathered to escape the heat of the city's buildings and sat at round tables near the bandstand. *Mütti*, however, chose a place on the soft grass away from the tables. There they spread a blanket and ate their meager fare while enjoying the music. At times the wind blew them a taunting whiff of the food that covered the tables of those wealthy enough to purchase a prepared meal. Louisa dared not mention how she longed for just a taste of whatever smelled so delicious. She knew they had all worked hard to earn the money that had purchased their picnic meal.

After dinner Henry and Louisa walked to a huge wooden flower bucket near the bandstand. From that spot Louisa watched *Papi* as he joined in the festive music. She was convinced she could pick out his instrument from among the others. Certainly it sounded the sweetest of them all!

As summer's reluctant darkness fell, ropes of lights twinkled above the round tables where ladies and gentlemen lingered to relish the gaiety of friends. Soon the band played their final number, and *Papi* came down to meet his son and eldest daughter. He handed his horn to Henry and accompanied them back to the family's picnic spot.

Louisa helped *Mütti* fold the quilt. As they moved together to double over the blanket and then apart again to stretch the remaining length, their movements reminded Louisa of a dance she had observed earlier in the evening. Festive fun filled this place. How Louisa wished life offered more carefree moments like the ones enjoyed under those lantern-lit trees!

Soon they had packed everything away, and the sleepy-eyed family headed to the streetcar stop. "Do you know what these late streetcars are called?" *Papi* asked as they waited.

"What, *Papi?*" Louisa inquired in return.

"Owl cars," Papi replied.

"That's because only owls are awake at such a late hour," said *Mütti* with a yawn. "I'm afraid we'll all want to sleep all day tomorrow, but unfortunately we will not be allowed to be like owls when the sun rises!"

CHAPTER TEN

~

The Chill of Winter

Fall—Winter 1894—1895

As the sun continued its southward march in September, pleasant days intermingled with the sweltering ones. The Shumakers, who were unaccustomed to the St. Louis heat, welcomed this relief.

The altered weather, however, brought a challenging change for Dorothy. Early one morning Louisa escorted her sister and Amalie Weiss to their new school. There they discovered a community resembling the one that had slept in the steerage hold on the ocean liner. Children of German, Irish, Russian, Polish, and Austrian immigrants daily shared dreams of education carrying them to wealth and success. These youths quickly learned the language of their adopted country and readily used it to form alliances, often with children of other nationalities. Amalie jumped into the scene with enthusiastic joy, while Dorothy hung back in trepidation.

When Louisa left the two girls in a class formed to teach English quickly to the newest immigrants, she saw tears in Dorothy's eyes. It was not until winter with its icy fingers had settled among the inhabitants of St. Louis that Dorothy declared she liked school. This announcement provided a welcome reason for rejoicing in the midst of a difficult season.

As the cold weeks went by, the fire remained stoked in the Shumakers' central room in spite of the meager money supply. *Papi* often rose during the night to feed the fire's insatiable appetite. Even so, the air remained chilly.

In the bed that Louisa and Dorothy shared, the cold intensified a long-standing battle. Despite Dorothy's small frame, she
always took up more than half the bed space. This was because of
her maddening habit of curling her knees toward her face while
thrusting her back far onto Louisa's side of the bed. Moreover,
Dorothy tightly clutched all the blankets, pulling them about herself like a cocoon. This habit created an unsealed gap between the
blanket's edge and Louisa's side of the mattress. Each morning
before dawn a cold draft forced Louisa awake. Even a vicious tug at
the blankets would fail to release Dorothy's grasp, and she would
stubbornly refuse to stir if Louisa shook her. As the nights grew
colder and the frost spread further across the window with each
passing morning, the offense grew more exasperating.

"*Mütti*, my toes are going to freeze off!" Louisa complained one
morning. "Dorothy pulls the covers completely off me! I could wear
every piece of clothing I own and I would still get cold. Please make
her stop!"

"Louisa, I cannot punish Dorothy for something she is doing
in her sleep" *Mütti* replied. "Since she isn't aware of her actions, I
can't make her stop. What I can do is give you a blanket that is all
your own. You can wrap it around yourself so Dorothy cannot get
at it. Will that solve the problem?"

"*Ja, Mütti*," Louisa agreed, satisfied both with her own bar-
gaining ability and *Mütti's* suggestion.

When *Mütti* came home from work that night, she carried a
midnight blue wool blanket with her. Louisa hummed with delight
as she held out her arms to accept the wonderful gift.

"There you are, dear," *Mütti* sighed. "I hope your nights will be
warmer now."

That evening after family prayers, Louisa snuggled beneath her
new blanket. *Mütti* sat on the bed and passed a chilly hand across
her daughter's forehead. "Sleep well, dear."

"Oh, I will, *Mütti*!" Louisa exclaimed. "I won't be cold
anymore."

"I hope not, Louisa," *Mütti* answered with a tired smile.

Dorothy, who slept against the wall, scooted to the foot of the bed for her good-night kiss. "I love you, *Mütti!*" she chirped.

"I love you too, dear. Sweet dreams!"

As the girls snuggled beneath their blankets, *Mütti* returned to the table. It was not long before Louisa heard the familiar sound of wooden legs being dragged across the floor. She smiled. Every night *Mütti* and *Papi* talked at the table after the children had gone to bed. Louisa loved being lulled to sleep by the music of their whispers. *Papi's* deep, peaceful voice sounded reassuringly strong and safe, and *Mütti's* speech had a musical cadence that reminded Louisa of laughter.

Louisa rolled over so she faced the table. She opened her eyes ever so slightly, not wanting anyone to see that she was watching. From this position she could see *Papi's* arm around *Mütti* and her brunette head resting on his shoulder. What peace enveloped Louisa's heart at the sight! The months she had spent in America had not lessened the joy of seeing *Papi* and *Mütti* reunited.

Louisa strained her ears to hear what passed between them. Would *Papi* praise her for the kindness she had shown Henry that morning? Would *Mütti* comment on the fine stitching she had done on the blue dress? She longed for such words.

But instead of the hoped-for joy, Louisa's eavesdropping brought her sadness. For the first words she caught came from *Papi* were, "How much did the blanket cost, Sophie?"

Louisa could not hear the amount, but she recognized discouragement in her mother's voice as she explained, "Jakob, she was so cold. I can't blame her for complaining. Dorothy does take all the covers."

"But we have so little left, Sophie," *Papi* argued tersely.

"I've heard about some families taking in boarders—" *Mütti* began.

"No!" interrupted *Papi*, struggling to keep his voice low. "I don't want strangers sleeping in our home. Anyway, we don't have room."

"I know," murmured *Mütti* weakly. "It was just an idea. We have to come up with something."

Father sat quietly. He slumped forward, his elbows resting on the top of the table. *Mütti* watched in tense silence as he clasped his hands behind his neck and remained still for several minutes. Louisa, now staring with unrestrained wide eyes, had never seen her father so discouraged.

When *Papi* lifted his head from the table, his anger had faded. "Forgive me, Sophie," he pleaded. "I was wrong to talk to you so harshly."

"Of course you are forgiven," *Mütti* murmured.

"Our home is the one place in America where no one is foreign to us. We need it to stay that way. Besides, I would not feel safe having a stranger living among us. You will get some sewing money tomorrow, and we will just have to make it last. You did what you had to do. We'll just have to sacrifice somewhere else. I will wait until next month to buy a new hat."

Louisa's heart sank when she heard those words. *Papi* had talked for a month about the hat he was going to buy. He had even pointed one out to them in a store window. He definitely needed a new hat; the brim on the old one had almost completely separated from the top. *Mütti* had sewn it back into place several times, but the worn leather tore easily, and her efforts produced only temporary results. Louisa wanted to rush to *Papi* and give him back the blanket. If only that would fix things! But it would not. And besides, she could not let them know she had been eavesdropping.

"Things are harder here than we thought they would be, aren't they, Jakob?" *Mütti* asked.

"*Ja*. We heard such wonderful things from all the people who came here before us. Besides, when I arrived, things *were* better. We could not have known that the country would be hit by this terrible economic panic."

"You, unlike some, wrote honest letters, Jakob. I knew what to expect. Remember how people in our village carried letters in their pockets for days so they could show the entire town how wonderfully their relatives were getting along in America? I wonder how many women cried real tears as they wrote those false rejoicings. Most letters were too rosy to be true. We should have realized that. No doubt the writers didn't want people in the village to laugh at them for having left home only to find themselves living a harder life."

"We can't blame others for writing good things," *Papi* responded. "I know your letters to your mother contain reports of how well we are all doing. You would not write anything to make her worry."

"*Ja*, Jakob, you are right," *Mütti* agreed wearily. "I need to write again soon, and of course I will send sweet tidings."

"Don't worry yourself about writing tonight, Sophie," *Papi* whispered. "You need to get some sleep. I will write the letter, and I will tell her about all the blessings we have experienced and how the Lord has certainly protected us from tragedy. When I think back to how lonely I was before you all came, I can hardly allow myself to complain today."

"Yes, dear," *Mütti* murmured, resting her head against her husband's shoulder for a moment before heading to bed.

Papi pushed himself up from his chair. Walking over to a cabinet, he pulled out a sheet of paper and a pen. He returned to the lantern-lit table to write the promised letter. As he began, Louisa drifted off to sleep.

Mütti employed every tactic she knew in her effort to spend as little as possible on food. She poured old milk into a bowl and left it on the table until it thickened and yellowed into curdled milk. Sometimes, as a special treat, the children were allowed to eat it with sugar sprinkled on top. More often than not, however, *Mütti* used the sour milk to make smear cheese, cottage cheese as the Americans called it. She accomplished this by placing the clabbered milk in a muslin bag that she hung over a pan. There it would stay, dripping steadily for several days. At last the excess moisture would be gone, and a smooth cheese would remain. The family smeared this on slices of homemade brown bread. *Mütti* also made headcheese, an entirely different food that took advantage of the low price the grocer charged for a cow's head. *Mütti* covered the seasoned meat with water and let it simmer on the stove for several hours. A thick stock resulted, which she poured into pans containing pieces of the cooked meat. Once the mixture had gelled, slices of the headcheese were served on bread.

This frugal cooking did not save enough, however, and soon *Mütti* began to work at a shoe factory during the day. She had been a respected cobbler in the old country. People had walked miles in worn shoes to purchase new comfort stitched by her hands. But her new job was vastly different. In the factory she performed a routine job for unknown consumers. Her work provided money for her family but no joy for herself.

Louisa worried about *Mütti* and voiced her concerns in her journal one evening.

December 12, 1894

Mütti now works at a factory. I wish she could stay at home all day because now she is so tired. Also, now I must do all the house-work and much of the work for the seamstress. I even help Mütti sew at night. I know Mütti must work. I heard Papi say one night that if she didn't have this job, Dorothy would have to go to work illegally like so many children that we know. Mütti and Papi would never allow that. We know little children who hide under tables or bundles of clothes when the inspectors come so they won't get caught. It's not right for little ones to work in the factories!

I also realize that Mütti is working in the factory so I don't have to. I am old enough to work, but Mütti will not even listen to the mention of that possibility. She says it would be cruelty to send me into such a situation—and yet she goes herself. I am thankful, but sad that she must make such a sacrifice.

The man who lives below us is very mean. At night after we have all gone to bed, I can hear him yelling at his wife. Right by our bed there is a register covering a vent. Papi says that this opening allows warm air from the room below to escape into our room (though our room still doesn't feel very warm). The problem is that it also lets noise up and stray coins down! I lost a penny the other day when it rolled to the register, fell through, and landed on the floor beneath us. Of course, I was too embarrassed to go and ask for it, and the people who live there never returned it.

Mütti bought an old, ragged woman's coat from the seamstress and cut it up to make a beautiful winter coat for me. Now Dorothy will wear my old coat that Oma made for me. How I miss Oma!

Oh, yes! I have some exciting news. Mütti told us yesterday

that a new baby will be coming in the spring! She explained that this
is part of the reason she is so tired. I hope it's a girl!

As winter wore on, *Mütti* weakened because of the extra burden
of carrying a child within her. By February she mentioned to
Papi that standing all day at the factory exhausted her. The next
evening *Papi* came home later than usual. He had remained at
the carpentry shop after closing time so he could build a stool
for *Mütti*. The next morning he and the stool accompanied
Mütti to work where *Papi* easily persuaded the sympathetic man-
ager to allow his worker to sit down. At last *Mütti's* legs were
able to rest.

Despite this partial relief, the factory work still took a toll. Her
ears had to endure the strain of relentless noise. She told Louisa
one night that she could feel the baby kicking within her more
often at work than at other times. "It is almost as though the baby
can hear the noise too," *Mütti* remarked with awe.

The worst torment of all, however, *Mütti* bore almost without
comment. Only to *Papi* did she whisper of the insult under which
her spirit strained. One night as Louisa listened from bed, *Mütti*
told of a sign that hung in the factory. "It is right in front of me,
Jakob, so that I must look at it day after day. At first I did not know
what it said because it is in English. Then a woman who sits next
to me told me. Now every time I see the sign, I am haunted by its
message. It says I am to ignore all my previous experience and per-
form only exactly what I have been told to do. It does not matter
if I know of a better way to stitch a shoe—it must be done the company's way! My skill is worth absolutely nothing! Worst of all, I
never have the satisfaction of meeting my customers and seeing
them pleased by my work."

"That is hard," sympathized *Papi*. "I often feel the same way at
my job. I rarely see the people who order the furniture I build. I
know I could make pieces that would suit customers better if I
could meet them, if I could get to know what style they really like.
I also never get to see my furniture in a home. It never looks as good
in the shop as it does in a decorated room, so I never really know
the quality of what I have created."

NEVER FORSAKEN

"I just wish things were different," *Mütti* moaned, tears flowing down her cheeks.

"But at least," *Papi* said, "you can still be creative with your sewing. The seamstress often praises your work, and I am sure you have made many people happy with the clothes you have produced." *Mütti* continued to cry softly. "Dearest Sophie," *Papi* murmured, "we cannot become discouraged. You must be brave. The Lord will take care of us, and it is His praise alone that we must seek."

CHAPTER ELEVEN

Sixth and Locust

Late February 1895

One grim and drizzly Saturday in February, *Mütti* took Dorothy and Louisa to a department store on the corner of Sixth Street and Locust. The day before, *Mütti* had pulled the family's summer clothes from a storage trunk and had quickly discovered that Dorothy did not fit into her old dresses. "Well, it's time for you to design and sew your first dress from beginning to end," *Mütti* had declared to Louisa. "Tomorrow we will go to the store to do some research." This prospect had excited Louisa. She had never entered one of the city's large department stores since the family could not afford anything sold within their walls.

When the trio stepped through the store doors, Louisa gawked at the beautiful decorations and merchandise. She would have happily spent an hour wandering aimlessly around the glass display counters. *Mütti*, however, marched straight to the area where children's clothes were sold. Dorothy immediately pointed at a pale yellow, checkered dress with a white collar and cuffs. "Look, *Mütti*," she whispered, walking toward it with obvious longing.

Mütti picked up the dress and examined its details. She ran a finger along the seams, then shook it inside out. After a careful examination of the pleats, *Mütti* motioned Louisa to her side. "I want you to look over every inch of this dress. Notice the way it is cut, remember where the pleats are placed, and determine how much fabric the sleeves and skirt will require. Create a pattern in your head."

Louisa looked at her in bewilderment. "How can I possibly remember all that?"

"Think of other dresses you have made with me. Compare this one to those," Mütti suggested. "I promise to help you, but I want you to remember as much as possible on your own." Louisa looked at the dress for ten minutes and then returned it, right side out, to its hanger. With a nod, Mütti took Dorothy's hand and began to walk away. A few feet from the dress she stopped, looked back studiously, and then left the department store with empty hands.

On the way home Mütti stopped at another store where bolts of wonderful fabric were stacked on shelves that reached to the ceiling. "Now, Louisa," began Mütti, "do you see any fabric that you like?"

"Shouldn't Dorothy choose?" Louisa suggested. "The dress is for her, after all."

"I'm glad to hear my daughter considering her sister's desires, but this time the choice is yours. We are going to buy enough fabric for you to make yourself a dress too. We will save money by doing both dresses out of the same material."

"Oh, thank you, Mütti," Louisa exclaimed. "I would love a new dress, even though my old ones still fit."

"I've noticed that they're a bit ragged," Mütti replied. "A young lady needs at least one dress she can feel beautiful in."

Louisa's eyes gleamed as she picked out a deep blue print. Never before had she worn a dress that she truly liked; now the perfect design formed in her mind. She was confident that with Mütti's help she could turn that lovely fabric into the dress she'd imagined. Moreover, with such a pleasant reward in sight, sewing Dorothy's dress suddenly seemed less overwhelming.

The only time Louisa's apprehension completely returned was when she began to cut the fabric. This step seemed so final; if she made a mistake, they would not have enough material. And Louisa knew they did not have enough money to purchase more. To her relief, Mütti oversaw the entire process, affirming most of Louisa's decisions and suggesting alterations to a few curves. When she began sewing, Louisa was thrilled to see the garments taking the desired shape. Nearly a week later, as Dorothy and she donned their new dresses, Louisa felt increased confidence in her ability as a seamstress. These homemade outfits possessed greater durability than those available at the store, and to Louisa's delight, none of the beauty had been sacrificed.

The Shumaker children had little time for amusement. Many of the household chores and errands were their responsibility since *Mütti* and *Papi* spent long days at work. Louisa and Dorothy did the cooking and much of the cleaning. Henry visited the grocery daily, carried water, scraped ashes from the stove, and kept the fire supplied with fuel. One afternoon when Louisa returned home with a load of sewing, she found Dorothy sweeping the floor with a fretful expression. Since she was alone and Henry's chores were obviously undone, Louisa immediately guessed the reason for Dorothy's agitation.

"Did Henry pick you up from school today?" Louisa questioned.

"Yes."

"Where is he now?"

"He said he had to meet some friends. He said he'd be back before you got home."

"I'm sure he hoped he would, but . . ." Louisa muttered. "Wait until *Mütti* hears about this!" Determined not to neglect her own work, she marched to her parents' room, sat down in the rocker by the open window, and began to sew.

It was a beautiful day, and Louisa could not keep herself from glancing out the window every so often to smile at the sun. Once when she looked down at a passing wagon, she sighted Henry darting into an alley on the other side of the street. He dodged behind a discarded crate, and a moment later Louisa saw two heads pop up from behind the makeshift shield. Beside Henry crouched Charlie, Henry's frequent partner in mischief. Both boys were staring at the street with ill-contained anticipation. What held their attention? Louisa wondered. She saw nothing more than the usual passing wagons and pedestrians. "Surely they're up to something," Louisa muttered.

As her eyes searched the street below, a wagoner suddenly

pulled back hard on his reins. As the creatures instantly obeyed, he jumped from his seat and dashed toward a wallet lying in the street.

Just as the man stooped down to clasp the wallet, Henry hollered, "Hocus-pocus, Sixth and Locust!" To Louisa's amazement, the wallet leapt to life and began to race down the alley. As the stunned wagoner stared after it, Louisa caught sight of Henry and Charlie racing around the corner at the back of the alley with the wallet following them!

"It's attached to a string!" Louisa exclaimed.

It took the angry wagoner only a moment to realize he had been duped. With obvious anger and little thought for his impatient horses, he stomped down the alley after the boys. "I hope Henry gets his due," muttered Louisa, knowing full well that the pranksters had escaped into the maze of alleys and small buildings that occupied the inner core of the block.

The wagoner did not pursue for long. As he raced after the pranksters, he wisely threw a quick glance over his shoulder and beheld a worse calamity. Two smaller boys, one of them Charlie's brother, had heckled his team until they began to dash down the street. In a fury the man spun around and raced toward his wagon. The boys scattered, and the tired horses came to a disinterested halt at the end of the block. The wagoner swung up into the seat and coaxed his team onward. No doubt his employer expected the load to arrive before nightfall.

For Louisa, however, the matter had not ended. She knew Henry would soon be climbing the stairs to start his chores. When she heard his laughter in the stairway a few minutes later, she bristled with anger and strode to the door. "How dare you act so foolishly?" she demanded, her eyes menacing. "Don't you know what *Mütti* and *Papi* would say if they had seen you? To tease that man when you should have been up here with Dorothy! And to shout out 'Hocus-pocus, Sixth and Locust'! Why . . ."

"You're being ridiculous! Those are just street names, Louisa!" he protested with a grimace as he placed a bucket of water near the stove.

"Not the first part," she shot back. "You know we don't believe in magic or superstition."

"And I suppose you're going to tell *Mütti* and *Papi* everything!" Henry snarled.

"Of course!" snipped Louisa.

"I doubt that," mocked Henry. "If you tell them about me, I will have to tell Charlie that you keep looking out the window just to catch a sight of him." Henry donned a smirking smile and blinked mockingly.

"I do not!"

"You were watching just now!"

"But you know I can't stand him!" shrieked Louisa.

Henry shrugged his shoulders, "Oh, I don't know. Maybe you're just faking that you don't like him, hmmm?" he taunted. Henry sauntered from the room, knowing he had effectively silenced his sister.

"How can you be so mean!" Louisa growled. She despised the injustice of his victory! Louisa ran to the kitchen where she began violently scrubbing potatoes while her tears plunked into the water basin. If *Mütti* had realized how clean those potatoes were that night, her praise would have been high.

CHAPTER TWELVE

Oma's Namesake

March—May 1895

By March St. Louis had claimed Henry and Dorothy's hometown allegiance. Even Louisa grudgingly admitted that she liked some things about America and did not feel quite as much like a foreigner as she had at first. The combination of English classes and daily conversations with friends and store clerks had enabled all three Shumaker children to master simple conversation in their new tongue. Dorothy had even thrown off any telltale traces of an accent that might have distinguished her speech from that of someone born in America. The family still spoke German, but only when *Mütti* and *Papi* were home. The flexibility of youth had allowed the children to embrace the new country much more readily than their parents did. Henry treated memories of the old country with scorn, and all Louisa's thoughts of Germany were thoughts of *Oma*.

A letter that arrived at the end of the month brought a smile to Louisa's lips the moment she saw it. The stamps were German, and the handwriting was definitely that of *Tante* Anna, *Mütti's* sister. When *Papi* arrived home that night, he disappointed Louisa by insisting that they wait and allow *Mütti* to open the letter. Louisa felt she couldn't contain her anticipation another instant! At last *Mütti* arrived home and tore open the letter with an eagerness that matched her daughter's. Louisa watched as her mother's eyes raced back and forth across the page until tears slowed their motion. *Mütti's* face turned ashen, and she dropped into the chair that stood nearby. Her arm fell to her lap, and a moment later she allowed both paper and envelope to flutter to the floor.

Louisa cautiously bent forward to pick up the letter. When she did not detect any protest from *Mütti*, she lifted the letter and began to read.

den 17. *Februar* 1895

Liebe Sophie!

 Mother has died. She breathed her last on February 10. This winter was harsh, and I think the cold and the constant wind were too much for her tired frame. She had been sickly during the months since your departure. We are weeping for her still, though it has been nearly a week now since her passing. Forgive me, Sophie, for not writing you immediately. My sorrow was too great, and I could not pen the words. We buried her next to Father. For me, it is as though joy itself has now left this village. Every house and tree holds a memory of Mother or Father or you, dear sister. Now only I am left. Johann will not leave the farm now, and I think it unlikely that he will ever want to come to America. I miss you so!

Deine,
Anna

By the time Louisa came to the last few sentences, she was reading through a blurry film of tears. When she looked up, she saw that *Papi* had moved to comfort his wife.

"It's spring," *Mütti* mourned. "Mother always loved this time of year—when everything comes to life again. How sad that she should die just before the coming of spring!"

Papi held her close, "Sophie, we must remember that she is now enjoying a far greater beginning than any springtime on earth." He paused, evidently measuring the effect of his words. When her choked agreement came, he continued, "Now the joy of heaven, which she has spent a lifetime anticipating, has begun." *Mütti* nodded, her head rubbing against his shoulder and her tears streaking his blue shirt. *Papi* encircled her with his arms and murmured, "Go ahead and cry, my love. Our loss is great."

That day St. Louis became Louisa's one and only home. All desire for Germany died with the passing of the dear old lady. Louisa's attachment to America grew even stronger a month later when Matilda Shumaker entered the world on May 28. At Louisa's suggestion *Mütti* and *Papi* chose to give their new daughter an American version of *Oma*'s name.

Henry, however, also had something to say about his baby sister's name. As soon as he saw her, he exclaimed, "She doesn't look like a Matilda to me; I'm going to call her Maddie. That sounds more like a little girl's name!" Everyone soon agreed that the name Maddie perfectly suited the alert newcomer.

In Louisa's eyes, Maddie was the most beautiful child ever born. The adoration Louisa felt for her grandmother, she now lavished upon *Oma*'s namesake. Louisa vowed that her little sister would grow up knowing her true name and hearing stories about *Oma*.

This commitment reminded Louisa of a neglected task. One afternoon she stopped at the hardware store on her way home from school. With a few coins *Papi* had given her, she purchased three pots and a small supply of soil. An hour later she stood at home, surveying a finished work. The pots were set in a row on a shelf beneath the window in the main room. Safely planted within each were some of the seeds *Oma* had entrusted to her granddaughter's care.

Louisa had forgotten how quickly seedlings begin to search for sunlight. When she first saw the green sprouts lifting their heads from the soil several days later, tears welled in her eyes. *Oma*'s seeds were thriving in this new land. With surprise, Louisa realized that just as *Oma* had foretold, she too was now firmly planted in America.

PART TWO

CHAPTER THIRTEEN

An Unwelcome Visitor

Early April 1896

The year between May of 1895 and April of 1896 rolled by uneventfully for the Shumakers. Although they continued to suffer the effects of a nationwide depression, their continued joy at being reunited more than made up for their lack of possessions.

On April 17, 1896, Louisa became a young lady of nineteen. Her appearance had undergone drastic changes since her arrival in America. A full skirt swished below her ankles in ladylike fashion, and her hair twisted upward into a bun instead of downward in pigtails. She enjoyed these new trappings of womanhood, but at times she cast wistful glances back to the carefree, frolicking days of childhood that had so quickly slipped behind her.

Louisa peered in the mirror on her birthday evening. The night before, *Papi* had told her that she was growing more like *Mütti* every day. Was that true? It did not occur to her to search for ways she mirrored *Mütti's* inner beauty; her desire for a beautiful face filled her thoughts. Sometimes she glimpsed a shadow of *Mütti's* features in her own, but no strong resemblance was apparent.

A voice interrupted her thoughts. "Louisa, please help Maddie wash her hands for dinner," *Mütti* called from the door. Henry had just returned home with their littlest sister, who spent her days with *Tante* Joanna. Retrieving Maddie was generally Louisa's responsibility, but as a birthday treat Henry had offered to go in her place that afternoon. Quite a gift, considering the numerous chores that Henry had himself!

Louisa glanced toward *Mütti*. "*Ja, Mütti*, I'm coming." When *Mütti* returned to the kitchen, Louisa thought to herself, *Why haven't I noticed how much older Mütti looks than she did a few months ago? She looks tired, and the color is gone from her cheeks!*

Louisa pushed aside such harrowing reflections. "It must be because of the baby she is expecting in October," she whispered, arguing with her misgivings. She had to admit, however, that *Mütti* had not looked so pale and weak when she was carrying Maddie. Nor had she paused halfway up the stairs to catch her breath as she now did each evening.

I must ask Dorothy to wait outside on the doorstep for Mütti when she comes home, Louisa reflected as she headed toward the kitchen. *She can help Mütti carry any packages up the stairs.*

The next evening when Louisa explained her plan to Dorothy, the eight-year-old girl solemnly agreed. *Even Dorothy has noticed Mütti's weakness!* Louisa reflected, her own strength draining at the thought.

By the time Dorothy ushered *Mütti* into their home that evening, Louisa had supper waiting on the stove. One task at a time, Louisa had learned how to manage the household and had won quiet murmurs of approval from her weary mother. *Mütti* was gently passing to her eldest daughter all her knowledge, from practical cleaning techniques to principles for training Maddie in obedience. What a blessing *Mütti's* foresight would later prove to be!

A few evenings later, a gray-haired woman came to call after *Mütti* had returned home. Although Louisa recognized the lady as the grocer's wife, she noticed that *Mütti* seemed reluctant to invite her to enter. "Good evening," greeted *Mütti* softly.

"Good evening, Sophie," replied the woman. "I've noticed you recently when you've walked by my husband's store. You're tired and worn-out. I thought maybe I could be of some help."

"No, this is just a spell I will have to go through," stated *Mütti* calmly.

"Oh, you are expecting a child then?" asked the woman with an apparently insincere innocence.

"*Ja,*" replied *Mütti* shortly.

"But you are not well. That I have seen for myself. This is not the normal weariness that a child brings. You must take care of yourself or you may risk death."

"I *am* taking care of myself," Mütti answered. "And now, if you will please state your business in coming here . . . I don't believe we have built up enough of an acquaintance to merit a social call from you." The curtness in Mütti's voice startled Louisa.

"I was just wondering . . . Might I provide you with some medicine that would take care of your problem?" wheedled the woman.

"How dare you . . . It is just as I thought!" Mütti declared with vehemence. "I do not have a *problem*. I have a child whom I love! Now I think it is time for you to leave."

Mütti strode to the door with remarkable energy and lifted the latch. With a resolute motion, she silenced the protest evidently rising in their visitor's throat. "Please leave us," Mütti demanded. Given no other choice, the woman wobbled out the door.

As soon as the door had shut and the woman's footsteps sounded from the stairwell, Mütti sank onto Henry's bed. All show of vigor disappeared, and Mütti's face once again became pale. Louisa rushed to her side and nestled against her.

"Why didn't you buy the medicine, Mütti?" she questioned. "Is it because we don't have the money? If it would make you better, I'm sure *Papi* would pay any price. Please get the medicine," Louisa pleaded.

"Hush, my dear," Mütti whispered. "You don't understand. What she offered me was not medicine." She stopped for a moment, and Louisa sensed that she was pondering whether to continue. At last she sighed and explained, "Louisa, she wanted to sell me a drug that would kill the baby that is within me. It is true that I might be healthier if I were not carrying a child, but it is not my place to decide that this baby should not live. God has given me . . . He has given our family this little one, and it is my job to bring this baby into the world no matter what sacrifice is required of me."

"But, Mütti," cried Louisa, lifting a tearstained face toward her mother, "you might die! What would we do without you?"

"Louisa, dear," Mütti replied as she stroked her daughter's face, "we are in the hands of a wise and loving God. The Bible says, 'There is a time for everything—a time to be born and a time to die.' It may be that when the time comes for this child to be born, it will be my time to die. If that is God's will, then I am ready. And you, my dear, must be ready too. You must be brave, no matter what happens."

Louisa could not promise courage. Her mind was confused and fearful. Her idle worry about *Mütti's* weariness had been confirmed by the harsh truth that death might be near. Louisa tried to push that possibility far from her mind's reach but found that to be impossible.

Mother and daughter sat together in silence. Louisa cried, and *Mütti* comforted. Burying her face against her mother's shoulder, Louisa wondered how *Mütti* could be so calm as she spoke of death. Then, as she brushed the back of her hand across *Mütti's* neck, she felt the wetness of the tears rolling down her mother's cheeks.

CHAPTER FOURTEEN

Greenhouses and Lily Pads

Late April 1896

Papi came home one April evening with a light step and a smile that betrayed a hidden delight. "Sophie!" he cried as he burst into the flat. "At last I have found some medicine for your weary heart." Louisa glanced inquiringly toward *Papi* as he continued, "I know how you long for all the trees and flowers that grew near our home in Germany. How would you like to visit a place just as green and beautiful? A man at work told me about a wonderful garden! A man named Henry Shaw died a few years ago and left a huge garden and park to the people of St. Louis. Anyone can visit! It's amazing, isn't it?" he raved, desiring her response but being too enthusiastic himself to pause. "This sounds like the America we dreamed about—a garden for everyone!"

"*Ja*, Jakob, it sounds wonderful," *Mütti* replied softly when he stopped for breath.

"Very well then!" *Papi* exclaimed. "On Sunday, after church, we'll all go to Shaw's Garden. An excursion like this is just what we have all needed. I don't want little Maddie to grow up thinking there is nothing more to this world than muddy streets, brick buildings, and black smoke. And most of all, I don't want us to forget the beauty of God's creation."

"It will be marvelous," agreed *Mütti*, a light glowing in her weary eyes. "Are you quite certain that anyone can go to visit? That sounds too good to be true."

"That's what I thought, so I asked several men at work, and

they all agreed. One even has a son who works there as a gardener. Who would know better than he?"

"Oh, it will do the children such good to be in a green garden with fresh air," murmured *Mütti* happily.

"It will do you good too, my love," replied Jakob, gently stroking her cheek. "That is what I am most happy about."

Sunday finally arrived. When the family alarm clock went off, Louisa jumped from bed and rushed to the window. Relief and excitement flooded her when she saw the sun shining brightly. Rainy weather would not keep them from their special day! She put on her Sunday dress and hurried to help *Mütti* pack a picnic lunch.

Louisa loved Sundays. Going to church seemed like a return trip to Germany. The building itself reminded her of her dearly loved *Kirch* in the Bramwald. And the hymns were the ones *Oma* had taught her to love, with the same rich German words that she knew by heart. When she sang with her eyes closed, Louisa could picture herself nestled among family and friends in her German village. Louisa's favorite hymn was *"Ein' Feste Burg"* by Martin Luther. One morning when Louisa had been nearly seven years old, *Oma* had noticed her granddaughter's silence during the singing of this hymn. Immediately following the service, *Oma* had taken Louisa by the hand, led her outside, and pointed to a castle that stood high above them on a hill. "Do you see that place, *mein Kind?*" she had asked. "That is a fortress. As long as it has stood, no one has overtaken it or harmed it. The people living within its walls have always been safe. When we sing 'A mighty fortress is our God,' we declare that nothing can ever defeat us because God is our protection, and he will never forsake us. How can you be silent when we sing to praise such a God?"

In the years since that reproof, Louisa had grown to share *Oma's* love for hymns and their familiar words of praise. Henry had recently angered her with his assertion that their American congregation should sing in English. Louisa had confidently declared her belief that such a change would never happen since most of the adult members, including *Mütti* and *Papi*, could not speak English.

Many of these adult immigrants lived their entire lives within a circle of German friends, employers, and shopkeepers. Finding a German church had been one of *Papi's* first priorities after he arrived in America. Two years later, when his family had accompanied him for the first time, *Mütti* had said, "Church makes me long for home."

"Yes, dear," *Papi* had answered, "for Germany, and for heaven where we will no longer be strangers and aliens in a foreign land."

As Louisa entered church with her family on the day of their planned excursion to Shaw's Garden, she remembered *Papi's* words and marveled at how content she had become in America during the past two years. This land was no longer unfamiliar, and that afternoon they would visit a beautiful place in their own city!

As soon as the service ended, Dorothy grabbed her father's hand in excitement. "Please, can we go right now? Don't spend a lot of time talking to people today," she pleaded.

"All right, my eager one!" *Papi* smiled and nodded to *Mütti* to lead the way out of the pew and to the back of the church. Soon the Shumakers reached the sunny outdoors.

The family had to ride several different streetcars on the way to the park. When they boarded the Manchester Road car, *Papi* told the children they had almost reached their destination. As they traversed Tower Grove Avenue a few minutes later, *Papi* exclaimed, "There is Shaw's Garden! That's where we're going after lunch."

"All I can see is a tall stone wall with trees on the other side," complained Henry. "Will they really let us go in?"

"*Ja*. Look, we have reached the gate." At this point the stone wall's level course rose into a stately entrance. Two-story, symmetrical rooms flanked the center section, providing a view of the garden through square pillars and wrought-iron gates. A magnificent stone pediment roofed the opening. Three large urns crowned each point of the triangle, and the base bore the garden's official name: Missouri Botanical Gardens 1858.

"Is that where Mr. Shaw lives?" Dorothy asked as she eyed the large structure.

"No. He's not alive anymore, and I doubt he ever lived there during his life," laughed *Papi*. "I imagine that's just where the gardeners have their offices and keep their things. I've heard there's a beautiful house on the grounds. We may even get to see it."

Just then the streetcar came to a halt. *Papi* swung Maddie into his arms and led the family onto Tower Grove Avenue toward a nearby intersection. There they stopped. On the other side of the street, a green expanse rose before them.

Mütti breathed a deep sigh of contentment. "It's like being on the edge of another world," she whispered. "I had almost forgotten."

"Forgotten what, *Mütti*?" asked Henry.

"How beautiful trees are when they are all gathered together in one place. How I miss home!"

"Today, Sophie, we will enjoy the beauty of our *new* home. It can be beautiful here. We have just not looked in the right places."

"*Ja*, Jakob," *Mütti* agreed a little mournfully. "You are right, I'm sure."

"This street must be Magnolia Avenue," *Papi* observed, "and there on the other side is Tower Grove Park. A man at work told me that the best place for a picnic is under those trees." After a group of carriages clattered by, *Papi* hurried his family across the street.

It seemed that all of St. Louis had decided to take advantage of the park that day! The ground under the trees displayed a painter's palette of colors. Women in gaily-hued dresses and lace-fringed parasols walked with dapperly dressed men. Children chased one another around trees. In the shade many families had laid down blankets for their picnic feasts. The most wonderful thing of all was that anyone could enjoy the park.

The Shumakers started down a path, and soon *Papi* pointed to an old oak tree towering above a stretch of unclaimed lawn. "How is that spot?" he shouted.

"Perfect!" Louisa declared as Henry and Dorothy raced toward its shade. Moments later Louisa and *Mütti* spread a quilt on the ground, and as soon as *Papi* said the prayer, Louisa and Henry began rummaging through the basket. Soon they had equally divided the food, and the family happily ate their lunch in the idyllic setting.

What fun they had! *Papi* entertained his family with humorous stories, and when *Mütti* laughed, she looked younger than she had for many months. But despite the enjoyable circumstances, the children ate rapidly. *If this park is so wonderful,* Louisa reasoned, *I can't wait to see what Shaw's Garden is like!*

She peered toward Magnolia Avenue. Beyond the street she could just get a peek at the first floor of the buildings that lined the other side, but she could not see the wall of Shaw's Garden. Her impatient eyes finally located a small bed of flowers nearby. "Oh!" she cried, pointing in the direction of her gaze. "*Papi*, can I please go look at the flowers?"

"*Ja.* Why don't you take Dorothy with you?"

"Please?" the younger girl begged.

Louisa nodded, and together they visited the brilliant blooms. It was not long before they returned. "They make my small plants at home seem so plain," Louisa admitted.

"Yours just don't get enough sun, dear, but they do indeed brighten our room!" *Mütti* replied as she finished repacking the lunch basket. After the last item was put away, *Papi* helped *Mütti* to her feet, and they were on their way at last.

Shaw's Garden surpassed the Shumakers' expectations! The roses smelled sweeter than anything they had previously encountered in America, a perfect antidote to the sour scent of the city. The bees and butterflies fascinated little Maddie, and the large greenhouses awed Henry. Many of the windows were opened wide, but *Papi* explained that they would be closed during cold weather. "The flowers here grow year round," he said. "The gardeners keep large fires going in the furnaces. Even in the middle of the night, someone stokes the fires. Because of such faithful care, these plants can live even on the coldest winter night."

"That doesn't sound like a very fun job," remarked Henry. "I'd rather sleep at night."

"Well, I'm glad someone is willing to do it," noted *Mütti*. "Because of his work, we get to see these beautiful flowers!"

After visiting the greenhouses, the family walked to the Observatory. The tower rose two levels beneath a fancy cupola.

The shape of the modified onion dome and its lacy woodwork fringe made Louisa chuckle as they approached; it looked very much like a stocking cap!

The intriguing tower captivated Dorothy. When the family drew near enough for her to safely strike out independently, she raced toward its shelter. Then she disappeared, only to emerge a moment later on the top level. Henry and Louisa, observing her excitement, hurried after her. When they reached her side, they were able to view the entire garden. Splashes of color and marvels of garden symmetry surrounded them.

"Come up, *Papi*! Hurry, *Mütti*!" they yelled. "It's wonderful!"

"I'll wait down here with Maddie," *Mütti* called up, waving *Papi* forward. Their father bounded up the stairs and soon stood beside them.

"*Papi*!" Louisa chattered, pointing toward a part of the garden they had not yet visited. "Look! That's where I want to go next!" When *Papi* agreed, Louisa rushed down to *Mütti* and Maddie. "They have ponds here!" she breathlessly disclosed.

The ponds were even more wonderful than Louisa had anticipated. "Water lilies!" she gasped as they approached. "One of my friends tried to describe them to me, but I didn't imagine they'd be so large!" The Shumakers found to their great delight that wooden planks braced the mammoth lily leaves so people could walk onto them. "Oh please, *Papi*, let me go first," Louisa begged. When he consented, she carefully balanced herself on a plank and walked onto the nearest leaf.

"You'd better not fall," called Henry. "You'd look funny riding home on the streetcar with water dripping from your hair and dress."

Louisa smirked and safely seated herself in the middle of one of the largest lilies. The naturally rimmed edges kept her dry; and thanks to the support of another board, the flat surface easily supported her weight. "It's like having my own boat!" she exclaimed. "*Oma* would have loved this!"

"It's my turn!" Henry insisted at that moment. Louisa returned to solid ground, allowing both Henry and later *Papi* to shuffle along the boards to the lily pads.

As *Papi* stepped back onto the path, he declared, "It's time to head home. It will be nearly dinnertime when we reach our doorstep."

How could an afternoon pass so quickly? Louisa could hardly believe their time in the garden had reached an end.

Later that night, she wrote about their wonderful excursion.

April 26, 1896

I never want to forget today—I doubt I ever will! We went to Shaw's Garden, the most beautiful place in this city, I think. For a few hours I forgot how dirty and smelly the rest of St. Louis is. I felt rich! Queens must spend their lives walking around in beautiful gardens. How nice that would be!

CHAPTER FIFTEEN

Tornado!

May 1896

On May 27 Louisa could not maintain concentration on the bead-work she was stitching onto a fancy dress. Her determination to fin-ish before *Mütti* came home that night failed to keep her from being repeatedly distracted by apprehension and curiosity. All too often her gaze involuntarily drifted out the window nearest her rocker; and at least once an hour, she walked to the window in the main room to determine the state of the westward sky. Maddie, playing near the kitchen table, looked at her older sister curiously each time she enacted this unusual performance.

That morning the St. Louis Weather Bureau had warned of severe afternoon storms, and schoolboys with their flair for exag-geration had added further drama to the forecast.

As Louisa had gathered the laundry from the alley that morn-ing, two neighbor boys loitering on a back step had piqued her interest. One lad boasted to his chum, "My uncle read months ago that a disastrous storm would hit St. Louis this month!"

"Well, my daddy said the same thing, and he's nearly always right," the friend had agreed. "Said the rain might hit us with both fists sometime later today!"

The ominous words made Louisa tremble. Yet that morning the sky appeared unaware that St. Louis's citizens were preparing for a storm. Each time Louisa looked out the window, a clear and bright day greeted her. Yet she couldn't shake the feeling . . .

Since she found it challenging to shop with Maddie, Louisa had arranged for her sister to stay with *Tante* Joanna during the afternoon. When they arrived at their aunt's home around noon, the weather changed. A heavy thunderstorm forced Louisa to delay her departure. When the rain finally subsided, Louisa faced soupy streets and snarled traffic—conditions unfavorable for an expedient shopping excursion. After visiting three different stores, Louisa returned to *Tante* Joanna's much later than she had hoped.

The weather had not improved, but the late hour concerned Louisa more than the gathering clouds. Despite *Tante* Joanna's suggestion that they wait for clearer skies, Louisa insisted that she and Maddie return home immediately—her hungry family depended on her for supper. "We'll take the streetcar," she promised as they rushed out the door.

Before they reached the streetcar stop, Louisa inwardly admitted her foolishness. Her worst fears were beginning to take form as clouds cast shadows of premature dusk upon the city. The mud that had impeded her progress earlier continued as an adversary, and the clouds threatened to throw more rain down to earth momentarily.

Maddie gripped Louisa's neck. Though the little girl had not yet reached her second birthday, even she seemed to sense the eeriness in the still air, and her eyes were wide with concern. "I know," Louisa muttered, "the sooner we're home safe and dry, the happier I'll be too!" The sky reminded Louisa of the Atlantic and of her old fear that the water would overtake their ship. The gray expanse above her now, however, appeared even more ominous than the ocean she remembered.

By the time they reached the streetcar stop, Maddie began to whimper. Louisa hugged her sister tightly against her as they both eyed the sky warily. The sky had turned a jade green. The abnormal hue was disturbing and sickening.

"We'll be okay," Louisa reassured the toddler. Yet as she glanced at the sky, she felt a queasiness in her stomach.

The air had remained still up to that point; nature was holding its breath. Louisa noticed that even the dogs were cowering beneath porches and hollow steps, so different from their usual feisty activity! Louisa began to wonder where Maddie and she could take cover if a downpour began.

Before she could come to a decision, the wind began to blow with an utter recklessness that snatched away all of Louisa's courage. She stepped forward, then halted, momentarily held back by the imminent nightmare. Suddenly she became aware of dampness on her shoulder, but she searched vainly for raindrops. Then an ache in her arms reminded her she was not alone. Maddie, clinging to her desperately, was sobbing. The sound of the little girl's wailing, so near Louisa's ear, had been lost in the noise of the storm. Only her wet tears had at last caught the attention of Louisa's overwhelmed senses. This reminder of her sister's fear jarred Louisa from her numb state, and she realized tears were welling in her own eyes as well.

Soon a hard rain began to fall; yet Louisa stood unmoved in the middle of the street. A man bumped into her, nearly knocking her down and effectively rousing her from her stupor. She frantically glanced at the faces of the few people who remained on the street, noting fear in the eyes of even the strongest men. Everywhere people staggered drunkenly, dodging flying trash and struggling against the wind that tossed them about in violent anger. As lightning flashed brightly upon the scene, Louisa sank to the ground in despair and wrapped herself around Maddie.

As they collapsed onto the mud, Louisa perceived a human hand clutching at her arm. How pleasant the warmth of flesh felt compared to the cold grip of the storm. But in fear Louisa tried to pull away from the woman who held her. "Let me go! We must go home!" she screamed. But the sound of the storm muffled her cries, and her strength failed. The struggle against both the wind and the woman seemed futile, and as the rain became torrential, Louisa gave in to the tugging hand. The woman guided the two Shumaker sisters toward shelter.

In the midst of this scramble, Louisa vaguely recognized that they had entered a store. A gruff-looking man helped push Louisa and Maddie to the back of the building where they were stuffed through a hole in the floor. Their female rescuer and the man who had assisted her immediately followed them. An instant later the man, who Louisa later learned owned the store, shut the hatch, sealing them beneath the ground in a crowded cellar.

A dim light from a solitary lantern allowed Louisa to survey the odd collection of people who surrounded her. Obviously few were acquainted, for a silence hung over the group, and blank stares met her at every turn. At last her eyes rested on the woman who had led them to safety. Here was a pair of kind eyes. At that sight, Louisa began to sob.

Her tears served to bring the others to life. "Don't cry," consoled the girls' rescuer. "All's going to be all right. You are safe now."

"But I must get home to my mother," moaned Louisa, beginning to realize these people were kind, but still wanting to be with *Mütti* and *Papi* during the crisis.

"If we had let you keep going, chances are you would never have made it home. As soon as it's safe to go out again, you can be on your way."

This comfort silenced Louisa but did not calm her fears. From beyond the cellar door came the noise of the storm's tantrum. Maddie buried her head in Louisa's dress, her whimpers just audible above the storm's muffled din.

A second glance at the others' expressions chilled Louisa, unaccustomed to the sight of terror in adult faces. The gentleman nearest her on the left bowed as though in silent prayer. A woman against the wall kept her head buried against her husband's shoulder. Others stared solemnly at the bare walls—every ear focused on what they could hear from above, every mind preoccupied with thoughts of loved ones who were not in that stuffy cellar.

Louisa shared their fear. Had *Mütti*, *Papi*, Henry, and Dorothy found shelter? Or had they been caught with nowhere to run?

A sudden silence replaced the storm's howl, but it did not bring them any peace. Those assembled in the cellar began to shoot darting glances toward one another.

At last the shop owner spoke grimly. "I'll go up and survey the situation."

Everyone nodded in relief at his offer. "Who knows what he'll find," one man muttered, voicing the concerns of the entire group.

It took a few men to push the hatch upwards. Then the shopkeeper climbed up into the gray light. The noise of his hollow footsteps resounded in the cellar. The assembled group traced the man's progress to the front of the store, waited through a moment of silence, and listened as he returned to the opening.

"It's over," he announced with the weary solemnity of a pallbearer. "It'll take a week for me to clean up the store. My windows are gone, and the street . . . Well, I suppose you had better come and see for yourselves."

The group below hesitated. What was it about the street that defied description? Louisa wondered if she really wanted to go up the ladder to see the disorderly world the storm had made. She thought of the storm as a wet and windy artist who was consumed by madness.

But she knew she couldn't remain down there forever. So she and Maddie climbed out of the cellar and onto the store porch. The sky's meanness had been tamed, its greenness drained to a dreary gray. Now repentant tears drizzled onto the earth instead of the pelting darts the clouds had flung down only a half hour before. The sky presented a much more appealing visage than it had when Louisa had last seen it, but she barely noticed because that was not what kept her attention. Instead she, along with the others from the cellar, stood on the porch and gawked at the street. She would not have recognized the place had she not known with surety that she had stood on this same street just twenty minutes before.

The awning that had shielded the storefront was missing, having been carried out of sight. But every other imaginable item littered the street. Wagons lay on their sides—some completely abandoned, others still holding frantic horses captive. Signs had been snatched from storefronts and smashed onto rooftops. A two-story building on the corner had been reduced to one story. Its jagged ruins stood out like a roughly built fence. On the porch a woman called out, "Help me! Oh, please help!"

Louisa did not wait to discover why help was needed. She snatched Maddie from the porch and began to run. She scrambled over slippery piles of lumber and fallen trees. Not entirely aware of where she was or what she was doing, she gripped projecting pieces with her free hand to steady herself. Carrying Maddie made progress difficult. Every few feet one of Louisa's legs would slip through a gap in a pile, but fortunately the debris did not shift and she was never trapped. Fear propelled her forward. What had happened to Mütti, Papi, Henry, and Dorothy?

As she rounded a corner, a tall man held out his arms to stop her. "You can't go that way, miss," he declared with somber, gray eyes.

"But I have to . . . I must see my family . . . must know if they are safe!" Louisa insisted.

"I tell you, miss, you'll have to go around another way. There's a dead man down this road. A tree fell on him during the tornado, and he's not a pleasant sight. I can't let you see that."

Louisa froze and nearly dropped Maddie. "Papi!" she screamed, tears streaming from her eyes. She struggled against the man's arms, but he succeeded in pushing her over to a porch step. Once he had her seated, he crouched down next to her.

He patiently waited until she calmed down. "Does your papa work on this street?" he questioned. Louisa shook her head. "Well then, that man can't be your papa. I'm sure he is somewhere safe. Now, I'll walk you over to the next street; then you can go home to see your papa." Louisa nodded tearfully. She allowed the man to help them around the block, and they were soon on their way again.

Although they had only nine blocks to travel, on that day the journey home seemed overwhelming to Louisa. Despite the tall man's attempts to shield the girls from one death, Louisa saw several dead bodies pulled from rubble on other streets.

They walked along a block of once elegant homes. Many times during the year before, Louisa had enjoyed strolling along this shaded avenue and gazing at the towering residences. She had always slowed her pace on this street, dreaming of one day seeing inside these homes. Now her desire was granted in an unwelcome fashion since several houses had been unmercifully ripped open and exposed to the world. It was eerie to see such beautiful decor alongside such destruction. In many places furniture had been flung about as though a great fight had taken place. However, Louisa did notice one room where everything stood neatly in place, including a desk resting on the edge of a storm-created precipice.

The wrought-iron fences along the street had borne similar destruction. Only a few sections remained where the original intricate designs were evident; in most places the iron bars twisted in mad tangles or protruded from tree trunks. The sight of some fence stakes imbedded in the ground or in huge trees like harpoons caused Louisa to scurry to the end of the block.

As Louisa and Maddie neared their home, the rampage of the storm became less evident. They were apparently straying from the path the tornado had carved through the city. However, the solid, erect buildings that still lined these streets did nothing to allay Louisa's fears. She remained convinced that tornadoes were capable of unbelievable madness. On some streets Louisa had seen only one or two damaged houses. "Almost as if the twister had singled them out," Louisa muttered. "Please, please, may our home be standing!"

At last, treading even more cautiously, Louisa rounded a final corner and stepped onto their family's street. Louisa clutched Maddie tightly as she strained her eyes toward the spot where their flat stood.

"Maddie! Oh, Maddie," Louisa panted, "it's still there!" Maddie looked searchingly at her relieved sister. Somber fear still swam in the toddler's blue eyes; the experiences of that afternoon had laid too heavy a blanket of fear over the little girl for it to be so easily removed.

Louisa raced toward the building. A few minutes later they burst through the door. "*Mütti! Papi!*" Louisa yelled.

Silence.

"Oh, where are they?" Louisa wailed. How quickly terror returned to her heart! Louisa ran to her parents' bedroom and knelt beside the window, pressing her face to the glass. Maddie slipped down by her side and nestled against her arm.

"Dear Lord," Louisa pleaded silently, "please bring them home quickly. Oh, please let them be safe. Don't let them be dead. I could not stand to lose them! Please, Lord—" A sob suddenly interrupted her prayer. Turning around she saw eight-year-old Dorothy standing in the doorway.

Louisa jumped to her feet and rushed to embrace her sister. "You're safe!" she exclaimed. "Where were you? I thought you'd be home before us." Dorothy regarded her numbly and continued her weak sobbing. "What is it, dear?" Louisa asked. "Are you still frightened?"

Dorothy nodded.

Louisa clasped her sister closely, smoothing her hair with a gentle hand. "The storm's over, and I'm sure everyone else will be home soon. You're safe, Dorothy. God protected you."

Dorothy finally spoke. "I was all alone and so frightened. I hid downstars under a blanket. Everything was so dark and loud and scary . . . I thought the house would be blown apart!"

"I know," Louisa agreed softly. "I was afraid too. It must have been terrifying to be here by yourself." Dorothy nodded and with a final sniffle ended her tears for the moment. "Let's go watch for the others," Louisa suggested. "They should be coming soon."

The girls joined Maddie by the window and soon sighted *Mütti* coming up the street. Unmindful of their youngest sister, Louisa and Dorothy dashed from the flat and down the stairs. When they flung open the door, *Mütti* was only a few feet away. With a shrill cry of joy, Louisa hurled herself into *Mütti's* arms.

"Louisa! Dorothy!" *Mütti* gasped, embracing her daughters. "But where is Maddie?" she asked with fear in her voice, her eyes searching the empty doorway.

"She is safe!" Louisa exclaimed. "I . . . I left her up in the flat—I was too eager to see you!"

They ran up the stairs and quickly located Maddie by following the little girl's forlorn wails. "Oh, my dear child!" *Mütti* murmured, racing forward to pluck Maddie from the floor. "Praise God! You're safe!"

The four Shumakers celebrated their reunion with tentative joy as they all peered out the front window, searching the street for the rest of their family.

While they waited, *Mütti* told the girls that she had huddled against the wall in the factory with a group of fellow workers. The storm had threatened great violence in that area but had done little damage.

"*Mütti*, it was awful," Louisa whispered, fear gleaming in her eyes.

"What did you see, child?" *Mütti* asked.

Louisa told of crumbled buildings and toppled trees before adding, "*Mütti*, worst of all were the dead people. What if *Papi*—"

"Hush!" *Mütti* commanded. "You must not imagine the worst. My poor dears—young eyes should not see such horrors." She hugged her daughters as though to shield them from any further dread.

Henry returned ten minutes after *Mütti*. He had just finished delivering a watch when the storm struck. He had found shelter in the back of a hardware store. "Buildings all around us fell down," Henry recounted with awe. "But that store only lost its roof. Everyone inside was safe. *Mütti*, if I had gone in the shop across the street, I might have been killed! The whole building caved in. I heard them say that at least one man died and several others were wounded. It could have been me!"

"Hush," *Mütti* commanded once again. "That is enough of such terrible descriptions. Praise the Lord that all my children are safe. The Lord has preserved us in the midst of the storm. Let us pray that your *Papi* is safe as well." She bowed her head and with closed eyes began to pray, "*Unser Vater im Himmel*, watch over my husband. Bring him safely home. Thank You for hearing my prayers and saving my children. Amen." The children, who had bowed with her, echoed her closing.

When *Papi* opened the door five minutes later, the thunder of five pairs of rushing feet greeted him. "Praise God," he murmured as the entire family sank joyfully into an embracing huddle on the floor.

That day was tragic for many in St. Louis. Over 100 people died, and many others were injured. On the day after the storm, most businesses closed so all citizens could aid with storm recovery. There were piles of debris to clear, wounded to treat, buildings to repair, and homeless to shelter. Even children helped in small ways.

Louisa and Henry walked with *Papi* to the carpentry shop. *Papi's* boss was the only one there when they arrived.

"Bad business, this storm," he remarked, shaking his head. "I have a brother who was killed . . . smashed when half his house collapsed." He stopped to wipe a tear from his eye. "People will be needing carpenters today. It would be wrong for me to have you work here. You go ahead and help on the streets. Take what tools you think you'll need. You can bring them back at the beginning of next week. Until that time, we'll try to help whomever and wherever we can."

Papi nodded. He strode to a box in the corner and began to select tools to place in a pack he had brought.

"And don't you worry," the owner added, "I'll pay you for these days. I can afford that, and I know you've got little ones to feed."

Papi thanked him and ushered the children out the door. "He's a good man," *Papi* remarked as they began to walk down the street. "I hope you will both treat people as kindly as he does."

They walked to *Onkel* August and *Tante* Joanna's building. Their aunt met them at the door. "Oh!" she exclaimed when she heard they had all survived the storm. "Such joyous news! I am so thankful! Last night we could not come to check on you because we were so busy cleaning up after the tornado. I could not sleep— I was so worried for your dear family. August left an hour ago to visit you. He is probably talking to Sophie right now. He wants to go out to work with you, Jakob. Tell me where you're going to be, and I'll send him in your direction when he returns."

Papi explained that they would go to the area where Louisa and Maddie had seen the worst damage. *Tante* Joanna noted the street names and commanded, "Come back here at lunchtime; I'll fix some sandwiches for you. And make sure the children don't get hurt."

"We'll all be careful," *Papi* assured her.

Papi and the children went down to the riverfront on Saturday. They were amazed to see that part of the great Eads Bridge had collapsed into the river. The storm had dashed so many boats upon the shore that the levee along the river had become a steamboat graveyard. "It's sad to see so much destruction and to know that many people have died," *Papi* commented as they surveyed the destruction. "Despite man's confidence in his own strength and his impressive new inventions, we are still absolutely powerless against a storm. All we can do is scatter for shelter like mice. Only God can control the winds."

The next day tourists filled the city. They had ridden trains into town to see the destruction. *Mütti* was not impressed. "It's one thing for the people of St. Louis to view the damage. It's quite another for others to travel into town just to gape at our tragedy!"

CHAPTER SIXTEEN

A Time for Everything

October 1896

On Sunday, October 11, a jarring shake roused Louisa before dawn. She immediately recognized Henry as her disturber and, giving a weak sigh of protest, rolled inward toward Dorothy in hopes of discouraging his efforts.

"Don't be so difficult, Louisa!" he pleaded in her ear. "*Mütti* says the baby's coming! We must go for help. Get dressed quickly!"

This revelation goaded Louisa into action. A few minutes later she met Henry at the front door. The pair quickly accomplished their first mission, which entailed racing half a block down the street to summon the lady who had helped bring Maddie into the world. Next they hurried to fetch *Tante* Joanna.

As they returned with their aunt, she reminded them of their last duty. "When we get home, you are to take Dorothy and Maddie downstairs. You may wait in the hall or on the doorstep, but you must not bother us until we call for you."

Henry and Louisa had expected this command because they had waited outside during Maddie's birth. However, when they reached home, their younger sisters were not pleased when Louisa guided them down the stairs and out the front door. Once they were outside, Louisa had to seat herself in front of the door to bar any attempts at reentry.

"Maddie see *Mütti*!" the youngest protested as she pushed her way onto Louisa's lap.

"I know, honey. I'm sorry, but you can't see *Mütti* right now," Louisa murmured as she hugged Maddie.

"Why do we always get pushed out whenever anything exciting happens?" grumbled Dorothy, throwing herself onto the stone doorsteps.

"You know we can't be in the way when a baby's being born," snapped Henry. "The last thing we need is for you to keep complaining."

Without reply, Dorothy shivered and snuggled close to her sisters. During Henry's rebuke, Louisa had observed her sister. Certain that fear lurked in Dorothy's eyes, Louisa slid an arm around her sister.

"*Mütti* has seemed so weak," Dorothy whispered, warming to Louisa's gentle gesture.

"Yes," Louisa admitted. "I've been worried about her health too." She paused thoughtfully. "I think that if *Mütti* could send a message to us right now, she would tell us to pray." She glanced at Henry who bowed in agreement.

"Father in heaven," Louisa prayed, "please give *Mütti* strength. Please bring the baby to us safely. Amen."

Four heads raised in silence, and the wait continued.

After a few minutes Henry bent down and picked up a pebble. With a quick downward thrust of his arm, he flung it against the cobblestones that lined the gutter. When it weakly ricocheted back toward him, he stretched forward to retrieve his toy and repeated the action. This diversion may have relieved some of Henry's tension, but the noise increased Louisa's agitation. She determined to remain silent, however, reasoning that an argument would only make them all more unsettled.

Eventually Dorothy exploded. "Stop it, Henry!" the eight-year-old hissed. "If you throw that rock one more time, I'll scream."

"You're already screaming," Henry observed blandly. A few minutes later, however, he did stop, contenting himself with rolling the rock between his two sweaty palms.

Louisa had nearly drifted to sleep by the time she received her summons. Just before noon *Tante* Joanna raised the front bedroom window and thrust her head beneath the sash. She appeared directly above the children, so they easily heard her quiet command. "Louisa, I need to see you." Louisa's heart sank as she noted her aunt's face. No joy shone there.

As Louisa rose, Dorothy began, "Oh, please—"

Louisa interrupted her. "Now is not the time to beg, Dorothy," she insisted. "Sit here and wait."

Dorothy dropped her shoulders and rolled her eyes but remained silent. *Tante* Joanna had disappeared, so protests would do no good anyway.

Despite Louisa's eagerness to see the new baby, she climbed the stairs with deep misgivings that held her advance to a cautious shuffle. When she rounded the corner at the landing, the sight of her aunt's frame on the top stair brought her to an abrupt stop. In the dim light Louisa noted her aunt's expression. As dusk heralds the coming of night, the sorrow shadowing her aunt's face was a harbinger of terrible tidings. Suddenly memories of two tiny babies engulfed her. Johann and Thomas—brothers born in the years between Henry's and Dorothy's births who had only enough strength to survive a few hours. Did another frail or dead baby await her? Louisa felt like fleeing down the stairs to avoid whatever awaited her upstairs. But she resumed her climb up the steps. She knew from what *Oma* and *Mütti* had told her many times that some things no human can outrun; neither ignorance nor absence can erase a tragedy that has already occurred. Sometimes the truth must be heard, and courage must be mustered. Was this such a time?

Tante Joanna stretched out her arms to Louisa, who surged forward to receive her hug. The grown woman clutched her niece closely. Louisa waited tensely for words that did not come. Instead, following a long silence, *Tante* Joanna began to sob, and Louisa felt the wetness of her tears.

After several minutes Louisa could wait no longer. "The baby . . . is the baby all right?" she pressed.

"*Ja*, the baby is fine," choked *Tante* Joanna. "A . . . a healthy little girl."

At these words Louisa lurched back from her aunt, a sharp pain stabbing her stomach. Her body instantly comprehended the terrible truth, but her mind refused to accept it.

"*Mütti?*" she shrieked, slumping to the floor.

Tante Joanna knelt beside her. "She is gone, dear. There was nothing . . . nothing we could do," she whispered in anguish. She gripped Louisa's arms and drew her niece back toward her chest. Like a doll, Louisa slouched against her aunt, all strength drained from her body. Every nerve screamed inwardly in anguish, but her voice could not speak. She choked and sputtered, gulping for air like one drowning in swirling waters. Even *Tante* Joanna, whose nails dug into her arms, seemed distant and removed.

After a long, anguished cry, shock and exhaustion overtook Louisa. Her mind raced to other occasions, times when peace had followed tears—the day she had left the Bramwald, and the afternoon of the tornado. *Mütti* had loved and encouraged her during every trial. Her mother's oft-repeated words echoed now in Louisa's mind: "*Take courage, dear one. The Lord does not forsake His children.*"

Louisa stared blankly at the wall. How utterly forsaken she felt! Numb. Alone. No comfort was possible, for *Mütti* was gone. She felt *Tante* Joanna's arms encircling her again and pulled away. She did not crave arms of comfort!

Gone! a voice kept screaming deep within Louisa. *You will never be with Mutti again—never see her or talk with her!* The tears flowed down her cheeks as she sat in hopeless silence. The one who could have restored her joy had been stolen away from her.

Finally Louisa allowed *Tante* Joanna to help her from the floor and lead her into the flat. *Papi* slumped at the table. Louisa longed to run to him, but *Tante* Joanna held her back, and *Papi* did not look up to accept her intrusion upon his grief. *Tante* Joanna steered her niece into the front bedroom where *Mütti's* body lay.

Louisa cautiously stepped to the bed. *No!* a voice within her screamed. *She cannot be dead, I refuse to believe it.* She reached out a timid hand to brush *Mütti's* forehead and drew it back instantly. The cold skin was proof that could not be refuted. *Mütti* was truly gone!

After a moment of stunned silence, *Tante* Joanna led Louisa back to the main room. In a rocker near Louisa's bed sat the woman who had assisted with the birth. In her arms slept a tiny child. The baby lay as still as *Mütti*, her eyes closed gently like her mother's, but Louisa knew that within her body flowed life and breath.

Curiosity drew Louisa toward her newborn sister. "My dear, would you like to hold her?" the gentle woman whispered. Louisa nodded. A moment later Anna Sophie Shumaker rested in her arms. The baby stirred and blinked. Had Louisa been less overwhelmed, she might have comprehended the irony of that moment as, so near *Mütti's* deathbed, she gazed into her sister's newborn eyes.

When Louisa looked up, she realized *Tante* Joanna had disappeared. Ten minutes later she returned with Henry, Dorothy, and Maddie. Louisa noted only Henry's shocked pallor and Dorothy's uncontrolled sobbing. On that day Louisa was incapable of detailed observation; death had muddled everything. Louisa tried to concentrate on *Tante* Joanna's words as she explained, "As soon as your dear mother knew it was a girl, she whispered, 'Her name is Anna' . . . Her sister's name, you know. I'll have to write your *Tante* Anna. It was later that your *Papi* decided baby Anna was to have a middle name."

"After *Mütti* died?" Henry stated dully.

"*Ja*, after she died," *Tante* Joanna confirmed softly. "Little Anna Sophie also bears her mother's name."

Tante Joanna took the children, including the newborn, back to her flat that afternoon, and they remained there that night. There were a few pleasant moments—those rare occasions when Anna awoke and treated her siblings to an amusing and rapid parade of expressions as she'd frown, then smile, then grimace in fluid succession. In the end, her lips always melted into a placid rest, and her eyes closed in perfect contentment. How Louisa envied her!

That night *Onkel* August stayed with *Papi* during *Mütti's* wake. As the elder brother and fellow mourner, he comforted *Papi* and helped guard the body from rats and mice. He returned to his home late Monday morning to escort the three oldest children back to the wake. Inside the main room of their flat, *Mütti's* body lay in a casket. Two bouquets of flowers stood nearby, but they failed to add any cheer to the dimly lit scene. Despite the presence of several friends and neighbors, silence prevailed. As the children entered, *Papi* lifted a haggard face toward the door. With apparent effort he rose to hug his children and weep with them.

After allowing the family a few minutes together, *Onkel* August drew *Papi* back to his seat and led the children to the table. Neighbors and friends had provided a midday meal that far exceeded any that the humble Shumaker table had supported before. Cakes, cold ham, bread, and beans were in abundance. Once the children had filled their plates, *Onkel* August sent them to Henry's tiny room to eat. He reminded the children that he expected them to remain silent. Louisa found his warning needless, for the sight of *Mütti's* body and the solemn surroundings had taken away her voice.

When it was finally time to return to *Onkel* August's flat for the night, Louisa rejoiced. The cold body in the casket looked unfamiliar to her, and she did not want to remember *Mütti* in that way. *Papi's* expression also scared her; she had never seen him look so sorrowful. She feared that the *Papi* she loved might have changed forever. How could she stand that loss while also enduring *Mütti's* death?

On Tuesday, the morning of *Mütti's* funeral, a rainy fog enveloped the city. *Papi* knocked at his brother's door just as his children began breakfast. He silently waited in an extra chair until they finished eating, and then he and *Onkel* August led the sorrowful children to the cemetery. *Tante* Joanna remained behind to care for little Anna.

Since most of the family's acquaintances were at work, only a small group joined the black-clad family among the gray stones. *Frau* Weiss attended the funeral, and Louisa knew that Elsa would have come if she had not had to work. Deep down she felt thankful that her friend could not observe her weeping. So constant were the tears she shed that her memories of that morning were merely blurred images.

When the funeral ended, *Onkel* August gathered the children together to take them back to his flat. "Louisa, your father needs to speak with you," he stated, nudging his niece. "You will walk home with him."

Louisa nodded and walked softly to where *Papi* stood before *Mütti's* grave. "*Papi?*" she whispered.

His head jerked slightly upwards, and he turned toward his daughter with startled eyes. "Oh!" he gasped. "Louisa, I'm sorry . . . I'm afraid I drifted away for a moment." He cleared his throat and turned back to the grave site in silence.

Louisa stood tensely at his side, wondering what would happen next.

At last he inhaled deeply and set his head squarely over his shoulders. "Come," he sighed. "We must talk about what is in store for you now that *Mütti* is gone."

His words chilled Louisa. Since *Mütti's* death, feelings of desperate loneliness had consumed her. The thought of going through even a normal day without her mother had brought tears to her eyes many times. Upon hearing *Papi's* comment, Louisa began to comprehend that the life she had considered normal before *Mütti's* death did not exist anymore. Circumstances would not allow her to slip back into familiar activities and routines; nearly every aspect of life would undergo some alteration. What would her new life be like? She did not know, but she was sure that before they reached *Onkel* August's doorstep, *Papi* would tell her.

Papi led her in a direction opposite to the one the others had taken. They strolled for several blocks in silence. The morning fog and rain had disappeared; although the sun shone brightly, the bright rays failed to warm the air, and a crisp coolness surrounded them. How Louisa longed to hurry home to indoor warmth!

Papi did not seem to notice her shivering. When they reached a park, he turned onto a gravel path and began to wind through the trees until they reached a beautiful bandstand where he sat down on the steps. As Louisa sank onto a step just below him, she noticed that sagging, weary skin framed *Papi's* eyes. How old he looked! For the first time in her life, Louisa felt uncomfortable in his presence. She glanced nervously about the park. Autumn colors adorned each tree, but even that lovely scene failed to bring her joy.

At last *Papi* spoke. "*Mütti* was so proud of you, Louisa. She boasted about your helpfulness and how quickly you have mastered new skills." His eyes began misting as he continued, "Louisa, I think *Mütti* knew she might not survive Anna's birth. She made sure I knew the name she wanted her daughter to have if it was a girl, and she prepared you and Henry to take over her work. I could tell that she was trying to fill her last few months with several years worth of lessons for you both. I wanted to deny her ailing strength, but she faced the truth with boldness and did everything she could to make sure her family would be able to continue without her if that became necessary."

Papi paused, wiped his eyes, then continued with newfound composure. "Louisa, we will survive. We all loved her, but God will grant us the strength to continue in life even though she has passed away. I have full confidence in your ability to manage the household chores. We will all rely on you; it is a burden the oldest must bear in such circumstances. I promise to help you however I can, but most of my hours will be spent at work, so some duties will be solely yours." He smiled, his sense of humor returning for a moment. "I am a woeful cook, Louisa. I did cook for myself while you were still in Germany, but I'm afraid that none of you would want to eat the food that comes from a pot I have seasoned!"

"I have done most of the cooking recently anyway," Louisa whispered, "and I will help as much as I can."

"Louisa," *Papi* said with a sigh, "it is the others who will help you. You and Henry will be in charge when I am not home. Henry will have as many responsibilities as you do, and you two must work together. Dorothy will take over many of the tasks you have done in the past, and little Maddie, though she's not yet two, will soon be able to help with the simplest tasks."

Louisa nodded, wondering how she would possibly manage such heavy responsibilities.

Papi continued, "Anna—praise be to God—is a healthy and strong baby, but she will need a great deal of care. *Tante* Joanna has vowed to lend a hand with that. I have decided to move our family into the third-story flat above *Onkel* August's shop. He owns the building and will rent the space to me for an affordable price. Besides, during *Mütti's* last days she made me promise that I would move the family to a new home. Too many taverns and other evils have established themselves near our flat. It will be a comfort to me to know that when I am not home, my brother will be near my children."

"I'm so glad," Louisa murmured, relieved that she would not be completely alone with the younger children.

"The move, however, will necessitate another change that will not be so easy for you to hear," *Papi* continued. "I insist upon paying my brother fairly, although I know he would accept much less. Rent in his part of town is higher than what we have been paying, and I cannot pay him and still put food on the table without additional wages. Henry, Dorothy, and you will all have to help. You must ask the seamstress if you can continue doing the work that *Mütti* did in the evenings, but that alone will not be enough. You must also find a daytime job. Henry will remain with *Onkel* August, learning the watchmaker's trade. He has become quite skilled, and my brother is going to increase his pay. Dorothy will be able to help you with the sewing, but she is still young and must attend school during the day."

"Yes, *Papi*," Louisa replied, tears trickling down her cheeks at the thought of taking on an extra job. Her fear was almost too great! How could she bear this challenge so soon after *Mütti's* death?

Papi looked deep into Louisa's tear-soaked eyes. "I am so sorry, Louisa!" He drew her to him. Louisa rested limply against him, sobbing as she had when she first heard the dreadful news of *Mütti's* death. As *Papi* comforted her, Louisa sensed a change in him. Forsaking his own grief, he focused his attention on her, and his strength renewed her courage.

That evening *Tante* Joanna and *Onkel* August encouraged Louisa to spend an hour alone in their bedroom. She gratefully agreed, relieved that they had noticed she needed time away from her younger sisters. While the others cleaned the kitchen, Louisa slipped away with her journal. She had brought this with her when she left home, hoping that writing would help her make sense of her emotions. And so, for the first time in many months, she began to write.

October 13, 1896

Mütti has died. I wonder how I'll live without her. I miss her terribly already, and it's only been two days. When I think of all the work she did each day, I don't know how she managed. Now I have to do almost everything! Papi said I will be cooking and cleaning and taking care of the little ones now. They will help with the chores, but I must be the overseer. I can hardly think about it—it's too much! Henry is supposed to help, but will he? That's a big question! I miss Mütti so much. Why did she have to die? I need her. But then, when I think of Anna and Maddie, I try to tell myself that I should really be thankful. I had Mütti for nineteen years; Anna never even knew her. What an awful thought! Now I must do for her all the things that Mütti did for me. I will tell Maddie stories at night and will press Anna's clothes when she is old enough to go to school. And I don't even know what I'm doing!

Help me, Lord! I am so confused. I am not ready for what I must do. I must find a job. It's dreadful—I don't know if I can bear factory work. The worst thing though is that Mütti is gone—gone forever. I can hardly believe it. How can I care for Maddie and Anna? It's true that Tante Joanna will help. I know she will be wonderful, but I still feel so scared. If I can just show Maddie and Anna half the love that Mütti gave to me!

CHAPTER SEVENTEEN

Seamstress Shop Surprises

On Wednesday, the day after the funeral, Henry headed downstairs to the watch shop with *Onkel* August. An hour later *Tante* Joanna took the girls to their new home. It was a short trip—out the door of *Tante* Joanna's own second-story flat and up one flight of stairs. "How nice to have you girls just one floor above me!" *Tante* Joanna exclaimed as she swung open the door at the top of the stairs.

The girls had never been in this part of the building because another family had occupied the upper flat until a month before *Mütti's* death. Louisa could hardly wait to see the inside; but even before she looked, she knew these quarters would suit them well. Because the building sat on the corner, a side entrance allowed the occupants to step directly from the street into the stairwell that led to the two flats. This arrangement made it unnecessary for the family to pass through *Onkel* August's shop each time they came home. It also meant they would not have to walk down a narrow back alley to reach a rear door.

Louisa's first glance inside only increased her satisfaction with her new home. "Our own water faucet!" she cried. "Never again will we have to haul water up the stairs!" Her eyes quickly took in everything else, including an ornate iron stove in the corner and white cabinets that lined one wall. "I will love cooking here!" she declared.

Tante Joanna laughed at her enthusiasm. "None of you will be able to eat much, I'm afraid. With your table and chairs in here, it

149

will be a tight squeeze. Anyone who gains a pound won't be able to sit down!"

Louisa had to admit the truth of this comment. The table would barely fit, and it would block the most direct path between the entrance and the door that led to the rest of the flat. "We'll have to walk with one shoulder rubbing the wall just to pass through!" she observed. "But I'd rather have running water than a large kitchen!"

Tante Joanna led them across the kitchen to a hallway that provided access to the four other rooms. She said that *Papi* had decided where everyone would sleep. Henry and *Papi* would each have their own tiny room. *Papi's* lay at the front and had a window. Henry's received no natural light and was situated in the rear part of the building next to the kitchen. The girls were given the largest bedroom; but even so, little floor space would remain once the bed Louisa shared with Dorothy was squeezed in along with Maddie's tiny bed, Anna's cradle, and a dresser. This room, like *Papi's*, had a window that overlooked the shop's awning and the street. In the corner, a pipe from *Tante* Joanna's and *Onkel* August's potbellied stove stretched from the floor to the ceiling. "The sparks that fly up from our stove will heat the pipe and give you some extra warmth," *Tante* Joanna explained. "Be careful not to touch the hot metal in winter!"

When they entered the last room, *Tante* Joanna announced, "This will be your parlor. I told your *Papi* that you needed a room for the family to gather and a place for the sewing machine. The fireplace in this room burns coal instead of wood, and it will keep you quite warm. For now the room will be sparsely furnished, but your *Papi* will make some chairs as soon as he can."

"There's a large window!" Louisa exclaimed. "My plants will help brighten the bareness!"

That night *Papi*, Henry, and *Onkel* August borrowed a wagon and spent the evening transporting all the Shumakers' possessions from the old flat to their new home. As the men lugged bundles, baskets, and furniture up the stairs, Louisa and Dorothy rushed about positioning chairs, unpacking dishes, making beds, and filling drawers. Louisa wanted to get everything in order as quickly as possible; their lives had been too chaotic recently. Soon her potted garden stood along the parlor windowsill, and her *Wilkommen* stitchery decorated the wall beside the door. Louisa felt settled in their new home.

The last bundle Henry carried in was a bag of uncompleted sewing work. When he dropped it onto the floor near the sewing machine, Louisa released a pained gasp. "I had forgotten!" she wailed. "What will I do? Mrs. Noltham is expecting the finished clothes back in her shop tomorrow afternoon!"

Papi put an arm around her shoulder. "You will do your best to finish, Louisa. What you cannot finish, must wait. *Mütti's* death should be an adequate explanation for any late work."

"I will work all night if I have to," Louisa declared, dropping to her knees and frantically unwrapping the sheet from around the fabric.

"No, Louisa," insisted *Papi*. "You will go to sleep now. Then tomorrow, when you are rested, you will begin."

When Louisa returned to the bundle of sewing after breakfast the next morning, the frenzy she had felt the night before had disappeared. She began by sorting the completed garments and remaining fabric to determine what work she still needed to complete. A slip of paper with instructions from Mrs. Noltham also guided her. Her first pile contained the work *Mütti* and she had finished—a wool coat and a pair of boy's trousers. The second consisted of partially assembled pieces for another coat. The last pile contained several yards of uncut green velvet and a roll of beautiful black ribbon. The instructions provided all the information Louisa needed. The details of the coat order were clearly described, and a drawing of a girl's party dress followed.

"That's what the velvet's for," Louisa muttered. "I think I can handle both the coat and the dress. Thankfully, I've done similar work before!" During the past two years, *Mütti* had been a demanding tutor, requiring detailed work and near-perfection. Louisa had been told to rip out many seams that were not satisfactorily straight. How gratefully she now recalled that preparation!

By mid-afternoon the coat lay in the pile with *Mütti's* completed work. Louisa had planned to finish before noon, but that
goal proved overly ambitious. Too often her progress had been
slowed by the tears that blurred her eyes as she placed her own
stitches near the neat work *Mütti* had done before her death. It was
four o'clock before Louisa began to cut the green velvet fabric. As
she began stitching the dress, Dorothy came home from school.
Louisa rushed to meet her. "You must take these coats and trousers
to the seamstress's shop," she commanded. "I have drawn you a
map; here's money for the streetcar. Explain to the owner, Mrs.
Noltham, that *Mütti* has died and that I'll have the dress done by
tomorrow." When Dorothy began to protest, Louisa cut her short.
"Dorothy, don't argue—you must go now or the shop will close!"

When Dorothy returned, Louisa pressed her for information.
"What did she say?"
     "She was mad."
     "What did she say when you told her *Mütti* had died?"
     "I didn't tell her."
Louisa stepped forward and grabbed Dorothy's shoulders.
"What?" she screamed. "Don't you understand? She may never let
me do work for her again. Why didn't you tell her?"
     "She . . . she frightened me," Dorothy stammered, her lower lip
trembling. "She almost yelled at me."
Louisa sank to the floor and began to cry. Her thoughts soon
left the situation at hand, and she began to long for *Mütti*. Sorrow
overwhelmed her, and she continued to sob, unmindful of
Dorothy's presence.
Nearly half an hour passed before Louisa began to consider that
Mütti would have wanted her to respond to Dorothy's timidity with
compassion. Louisa wanted to scream, "But she's ruined everything.
I told her what to do!" Then she glanced toward Dorothy, rocking
nervously in *Mütti's* chair, and her anger melted. She noted the
tears falling from the eight-year-old's eyes. Louisa rushed to the
window and knelt at Dorothy's feet.
     "I'm sorry," Louisa murmured, reaching up to wipe a tear from

Dorothy's eye. "Mrs. Noltham is stern even in good circumstances. I would have been afraid too. Will you forgive me?"

Dorothy nodded and slipped from the chair into Louisa's arms.

After a late night of work, Louisa set out early Friday morning with the completed dress. Even though she planned to utilize the street-cars, she knew that at that busy morning hour she had to allow plenty of time to reach the esteemed avenues of the West End where Mrs. Noltham's establishment was located. Most of the shop's customers came from the wealthy ranks that lived in that section of town, and often the garments that *Mütti* had stitched had been finer than any the Shumakers wore.

Louisa reached the seamstress's shop soon after it opened. When she pushed the knob to enter, the door stuck. She knocked it loose with a kick, and the noise summoned Mrs. Noltham from the back room. "So you've come at last, I see," she exclaimed sharply. "You're late! Precious little care you have for what my customers think. What if they had arrived early this morning, asking for the dress? How do you think that would have made me look? I'll not risk losing good customers because your mother's late with her work."

In an instant the fabricated composure that Louisa had displayed when she entered the shop disintegrated. "My mother was never once late!" she responded vehemently. "How dare you accuse her when you know nothing about it!"

Mrs. Noltham drew herself up in disgust. "Well! Is that how your mother has taught you to speak to your elders? Really now, I had thought better of her. I know enough to see that this work is late, and your tirade has done little to soothe my opinion of your mother."

Under this attack Louisa wilted to the floor, her tear-covered face shielded behind her hands.

Though Mrs. Noltham was often easily offended, a softness lay beneath her bristles. In a moment she rushed to Louisa's side, put a reassuring arm about the girl's shoulders, gently drew her to her feet, and led her to a chair in the back room. When Louisa had calmed herself, she explained the family's loss.

"Oh, how terrible," Mrs. Noltham murmured, wiping a tear from her eye. "I had no idea she was so weakened. She's never failed to get her work to me on time. Such a wonderful woman . . . she'll be sorely missed!"

"Yes, ma'am," Louisa agreed, forcing herself into full composure. "I finished the work that *Mütti* had not completed. With the funeral and all the confusion, I just couldn't get it here any earlier. I worked as quickly as I could, and—"

Mrs. Noltham interrupted her, "Of course you did, my dear." She pulled the dress from the sheet that Louisa had wrapped about it. "Did you make this?" she inquired.

"Yes, ma'am."

"You do fine work. Your mother taught you well."

"If you would allow me," Louisa proposed, "I'd like to continue doing the work that *Mütti* did. I will be looking for a job that I can do during the day, but in the evenings I can sew. I will not disappoint you."

Mrs. Noltham examined the dress for a moment longer. "I will have work waiting for you each Thursday, as usual. Can you be here to pick it up?"

"Yes, ma'am!" she exclaimed in joyful relief.

"And I think I may be able to help you find other work," Mrs. Noltham continued, to Louisa's amazement. "Domestic work would be best for a girl your age, but I assume you will want to live at home with your family." Louisa nodded. "That makes things a little more difficult," Mrs. Noltham continued, "but I may know of just the place. Can you be here Monday at closing time?" she asked.

"Yes, ma'am," Louisa replied, nodding eagerly.

"Very well, I shall see you then," Mrs. Noltham stated crisply. "In the meantime I shall check out this possibility. I hope to have good news for you when we meet again." She waved cheerfully as Louisa lifted the latch, and her kindness ignited a joy in Louisa's heart that she had not felt since *Mütti's* death.

On Monday Louisa walked through the crowded streets with nervous anticipation. Her family needed money desperately, yet she feared the unknown job that might be offered to her. Her surroundings provided no comfort. The streets were dry and dusty; the whirl of passing streetcars and the rumbling of heavily laden wagons stirred up sufficient dust to choke even the hardiest of citizens. As Louisa walked, she held a damp handkerchief to her mouth to filter the air. It was impossible, however, to completely avoid affliction from the dust. By the time she reached her destination, the lower half of her pale blue dress had turned brown.

Mrs. Noltham greeted Louisa cordially and quickly locked up the shop. As she led Louisa through a lovely section of town, she described the possible employment. "Mr. Charles Hatterly is an older gentleman who wants to hire someone to look after his household chores—mostly cleaning and dusting, you understand," she prattled. "He is a widower, and his wife never could stand for things to be even the slightest bit out of order. He became accustomed to that, I suspect. And besides, if I had the money to have someone else do my cleaning, as he definitely does, I most certainly would not lift a finger to dust and scrub!"

She turned to Louisa with an amused smile. "I am quite certain you will find this job to your liking. He is a most kind gentleman and a well-respected businessman. He attends my church and orders his clothes from my shop. How perfectly wonderful that he is looking for someone just when you are in need of a position! And after the tragedy that you have been through . . . Well, this may be just the thing for you! I have told him you will not be able to stay there during the evenings as so many domestic servants do, and he said that is certainly fine with him. At any rate, he cannot imagine you desiring to dust by candlelight; that is what he said himself. And I would certainly agree!"

At this point they finally reached the Hatterly house, and the seamstress ceased her chattering. As Louisa surveyed the sprawling house before her, she understood why the owner required a house servant. Such a large residence certainly seemed capable of harboring great quantities of dust and grime!

Before ringing the bell Mrs. Noltham smoothed her skirt just below the waist and pulled herself up properly. About two minutes later a plump woman appeared at the door.

"Well, good evening to you!" she exclaimed. "I'm so glad to see you, Mrs. Noltham. And you must be Louisa!" she observed, turning her sparkling eyes toward the other visitor. "I'm Betsy, the cook. I'm so glad to meet you. Now, if you'll just come in, I'll run and tell Mr. Hatterly that you've arrived. He told me to be on the watch for you two!" As she spoke, she led them into the parlor and motioned toward two chairs. Louisa felt completely overwhelmed. Despite Betsy's friendly greeting, the cook's simple words had made Louisa nervous.

Mrs. Noltham, however, did not remain silent long enough to allow Louisa time to contemplate her fears. "They do without pretentious formality in this house," she whispered. "Mr. Hatterly will have nothing of the sort. I'm sure that you will like it here!"

At that moment Mr. Hatterly strode into the room with a ready smile and an exuberance that communicated that he expected to be impressed with the young lady who had come to seek employment. A well-groomed walrus mustache marked his face with distinction, and his clothes were entirely fashionable. He wore an elegant Prince Albert frock coat, apparently having just returned home from his West End business office.

An hour later Louisa hastened homeward with a smile on her face. What news she had!

Papi was waiting at the kitchen table when she arrived. "So how did it go?" he asked in his deep, warm voice.

"Oh, so well! I have a job as a domestic servant! The man I'll be working for is Mr. Hatterly. He will be a wonderful employer. I'm sure of it, *Papi*!"

"How thankful I am," *Papi* said. "I hoped you would not have to work in a factory. When do you begin?"

"Wednesday."

"Very good. You'll be needing a white apron, no doubt. All domestic servants wear them. Tomorrow you can go to the store and buy yourself a good one."

"But, *Papi*, I can make one," Louisa demurred.

"We can spare the money this time," *Papi* insisted, retrieving several coins from a box in the cabinet. "You have enough sewing to do without an extra project!"

As Louisa dusted Mr. Hatterly's library on the following Monday, she paused for a moment to lift the cover of a Charles Dickens novel. How she loved books! Her mouth whispered the opening words as she read just a few lines. Then she sorrowfully forced herself to close the book. Looking up she realized with horror that Mr. Hatterly, at home for his midday meal, stood in the doorway observing her actions. She inhaled sharply, embarrassment and shame flooding her.

"Louisa, you are employed to dust, not to read," he began.

"Yes, sir," Louisa replied. Raising her head as she spoke, she noted with surprise that Mr. Hatterly's eyes were twinkling.

"I cannot reprimand you too harshly, however," he remarked, "for I myself have often been guilty of reading when there was work waiting to be done. I can hardly stand the sight of an unopened book!" Louisa smiled unconsciously. Noting her expression, Mr. Hatterly continued, "I see that you suffer from the same love of literature that possesses me. Well then, you may borrow any of my books. You need only to ask me before you take one. How would you like that arrangement?"

"That would be wonderful, sir!" Louisa exclaimed with moderately controlled enthusiasm.

"Very well then. I would suggest that you start with the one I have just caught you reading. It is one of my favorites. Or perhaps you'd enjoy *Life on the Mississippi* by Mark Twain. I'm sure that you'd appreciate his references to life in our part of the country."

As the door shut, Louisa resumed her dusting with an unfading smile. Since the Shumakers had never been able to afford many books, Louisa had existed on meager rations of literature. Finally she had full access to all that she had so often longed to read.

CHAPTER EIGHTEEN

Christmas Joy

December 1896

By the beginning of December, winter's dull colors had shrouded St. Louis for over a month. Frequent rain had turned the dirt streets to mud and had rotted the leaves that had collected in the gutters. A rank smell permeated the air, and Louisa's stockings were soggy each time she removed her shoes. The nineteen-year-old had reluctantly realized that she must do something to lift her spirits. The approach of Christmas presented the perfect opportunity.

As she left home one morning Louisa walked through the watch shop instead of using the side door. She stopped beside Henry's workbench and addressed her brother in a low whisper. "I have a wonderful idea, but I need your help. We must make this a special Christmas. The weather has been so dreary, and we're all missing *Mütti* so much. Let's plan to make Christmas Day as joyful as possible, especially for Maddie's sake. She's too young to even remember last Christmas."

Henry readily agreed, and they conspired together for a few minutes before Louisa hurried away to Mr. Hatterly's house.

That afternoon she stopped by Mrs. Noltham's shop to exchange several completed garments for a new bundle of fabric.

"You have done good work, Louisa," Mrs. Noltham praised. "And what about the job with Mr. Hatterly? Are you getting along well there?"

"Oh yes, ma'am. I am so thankful to you, Mrs. Noltham."

"Hush, don't mention it, my dear. It's the least I could do in your poor mother's memory."

"I was wondering," Louisa ventured, "if I might buy some spare gold-colored buttons from you. I am making a coat for my sister, and I'd like to add the buttons as a Christmas surprise. She is pining for them . . . says all her friends have gold buttons."

"Well, I do believe I have just the thing. Right this way!" Mrs. Noltham led Louisa to the back room and pulled five large brass buttons from a drawer.

"Oh!" Louisa gasped. "Those would be perfect! How much are they?"

Mrs. Noltham pressed her to take them at no charge, but Louisa would not hear of it. They finally settled on a price that Louisa suspected was well below their actual worth. Louisa waltzed out the door, elated with this early success in Christmas shopping. An hour later the buttons were safely stowed in *Tante* Joanna's cupboard since Henry and Louisa had agreed to enlist their aunt as an accomplice in their Christmas schemes.

Two days after the purchase, *Papi's* gift, wrapped in pages from an old hardware catalogue, joined the buttons in the cupboard. Since October Louisa had been knitting new heavy, woolen socks for him. His warmest pair had holes that grew bigger despite Louisa's best darning efforts. She feared the bite of St. Louis winters and did not want her father to come home one evening with frozen toes.

A week before Christmas Louisa hid Maddie's favorite doll in the cupboard. The little one cried bitterly until Dorothy (who had lost a doll in December several years in a row) whispered enthusiastically, "Maddie, Christmas is coming, and you never know what wonderful things will reappear at that time! If I were you, I wouldn't worry about the doll." Maddie looked quizzically at Dorothy and then, to Louisa's amazement, quieted as if she understood Dorothy's explanation.

Christmas was only a few days away when Louisa finally had time to visit the Famous Department Store. Over the past year she had saved up a little bit of extra money. With *Papi's* approval, she planned to spend most of it on Henry. Inside the store most people milled between the counters near the entrance, but Louisa strode directly to the clothing department. There she found the perfect shirt for Henry. She admitted to herself that it was expensive, and the Shumakers never bought their clothes ready-made, but, a voice within her insisted, that was exactly why just this once she was buying a special shirt for Henry. Soon much of her precious money had passed from her hands, and she joyfully carried her package home. Those who sighted her on the streetcars must have wondered what brought such a satisfied smile to her face.

That night Papi brought home a rattle he had made at work. Henry later took the toy downstairs where Louisa had stashed a brush and paints she had borrowed from her friend Elsa. Louisa smiled as she thought of how her brother would bring the rattle to life in a blaze of color. Anna would be fascinated!

The morning before Christmas, Louisa pressed her remaining money into Henry's hand. With a smile he headed out the door to buy oranges, candy, and nuts for each member of the family. Louisa was determined that the socks and stockings that hung by the fireplace would not be empty even though Mütti could no longer fill them as she had each year previously.

On Christmas morning Louisa tiptoed softly from her room. She clasped her hands in delight when she peeked into the parlor. The socks and stockings on the mantel were bulging, and near the window a small tree spread its branches. Henry had set it up during the night and had decorated it with ribbons and tiny unlit candles. Louisa's gifts and others that she did not recognize rested beneath the first tree that had ever been part of a Shumaker family Christmas celebration. Papi sat in the rocking chair with a smile on his face. "Merry Christmas!" he declared. "You and Henry certainly know how to surprise your Papi!"

"Do you like it, Papi?" Louisa asked, confident that he would praise them.

"Ja, ja! Very much, Louisa."

Satisfied, she went to find her brother. "Oh, Henry!" she gasped when she entered the kitchen. "It is so beautiful. I've always wanted to have a Christmas tree. How ever did you afford the decorations? How surprised the others will be!"

Henry rose from the side of the stove where he had been scraping out the soot before starting a new fire. "Tonight I'll light the candles," he declared. "I couldn't afford the isinglass lanterns that would have kept the wax from dripping. We will just have to keep a bucket of sand nearby in case the tree tries to go up in flames!" A triumphant smile blazed on his face as he and Louisa shared the joy of the celebration they had prepared.

Soon Henry had a fire blazing in the stove. Louisa lifted the dishcloths from two pans of sugar rolls that she had set out to rise the night before. Satisfied with their puffiness, she placed them in the oven.

Moments later Dorothy came running from the bedroom, dragging Maddie behind her. "It's Christmas! It's Christmas morning!" she sang.

"Good morning!" greeted Louisa. "Maddie and Dorothy, you must get some more clothes on. It may be Christmas, but it is still cold." She herded the two back into the room where she picked up slumbering Anna. "You have no idea what is going on, do you, little one?" she said with a smile, softly tapping Anna's nose.

When Louisa led the girls to the parlor, Dorothy gasped in amazement. "Our own Christmas tree!" she cried with delight. Maddie ran up to *Papi*, wriggled her way into his lap, and began to chatter with excitement.

Soon *Papi* calmed Maddie and asked Louisa to bring him the family's large Bible so he could read the story of the Savior's birth. He began in Isaiah 9:6, "*Denn ein Kind ist uns geboren, ein Sohn uns gegeben . . .* For unto us a child is born, unto us a son is given. . . ." Then he moved to the story of the shepherds and the angels and the wise men all coming to worship the baby who was born King of all the earth.

"Baby," piped Maddie, pointing to Anna.

"Yes," answered *Papi*. "Jesus was a baby like Anna, but he grew up to be a man like me. Then . . . he died."

"Like *Mütti*," whispered Dorothy.

"Yes, Dorothy, like *Mütti*," he affirmed quietly. "And you know what? When Jesus died, some people were sad, just as we have been since *Mütti* died. But soon those people were happy again because Jesus didn't stay dead. He came back to life."

"I wish *Mütti* was alive," Dorothy murmured.

"Yes, we all do, and in heaven she is," sighed *Papi*. "But it is much more important that Jesus came back to life. Do you remember me telling you that *Mütti* is now in heaven?" The children nodded. "You see, God allowed *Mütti* to enter heaven because Jesus died and then came back to life."

"I thought *Mütti* went to heaven because she was good," Dorothy remarked.

"No, no one can get to heaven just by being good," replied *Papi*. "Although *Mütti* was kind, loving, and compassionate, none of that could have gotten her to heaven because she was a sinner, just like the rest of us. God is holy; that means there is nothing sinful about him. He will not allow any sin into heaven. The only way humans can enter heaven is to get rid of their sinfulness."

"Then why is *Mütti* in heaven? How did she get rid of her sin?" Dorothy pressed.

"That is an excellent question. For us to become Christians and go to heaven to be with God, our sin must be taken away. The problem is, we cannot do this on our own. Jesus, however, has provided a way for us to get rid of our sin. We must first admit that we are sinful and that we deserve to be punished by death. The amazing truth is, we do not have to receive that punishment. Jesus died in our place. We must believe that Jesus, who lived a perfect life, received our punishment for us when he died on the cross. We must rely on him as our only Savior. Then we can again have a relationship with God. *Mütti* knew she was sinful but also that Jesus died for her sins. She believed in Jesus as her Savior!"

"But *Mütti* did do lots of good things," Dorothy noted.

"Well," *Papi* replied, "two things happen as a result of salvation. The first one is that because Jesus came to life again, anyone who believes in Him will live forever in heaven. In other words, God takes away death and gives our souls life. A second result is that God changes us while we're on earth. He works in the lives of His children to make them more like Christ. That's why *Mütti* had become such a loving and kind person. God had worked in her life for years."

"I'm so glad we know *Mütti's* in heaven," whispered Dorothy. "It makes me feel better."

"Me too," murmured Louisa.

"Yes," continued *Papi*. "And all because Jesus came as a baby in Bethlehem. Don't we have something wonderful to celebrate at Christmas?"

"Yes, *Papi*," answered Louisa softly. "Thank you for reminding us." *Papi* smiled upon her warmly, but she noticed a touch of sadness in his eyes and knew he sensed the emptiness by his side.

Henry began to hand the stockings down to the girls. "Oh, how I love oranges!" Dorothy exclaimed, just as she did every year. "I always think I will save mine, but I can never wait! They're just too yummy!"

Louisa laughed. "Well, let's start breakfast then, so you can get on with eating that orange!" Dorothy gave this idea instant approval, and she led the family into the kitchen.

The sugar rolls, sausages, and eggs disappeared quickly. What a rare treat Christmas breakfast was compared to the usual oatmeal or biscuits!

Maddie did not allow the family to dawdle at the table. "Presents?" she suggested as she licked the last bit of sugar from her fingers.

"Why, it's you we've been waiting on!" *Papi* exclaimed, scooping up Maddie and lifting her to his shoulders. She giggled, ducking to avoid hitting the doorframe as *Papi* headed for the parlor.

What a load of gifts awaited them! There had never been such a Christmas in the Shumaker house. There were at least three gifts for each family member!

Louisa watched with contented pleasure as her family opened her presents. Henry stared at her in joyful disbelief when he saw what his package contained. Maddie squealed when Louisa handed her the doll that had disappeared the week before. Henry had replaced her missing eye, and Louisa had sewn a new, ruffled frock for Dolly. Dorothy, near tears at the sight of the golden buttons glistening on her newly finished jacket, hugged Louisa several times. *Papi's* jovial praise, however, warmed Louisa the most. "I thank thee, Louisa," he said jokingly, holding high his new socks. "From the bottom of my toes, I thank thee!"

The thoughtfulness behind each of the gifts Louisa received overwhelmed her. Henry handed her a round box that she found very curious. She thought it unlikely he would have selected a hat for her; he knew nothing of women's fashions! To her surprise, however, the box did contain a lovely bonnet. "Oh!" Louisa gasped. "It is absolutely wonderful. I shall have to wear it every Sunday. You must have saved for months!"

Dorothy presented her older sister with a knitted blanket. "How thoughtful!" Louisa exclaimed. "You obviously heard me complaining all last year about being cold in the evenings!"

"Yes," admitted Dorothy. "You did moan about it practically every night. This year too. And I've been laughing all along, knowing I had the perfect gift!"

When no more presents remained beneath the tree, *Papi* said, "I still have one gift left to give. It is for Louisa, but she must search for it in the flat below."

Louisa jumped up and headed for the door with the entire family following. When she reached the second-floor landing, *Tante* Joanna opened the door. "I heard you coming," she declared. "We've been waiting for you."

Louisa rushed inside, and there in the middle of the room stood an ornate rocker with a red bow. "Oh, *Papi*, it's perfect! How did you know this is what I've wanted for years?" she exclaimed.

"I didn't," *Papi* admitted. "Last summer *Mütti* told me that she wanted you to have a rocker of your own. This is to replace the one you gave to Margaretha years ago."

With tears in her eyes, Louisa threw her arms around *Papi*. *Mütti's* love had once again touched her!

What a marvelous Christmas morning it was! Even though Louisa's plan had been to create a special day for the younger children, she found that the festivities renewed her own joy as well. She recognized for the first time the deep love she felt for each member of her family. The next morning she took a few minutes to write down her thoughts.

December 26, 1896

I think I have spent so much time missing Mütti that I have not remembered how special everyone else in my family is. We had a wonderful Christmas together. I can hardly believe the gifts that Papi, Henry, and Dorothy gave me! Each one made me think of how much they do every day. Papi, of course, is as dedicated and hardworking as he has always been. But Henry has outdone anything I could ever have imagined. It's truly amazing! He used to mosey along to the grocery when Mütti sent him. Now he practically runs. He works so hard! He has even taken a job as a lamplighter's assistant and gets up before everyone else to extinguish all the gas lamps near our block. It's freezing cold and dark, but he does it anyway. A lamplighter's assistant doesn't make much, but every bit of money helps.

Dorothy works hard too. She's so quiet and diligent. She waits in the cold every morning for the milkman to walk by, then runs Anna's milk up to Tante Joanna. She is becoming a skilled seamstress too. Mütti taught her well. Now, after much practice, she makes nearly all the family clothes, just like I used to. She recently made a smock for Maddie, and we can hardly get Maddie to take it off! She loves it so much that she wants to wear it to church, to bed, everywhere! At least she happily wears it during the day and keeps her dress clean.

Tante Joanna is wonderful! I don't know what we would do without her or Onkel August. They are always ready to help with anything. God has surely been good to us.

PART THREE

Rudi's Reappearance

April—May 1899

Nearly two and a half years later, on April 17, Louisa turned twenty-two. Elsa's birthday occurred a few days later, but the two girls did not meet for a joint celebration as they had every other year since their arrival in America. Although Louisa had moved away from Elsa's section of town, that alone did not keep the girls from seeing one another. Rather, their interest in maintaining a friendship had waned because their lives had taken different paths. While Louisa had spent the past year consumed with managing her household responsibilities and two jobs, her friend had indulged in leisurely evenings after her shift at the factory. At their rare meetings, Elsa chattered about entertainment at local *Biergartens* and rides on horse-drawn merry-go-rounds.

Elsa had little use for a friend who refused to make time for visiting and fun. And to Louisa, ice cream and suburban trips seemed rather frivolous and trivial after the trials she had endured during the past three years. Louisa actually felt relief when Elsa finally stopped inviting her on excursions. Both Elsa's friends and her extravagance made Louisa feel uncomfortable. She preferred to spend quiet evenings at home sewing for wages instead of frolicking about spending money. Moreover, Charlie, Henry's childhood friend, often joined Elsa's party, and Louisa wished to avoid him at all costs. He seemed to enjoy her company a little too much, and she certainly did not savor his obnoxious ways.

By April of 1899, Louisa had nearly concluded she would never see Elsa again. But to her surprise, late one afternoon an energetic knock summoned her from the potatoes she had been peeling. There in the stairwell stood Elsa!

Once inside, Elsa plunged into an animated explanation of why she had come. "Well, Louisa, as you know, my birthday was two days ago . . . Had you forgotten?" she queried carelessly. "Well, anyway, I had a wonderful day! Guess what *Papi* gave me? You'll never guess, of course," she rambled. "He gave me his permission to get married, so long as I don't choose a bad egg. Well, of course, there's no fear of that! In fact, though *Papi* didn't know it, I already had the fellow picked out and nearly secured. That is to say, I knew he had his eyes set on me. He had told me as much himself! And oh, what a dashing fellow he is! Remember Jake?" she questioned, throwing enough of a glance toward Louisa to note her nod. "You've been in hiding for so long, it's a wonder you remember any-one!" she digressed. "Well, as I was saying . . . isn't this the most wonderful thing you've ever heard? Jake asked me to marry him! The wedding will be in a month, so he has time to save up a little money. That's all that Father asked. He and *Mütti* are so pleased. Isn't it exciting, Louisa?" she asked, demanding a response.

A bit dizzied by this unexpected news, Louisa required a moment to gather the right words. "W-why . . . why, of c-course," she stammered. "I am happy for you, Elsa."

Elsa spent the next fifteen minutes rattling off the latest rumors concerning several mutual acquaintances and a host of people Louisa had never met. When Elsa's well of words had run dry, an awkward silence ensued that prompted a hasty end to her visit.

After Elsa's departure, Louisa returned to the potatoes and con-templated her old friend's news. She felt misgivings that she voiced in her journal later that night.

April 21, 1899

Elsa is getting married. I suppose it's not surprising, even though I certainly would not want to marry anytime soon! It seems like only yesterday that we hid in tents on Elsa's fire escape and laughed at the boys showing off in the streets below. Surely, they knew we were there all the time, but they never paid any attention to us.

Now Elsa is actually marrying one of those boys who used to act so silly. He was always friendly and handsome, but I have never trusted him. He alone threw bold, flirtatious smiles toward us as we sat high above. He is German at least, and his family is fairly well off. I suppose Elsa's father liked that.

Elsa might at least have found someone worth marrying. It's difficult, I'll admit, but it doesn't seem like she waited very long. I suppose I could get married soon if I had that as my goal. Mrs. Noltham seems to think it's time I found a beau, but I refuse to even consider any of the fellows I currently know.

Tante Joanna is a comfort. When she heard about Elsa, she said, "Well, I'm glad you have more sense than that girl. She'll end up sorry one day, count on it. Now don't you go thinking you have to match her silliness. I have no idea what your dear family would do without you!"

Enough of this marriage talk! My family needs me now—especially Maddie and Anna. Sometimes I wonder if Maddie even remembers Mütti. There are times when someone mentions a memory of Mütti, and we all become a little sad, except for Maddie. She remains cheerful. She's so young, yet she always talks about joyful things. She laughs at bugs in the stairwell and notices the funny noises the wind makes at night. She is such an eager child. She knocks things over and chatters endlessly. Even when she had just begun toddling around our flat, Mütti predicted that Maddie would be the sunshine in our family. How right she was!

Storytelling is Maddie's great delight. True, her stories are the rambling, simplistic tellings of a three-year-old, but she makes me smile. She pulls herself into a kneeling position on her chair at the dinner table (I think this makes her feel bigger), then throws herself into the most lively tales of what she has been up to. At times I think it is this little one's cheer that keeps the rest of us trudging along through the difficulties that plague us.

A few days later another hand rapped at the Shumakers' entrance. When Louisa opened the door, a gangly boy who could not have been more than thirteen stood just beyond the threshold. He raised his blue eyes to meet hers and there, encased in a vaguely familiar squint, she found an odd mixture of desperate hope and careless laughter. The boy ran an uneasy hand through his tousled blond hair as he grinned sheepishly and said, *"Guten Tag!"*

"Yes?" Louisa prodded. "What do you want?"

"Louisa, don't you recognize me?" the boy asked.

Louisa looked more intently at those eyes that had piqued her interest a few moments earlier. "Rudi?" she exclaimed incredulously as her cousin broke into a beaming smile. "Why, it is you! We weren't expecting you to arrive here from Germany this soon! Where is your family?" She glanced beyond him, expecting to see her other relatives tromping up the stairs.

With the onslaught of these questions, weariness came over Rudi's expression. "Please, Louisa, may I come in? It's been a long trip."

"Oh, of course," Louisa agreed. She led him to a seat at the table and set before him a glass of water and a slice of bread. She then slid into the head chair and leaned toward him, hunched over her elbows in curiosity. With controlled impatience, she quietly observed him devour the food.

At last he spoke. "I've run away, Louisa. Please don't reprimand me—I could do nothing else! You see, I wanted so desperately to stay in America, and *Mütti* and *Papi* wanted to take me back. Louisa, you would have done the same as I did. I'm sure everyone else is mad at me. You mustn't be mad too, Louisa," he implored.

"Slow down, Rudi," replied Louisa. "I can't make sense of what you're saying. I am not yet sure whether I should be upset or not."

"Here," Rudi said as he slid a letter across the table to her. The envelope bore her address but had no stamps. It had been roughly opened. "*Mütti* gave this to me at Ellis Island and told me to mail it. I heard *Papi* telling her that our hope had vanished and we would all have to go back to Germany. I just had to know what the letter said."

Louisa pulled out the letter and began to read.

Ellis Island, *den 22. April* 1899

Lieber August, *lieber* Jakob!

    I write with tears in my eyes. I am scarcely able to believe we have been so cheated, and right here at the threshold of paradise no less. We had heard the horrid stories about Ellis Island, but we were so sure we would find only joy here. How wrong! I hope you count your families as blessed. Everything was so easy for you. Anyway,

I must tell you the entire story. Juliane's eyes began bothering her during the voyage. They seemed often to be red and sore. I thought she had improved as we neared America. Perhaps my excitement about our new life in America clouded my eyes from the truth. After we landed, we were taken to the inspection building and the doctors. One man pulled up each of our eyelids and rolled them back over a buttonhook. His actions were rough, and I was thankful when he pushed me forward. I turned back, though, when I realized that Juliane hadn't followed as quickly as I thought she should. Then I saw the man writing a large chalk letter on her jacket. A nice jacket too, one we had bought for her to bring to America. But now she will never wear it as an American. They tell us she must be sent back. Since she is under ten, one parent must accompany her. Of course, I would go even if it were not required. Since Wilhelm refuses to be separated from me, and I from him, we must all return home. That is not the end of our terrible misfortune. They say that Juliane may eventually become blind. Whatever will we do? She will be doomed for the rest of her life. I cannot bear to think of it. Well, we must leave soon. I wanted you to know not to expect us anymore.

Thank you for the money you sent to the island for us. We must now use some of it to purchase return tickets for Wilhelm and the older children. The owners of the ship must pay for Juliane and me. Apparently, it's their fault they did not detect her disease before we left. I wish they had; it would have saved us so much trouble. I wish none of this had ever happened. Now we have absolutely nothing. The ocean liner company will not return any of the money we paid for the trip here, so we will live in poverty when we reach home. But enough of our troubles. I am sending you the money that is left over after purchasing the tickets. Thank you for attempting to help us.

Deine,
Bertha

"And our money?" asked Louisa, looking up at the boy who had intently observed her pained expressions as she read the sad tidings.

"I had to use it for my train ticket. I promise, Louisa, I will pay you back every penny. I'll get a job as a newsboy or a bootblack or a factory worker . . . anything! You must let me stay with you! I have nowhere to go."

"The most logical place for you to go is back to your parents."

"I will not return," Rudi replied adamantly, rising from his seat. "If you mention that again, I will leave."

"Sit down, Rudi," Louisa commanded, her eyes flashing at his impertinence. "Nothing has been determined yet. *Papi* and *Onkel* August will decide what is to be done. They will be home soon enough." Rudi sank back into the seat, and Louisa continued, "How on earth did you find us?"

"An official from Ellis Island made sure I got onto the right train. Then once I reached St. Louis, I used the address on the envelope. I just kept showing it to people, and they pointed me in the right direction."

"And how did you get through the immigration inspection? I can't believe they would admit a lone thirteen-year-old boy."

"Many boys my age got through."

"But you disobeyed your parents, Rudi. Do you really care so little for them? They must be crazy with worry! If only I could be completely happy to see you, but . . . !" She stopped with a moan.

Later that night, as *Onkel* August and *Papi* talked together about Rudi, Louisa confided in her journal.

April 24, 1899

My cousin Rudi appeared at our door today. I doubt that I have ever been more surprised in my life. I mean, we were expecting him, but not alone! Tante Bertha, Onkel Wilhelm, Margaretha, and Juliane had to return to Germany. Rudi sneaked away without telling them of his plans. I can only imagine how terrified his parents must be—and how grieved! When I think of how much I miss Mütti, I know the anguish they must be going through not knowing if he is even alive. It's so hard to even be excited to see Rudi when I know the pain he has caused!

Anyway, he has caused quite a stir here. I don't think that Papi or Onkel August know what to do. They're talking about it right now.

I guess the truth is, I am glad Rudi is here. Over the past few years I have only been able to bear the pain of Mütti's death because I have had my family around me. I am glad to have yet another relative near.

Later that evening *Onkel* August told Rudi that he would be living in the second-story flat and working in the watch shop. Henry, at twenty years of age, had become skilled and too valuable to be sent on errands. *Onkel* August welcomed the opportunity to have a younger boy to help with deliveries and shop upkeep. Rudi would also help Louisa by transporting her seamstress work to Mrs. Noltham's shop. *Papi* wrote a letter to *Tante* Bertha explaining the situation and asking for any additional instructions.

A few weeks later an incident proved that Rudi's lonely journey to St. Louis had not extinguished his propensity for wandering. When Louisa returned home on May 11, Henry left his work in the shop and met Louisa at the foot of the stairs. "I want to warn you before you go to get Maddie and Anna . . . *Tante* Joanna's stirred up like I've never seen her before."

"Surely, Maddie didn't—"

"No, not Maddie. It's that scamp Rudi. He's up to no good, I tell you," Henry remarked, shaking his head. "*Onkel* August sent him on a delivery this morning, and we haven't seen hide nor hair of him since! *Tante* Joanna has tottered between anger and worry all afternoon."

"Maybe he got lost," Louisa suggested.

"I doubt it! Mark my words, he's up to no good!" Henry insisted.

At that moment Rudi himself burst through the door. Unchecked by the silent reception he received from his cousins, he plunged into an excited story. "You'll never guess what I saw today!" he shouted as the door slammed shut.

"No, we won't even try," Louisa stated flatly.

"Well," he continued in spite of his breathlessness, "as I went to make my delivery, I heard an incredible racket. All the whistles near the riverfront were shrieking and bellowing. I nearly jumped out of my boots, it was so sudden and all. I asked a man what all the commotion meant. 'It's a celebration of the arrival of the *U.S.S. Nashville*,' he told me. 'She's on a tour of inspection.' I bet you two don't even know what's so special about that gunboat. The man told me the whole story. 'Son,' he said, 'that boat's the one that fired the first shot in the Spanish-American War. Why, she played a great part in America's recent war victory!'"

Louisa and Henry regarded Rudi silently. Undaunted, he continued, "Well, as you can well imagine, I ran down to the levee to join the celebration. Boy, what a sight! Henry, you should have seen it! I sure wouldn't mind being a sailor on a ship like that!"

Louisa, unable to remain quiet any longer, cut him short. "Rudi, if you ever do decide to run away to be a sailor, at least do *Onkel* August and *Tante* Joanna the kindness of telling them your plans. I don't imagine you had instructions to go all the way down to the levee today?" She hoped to see him squirm, but he stood unaffected.

"Don't waste your energy cross-examining him," Henry advised. "*Onkel* August has words enough to say to him." Henry turned toward his younger cousin. "He's waiting in the shop. I wouldn't dawdle if I were you. You can explain to him what you spent the rest of the day doing. Seems to me that it doesn't take six hours to look at a boat!"

Louisa sighed as Rudi walked into the shop. "I loved him so dearly when we were both children," she remarked to Henry. "I still love him. But his behavior . . . I thought having him here would bring us joy, but instead he's brought us sadness."

CHAPTER TWENTY

Another Escapade

June–July 1899

Work filled every moment of Louisa's days. Since Sundays alone offered a reprieve from the constant scramble, the weeks passed quickly. Dorothy had hung a month-by-month calendar in the kitchen; and when Louisa remembered to look at it, it helped her keep her dates straight. One day, after ignoring the calendar for some time, Louisa glanced toward the wall where it hung and found herself confronted by the month of June. "Surely not!" she gasped, turning to face Dorothy who sat at the table. "You must have changed the calendar early!"

"Louisa, it's the twelfth of June!" Dorothy insisted with a laugh. "Have you had your head in a hole the first half of this month?"

"That's more true than you think!" Louisa muttered. "I do well just to keep the days of the week straight!"

A few days later when the sun began to bake St. Louis, Louisa had no trouble recalling that summer had come. How she hated hot weather! Even at night, she sweated as she slept. She felt like a wilting flower that is not allowed to die but must continue a miserable existence. Even the tepid water that flowed from their faucet offered no cool relief but merely reminded her of the steamy humidity that surrounded her. "If only we could have cold water in summer and warm water in winter!" she muttered to Henry one night as she finished the dishes. "When it's hot, everything's hot; and when it's cold, everything's frigid!"

"Fall will come soon enough," Henry encouraged. "Then we'll have a few wonderful months."

"It's only June," Louisa moaned. "This summer will never end!"

"Part of the reason you're so miserable is that you spend all day rushing around," replied Henry. "It's dusty and hot on the streets and steamy in front of the stove, even if you do get all the cooking done in the morning. Not to mention the fact that you spend every evening with extra clothes draped over your legs as you sew. You must be suffocating!"

"Can I help it that I have to do all those things?" Louisa snapped. "I have little choice!"

"Louisa, don't be angry," Henry entreated. "I only wanted to show that I understand how hot you must feel. I know you can't change anything."

Henry stood in thoughtful silence for a moment, then blurted out a sudden idea. "I know just the thing for you, Louisa! You need an evening off. Tomorrow we'll take the streetcar to the Fairgrounds. There's plenty to look at there, and trees shade much of the place. Besides that, there are wading pools. Your feet could cool down at least!"

Before Louisa could protest that she would never take off her shoes and stockings in public, Dorothy burst from the hall and exclaimed, "Oh, can I go too?" Henry and Louisa turned in disbelief; at age eleven, Dorothy rarely craved any outing that might involve crowds.

"Would you really like to go?" Henry pressed.

"Definitely," persisted Dorothy.

Louisa continued to survey her sister in amazement, suddenly realizing that Dorothy was hot and tired just like everyone else. What set her apart was the patient perseverance with which she bore her hardship.

"Well!" declared Henry, forgetting to wait for Louisa's agreement, "it's decided then. We'll leave tomorrow night right after dinner."

What a delightful evening they enjoyed! Louisa refused to wade, but Dorothy gleefully shed her shoes and stockings and, holding her skirt just above the ankle-deep water, began to romp. From time to time she sneaked behind Henry and with a flick of her toes sent tiny fountains of water rushing his way. He wisely counterattacked so weakly that Dorothy's dress did not suffer any watermark casualties.

Louisa observed their fun from a nearby bench. The sight of lush trees and the sound of laughter soothed her. When the shadows at last grew so long that they began to melt into a mass of darkness, Louisa reluctantly reminded her siblings that they should begin heading home. With twin groans and a final splash on Dorothy's part, the brother and sister withdrew from the pool to dry their feet.

"Well, do you feel better?" Henry asked as he shook his sock out to its full length.

"Yes," Louisa conceded with a smile. "You certainly picked the right remedy for my ailments."

"Well," replied Henry, "after twenty years of living with you, I certainly hope I know what will cheer you up!"

"Tonight you did anyway," Louisa admitted.

"And you had a pretty good time yourself, Miss Dorothy, didn't you?" Henry asked, pulling his younger sister's long braid.

"Oh, yes!" she answered, her blue eyes glistening.

When Louisa came home one early July afternoon, she found her aunt waiting for her at the top of the stairs. "Well, my girl!" *Tante* Joanna exclaimed with a huff. "Would you believe it?"

"What?" queried Louisa, fearful that her cousin had added another exploit to his growing list of disturbances.

"It's that lad Rudi. He has disappeared again, that's what. Your uncle sent him out on a quick delivery, and the rascal never returned!" *Tante* Joanna shook her head in disgust. "Don't we have enough worries without having that boy add to them?"

"Now, *Tante* Joanna," begged Louisa, "we don't even know what's happened yet. You mustn't accuse him so harshly until we learn the truth."

"Oh, I know," snipped *Tante* Joanna, shaking her head. "It's just that . . . oh, I just . . ."

"You just have grown to love him and are worried about him, right?" Louisa replied softly.

Tante Joanna allowed a smile to push its way onto her lips. "Yes, you have found me out. I'm really concerned about the boy. We have no idea where he could be."

"Well, I wouldn't worry," declared Louisa with forced enthusiasm. "A boy who can forge his way to our home all the way from the immigrant inspection gates in New York City certainly won't lose himself on the streets of St. Louis." She turned and walked up to the third floor, muttering to herself, "At least not for long! What can that rascal be up to?"

Tante Joanna's fears turned out to be more well-founded than Louisa's attempted optimism. Louisa had expected that her cousin would appear before sundown. But when *Tante* Joanna extinguished the lights at bedtime, Rudi's bed was empty. Louisa slept restlessly that night, her ears straining for the noise of footsteps on the stairs. All remained silent, however; and when the sun rose the next morning, Rudi had still not returned. As Louisa prepared breakfast, she found that *Tante* Joanna's fears had infected her own heart.

On the second morning after Rudi's disappearance, *Papi* began to express doubts that they would ever see Rudi again. "He probably headed west in search of gold or embarked on some other absurd adventure. That boy has no sense!"

Louisa mulled over *Papi's* comment while she walked to work. Endless questions assaulted her mind. Had some trouble befallen Rudi? Or was he cavorting about town? Was he really crazy enough to head west in search of adventure and excitement? Suddenly a shouted word drove all those thoughts away.

"Louisa!"

When the speaker darted from the alley, Louisa's fears vanished. "Rudi! You're safe!" she exclaimed. Then she noticed the amusement in his expression, and misgivings dampened her enthusiasm. "Where have you been?" she demanded. "We've all been worried sick. I've hardly slept the last two nights!"

Her rebuke did not dim the thrill that burned in Rudi's eyes.

"Oh, Louisa, I've had a bully of a time! I'll tell you, but you mustn't let the others know. They would never understand." Louisa glared at Rudi, but he failed to heed the warning in her eyes. "I've been to Chicago with some of the boys—saw the White Stockings play."

Louisa stood gaping as he told his story. But when Rudi paused to grimace at an annoying fly, Louisa's tongue came to life. "Do you think of no one but yourself?" she cried. "Do you expect me to stand here and listen to you gloat about such an exploit? Do you have any idea how much we worried about you? Does it even matter to you? You might at least have given *Tante* Joanna and *Onkel* August warning after all they've done for you. But not you! I suppose I should not be surprised; after all, you left your own family in New York."

Rudi winced at her final statement. "But, Louisa, I have always dreamed of going to see a baseball game," he stammered.

"I suppose a St. Louis Browns game wouldn't have been good enough?" stabbed Louisa. Rudi stared at his feet. "And the money!" continued Louisa. "I have not forgotten, Rudi, how much those train tickets from New York cost us years ago. I hope you at least paid for the trip honestly!"

"Don't be too quick with your rebukes, Louisa!" Rudi pleaded. "I didn't need to buy a ticket—we bummed our way to Chicago."

"Rudi, that's dangerous—you might have been killed!" Louisa gasped as she imagined her cousin hanging perilously beneath a railway car.

"Aw, I wasn't the least bit afraid!"

"That's only because you're crazy, Rudi," Louisa charged. "If you had the sense of a donkey, you would have stayed home and would not have even considered riding beneath a train!"

"You're sure sour today!" Rudi snapped. "It's not that bad, Louisa. There are bars under the train cars, and I just hooked my legs on one and held on tightly to the other. The dust and flying gravel gets bad, but I'd hardly call that dangerous!"

"I refuse to stand here and listen to your nonsense any longer, Rudi. The entire plan was foolish and thoughtless. Grown men have died while dangling beneath trains!" Louisa declared. "I recommend that you get home as quickly as possible, although at this point I don't much care what you do!" She turned and resumed her walk to the streetcar stop.

"Louisa," Rudi called after her, "you won't tell anyone else where I went, will you?"

Louisa swung around fiercely. "And just what story are you planning to tell them? Some lie that you concoct? Has it ever occurred to you, Rudi, that *Onkel* August and *Tante* Joanna have sacrificed a great deal for your sake? What you have done is a disgrace! They will know, Rudi. Whether they hear it from your mouth or mine is up to you!"

Louisa pivoted away from her cousin, joining the early-morning throng. She had only taken a few steps when a whistled melody reached her ears. She cringed as she recognized Rudi's carefree rendition of "There'll Be a Hot Time in the Old Town Tonight." How it infuriated her to picture him sauntering away with his hands buried deep in his pockets and his mind probably already pondering his next adventure!

When she returned home that night, Rudi's tune had changed. His exploits were known in detail, and she had never seen her cousin look so sober or *Tante* Joanna so hurt. Although she never heard the details of what had transpired, she was certain Rudi had received just discipline.

CHAPTER TWENTY-ONE

A Snowstorm Rescue

February 1900

By February of 1900 Louisa had begun to long for snow, but not for her own sake. Maddie awoke every morning, ran to the window, then turned back sadly with the news that no flakes were in sight. Louisa hated to see her repeatedly disappointed. How could a four-year-old wait patiently for a significant snowfall when the water in the gutters had been frozen for weeks? The light dusting they had received Christmas Day had not been adequate according to Maddie's standards.

Other than Maddie's unfulfilled hopes, Louisa was content with the cold weather. It had its advantages. The street mud had solidified into a frost-covered surface that rivaled stone pavement. Furthermore, only in winter, when street garbage froze, did the city air remotely rival the fresh air of Louisa's birthplace. After several years in America Louisa had nearly decided that winter cold was preferable to summer heat. She did not personally see any benefit in wet, slushy snow; but since Maddie thought snow was winter's greatest glory, Louisa desired a few white days for her sake. So both sisters hoped and waited.

"Brr-r-r-r-r! It's blustery out there tonight," called Louisa as she entered the empty front room of her aunt and uncle's flat at dusk one evening. She brushed some lingering snowflakes from her coat while she waited for Maddie to appear. Instead, Rudi stepped out of one of the back rooms.

"Did you get the clothes delivered to Mrs. Noltham?" Louisa asked, glancing toward Rudi.

"N-no," he stammered. "I had to stay here to watch Anna. *Tante* Joanna had to go to the store."

"Didn't you tell *Tante* Joanna you had to deliver the clothes?" pressed Louisa.

"No," Rudi mumbled. "Don't get angry, Louisa. Dorothy came home early and offered to take the clothes."

Anticipating her cousin's next confession, Louisa rushed forward and grabbed Rudi's shoulders. "Where's Maddie?" she demanded. "Surely you weren't crazy enough to let her go out in this storm too?"

"She wanted to play in the snow. You know how she's talked of nothing else for weeks. How could I keep her in?" Rudi shrugged carelessly.

"How could you?" Louisa shrieked. "On a night like this? They're probably lost and half-frozen by this time!"

"Stop it!" snarled Rudi. "They'll be all right. Anyway, I figured you'd want me to stay with Anna since I'm older than Dorothy."

"Rudi, don't even try to whitewash this one!" Louisa snapped. "I see the truth all too well! No doubt you played on Dorothy's noble sense of duty. I can hear you explaining that you would have to wait until tomorrow to deliver the clothes, unless of course she would like to take them tonight. You knew well enough that Dorothy would never allow the work to be late; she knows what that could cost us! But then to send Maddie besides! She's only four! Even on a good night, she should never be walking through the city!"

"I gave them money for the streetcar," Rudi protested.

"Do you care nothing for my sisters?" Louisa yelled. "Did it never occur to you that the streetcars can't run in heavy snow? There's a chance that they were able to ride *to* the shop, but you can be sure they're *walking* home!"

"Maybe they didn't go all the way. Maybe they turned back," Rudi suggested.

"Dorothy would never give up. She may only be twelve, but she understands duty better than you do at fourteen!" At that moment *Tante* Joanna returned home. Louisa sighed with relief as she pulled Rudi's coat from a wall hook and threw it toward him. "Come on, Rudi! You will at least help me search for them! We have no time to stand here talking any longer; the streets are getting darker and colder!" She grabbed Rudi's arm and, after a quick explanation to their aunt, pulled him down to the street.

The click of the fastening door, like the pistol shot that begins a race, spurred Louisa forward. Although gaslights lined her path, illuminating the snowflakes' dance, her eyes focused on the darkness that lurked just beyond the edge of the lamps' glow. Louisa tried to envision how Maddie and Dorothy would view the city. When she recalled her own journey through Bremen on that dark night years before, fear chilled Louisa through and through.

The icy wind felt like pine needles brushing against her face, and the cold air rushed down her throat like a searing fire. Louisa bowed her head to shield her face from the wind's direct onslaught, yet trudged on unbeaten.

Every few minutes Louisa looked back to be sure Rudi was still following. Each time his scowling expression reproached her, souring the gratitude she felt for his continued presence. Not a word passed between them until they reached the lovely, tree-lined avenues of the West End. As they began to pass landmarks that declared they had entered the vicinity of Mrs. Noltham's shop, Louisa trembled. "We should have found them by now," she yelled back to Rudi.

He nodded in silence.

A moment later they rounded the corner of a brick building and stopped. Across the street, guarding a long avenue of elegant homes, stood a pair of turreted stone gates. The frame of the entrance focused Louisa's eyes on the first house beyond its towers. The mansion blazed with electrical lights. In the street below, a sleigh waited, its horse pawing the ground impatiently. Nearby, just at the edge of a park that divided the avenue into parallel streets, stood a tiny figure.

"Maddie!" exclaimed Louisa. But she did not see Dorothy! Panic shot through her until, at last, her darting eyes located Dorothy waiting in a shadow a few feet from Maddie.

Louisa pointed. "There they are!" she announced to Rudi, who had surged forward to her side when she had spoken Maddie's name.

"Well, let's go get them," he replied brusquely.

As they started forward, a sharply dressed gentleman stepped onto the porch of the nearest house. Behind him a lady appeared in the doorway. Rudi and Louisa both stopped abruptly.

"I'll wait here," the boy mumbled, betraying a bashful hesitation that Louisa had never before witnessed in him. He leaned against a nearby brick wall, grabbed a stick from the street, and began to pry snow from the cracks in his boots.

Louisa remained near her cousin, but she returned her attention to the scene beyond the gates. The young man had drawn his partner's hand through his arm so that he might escort her down the icy steps leading to the street. As the young pair advanced, Louisa enviously noted the lady's elegant jet-black mantle and the lavish amount of fabric in her skirt. When the couple reached the sleigh, Louisa turned her attention back to her sisters just in time to see Maddie begin plunging toward the spot where Dorothy waited. Louisa knew that her little sister was afraid of the strangers. Maddie's dash soon ended when she stepped upon an exposed patch of ice and fell backward with a yelp.

Without hesitation the gentleman ran to where Maddie lay. For a moment the awkwardness of encountering such a wealthy, refined stranger kept Louisa from taking any action, but soon she summoned the courage to ignore her own shyness and rush to Maddie's side. When she reached her sister, both Dorothy and the gentleman had already knelt beside the little girl. The young man seemed oblivious to the snow that would certainly ruin his elegant trousers. He gently lifted Maddie to her feet.

"Maddie, are you hurt?" Louisa probed. Her little sister shook her head, though tears continued to fall, making small holes in the snow where they fell.

"Is your name Mattie, little one?" the young man asked. Maddie nodded, missing the minute difference in pronunciation. "Well then," the gentleman continued, "I think I should introduce myself, for we are twins of sorts. I'm Matthew. I'm afraid I've grown a little old for the name Mattie now, but that used to be my mother's favorite pet name for me. When this young lady . . ." He glanced toward Louisa with clear, gentle eyes. ". . . ran up and called your name, I almost answered. You can well imagine the confusion I felt at hearing my old name from a stranger!" He gave Louisa a friendly smile.

"Why were you standing out in the snow?" Matthew asked Maddie.

"The horse!" she explained.

"Oh!" Matthew laughed. "That's Lady. Would you like to meet her?"

Maddie looked up at her oldest sister with pleading eyes. Just then Rudi summoned them impatiently from across the street. "We must go quickly," Louisa murmured.

"It will take only a moment." Matthew grasped Maddie's waist, exclaimed, "Up we go!" and lifted her from the ground. As he carried her toward the horse with one arm, he brushed the snow from her coat with the other. "You look just like a snowman!" he teased.

Maddie's eyes glistened as she laughed and declared, "You too!" pointing to his black top hat.

"Why, you're right!" Matthew chuckled. "This hat would be perfect for a snowman."

After Maddie petted Lady, Matthew returned her to Louisa. "Good night, Maddie!" he cried, bowing to sweep the remaining snow from his knees. "Don't let the snow swallow you up later tonight! Good night to you all!" he added, lifting his hat in salute.

"Good night," Louisa whispered. As she watched Matthew climb into the sleigh, she cringed slightly in embarrassment. The beautiful lady glared disdainfully from the sleigh where she now sat. Louisa inwardly shuddered to think of how common her family must appear to the refined couple, but she quickly pushed such thoughts aside and turned her attention to her sisters. "How glad we are to find you two!" she exclaimed. "I was so worried!"

"I'm glad you came," whispered Dorothy, hiding her words from Rudi. "I'm afraid of dark alleys."

"I thought as much," answered Louisa with a grim smile. "Now, Rudi," she called after her cousin who had already begun tromping homeward, "would you be so kind as to carry Maddie home?" With a growl, their cousin retraced his steps, lifted Maddie to his back, and resumed his journey homeward.

CHAPTER TWENTY-TWO

A Noise in the Night

February—March 1900

When Louisa arrived home the next afternoon, Maddie complained of a sore throat. *Tante* Joanna explained that the little girl had spent most of the day curled up in a soft chair rather than playing energetically as she usually did. By evening Maddie's forehead burned with fever, and the little girl remained silent because talking hurt her throat too much.

The illness lasted over a week and caused several changes in the Shumaker household. At night Anna crowded into the bed Dorothy and Louisa shared so Maddie could have a bed all to herself. During the day *Tante* Joanna relocated to the third-story flat so Maddie would not have to move downstairs. And during every waking hour Louisa prayed continuously. She managed to keep her fears from her siblings, but she shared them with *Papi* and wrote of them in her journal.

> *February 23, 1900*
> *Maddie has been sick for more than a week, but I think she is finally getting better. Praise God! I was more afraid than I can explain. Every time I looked at Maddie's pale face, I thought of Mütti. I don't know why this sickness affected me so much; after all, we've all had turns at being sick in the three years since Mütti's death. Maybe it's just that I love Maddie so much, or maybe it's that she seemed so very sick and I've known so many children who have died. She had such a high fever!*
> *I was even afraid to leave her with Tante Joanna each day. I struggled against the fear that Maddie would die if I left, that I would*

*return home and find that grief had once again invaded my home.
Papi said he understood how I felt. For many months after Mütti's
death, he experienced fear every time we children were out of his
sight. He told me we must trust Maddie to God's care. I kept wish-
ing, though, that I could know for certain that God would choose to
heal Maddie!*

*Now she is so much better, praise God. She is starting to chat-
ter again, and that's a sure sign she's returning to normal. The fear
is slowly leaving me.*

For a few weeks happier days returned to the Shumaker household.
Maddie's laughter once again filled the flat, and a new contentment
settled upon Louisa. Her fear during Maddie's sickness had
reminded her how much she treasured each member of her family.

On March 16 the girls spent a peaceful hour together before
dinner. Since a stew was simmering on the stove and the rooms
had been tidied, no urgent chores compelled them to bustle about
the flat. Of course, Louisa and Dorothy did not sit idly; they sewed
with the diligence of those who know that stitches equal mouth-
fuls of food. Maddie knelt on a kitchen chair. In her characteristic fashion, she slid forward and stretched herself across the table,
leaving only her lower legs in place on the chair. After a contem-
plative moment she cradled her chin in her hands and announced,
"I want snow!"

"I'm afraid there's little chance of that now, you goose!"
laughed Louisa. "Soon it will be time for flowers. I can't wait! As
Oma always said, spring is the best time of year!"

Dorothy looked up from her work and peered across the table
at Maddie. "You wouldn't want to be lost in the snow again, would
you?" she asked in disbelief. "I'm thankful for the warmer weather."

"I want to see the horse!" Maddie persisted. "And Mr. Mattie!"

"You haven't forgotten him, have you?" Louisa questioned,
hiding her own vivid memories behind an incredulous tone. "It's
been over a month since that snowy evening!"

"He was like a prince. Like the one in the story you read to
me!" answered Maddie.

"Well then," commented Dorothy dryly, "the fancy lady with
him must have been his wicked stepsister."

"Dorothy!" Louisa murmured. "That's not a nice thing to say. You might at least mention that she was very beautiful."

"Not on the inside," said Dorothy. "All the princesses, fine ladies, and milkmaids in the fairy tales I have read are as beautiful as flowers or starlight, but they are also kind. Didn't you notice how that lady glared at us, Louisa? And she didn't even try to help Maddie. She was no princess!"

"America doesn't have princesses," Maddie declared. "*Tante* Joanna said so."

"Well then, there can't be any princes here either!" Dorothy replied.

"Anyway," Louisa observed with a laugh, "I doubt that either a prince or a princess would be tolerated in St. Louis for very long, especially on our street."

"Royalty would never want to come to our part of town. That haughty lady wouldn't be caught here either; that's as certain as spring!" Dorothy declared.

Maddie sighed. "But Mr. Mattie would come!"

"He would have no reason to," countered Louisa. "Can you think of anything that would bring him to our street?"

"He was nice," Maddie answered simply.

That night Louisa awoke at an unusual hour. Even in her groggy state, she knew that a single, unrepeated noise had beckoned her to consciousness. She pushed herself into a sitting position, her ears straining against the quiet. No unusual sound came from the bed that the younger girls shared; and beside her, Dorothy breathed with the steady rhythm of sleep.

"I must have heard something outside," Louisa told herself. As she settled back against the mattress, however, the noise came again. This time its unmistakable origin and meaning gripped Louisa with fear. A pained moan had come from the other bed.

Louisa leapt to her feet and lunged toward her youngest sisters. In the glint of moonlight that fell upon the bed, Louisa saw Maddie's glassy, frightened eyes. As the little girl's lips parted ever so slightly to emit another low moan, Louisa noticed a large bloodstain on her pillow. Placing a trembling hand on Maddie's brow,

Louisa read a terrible message in the simmering dampness she encountered.

"Just a minute, Maddie," she whispered hoarsely. She rushed into the hall, calling to *Papi* and Henry as she ran toward the kitchen faucet.

Papi appeared quickly. The desperate fear in his daughter's voice had brought him from deep sleep to full alertness in an instant. "What is it, Louisa?" he cried.

"Maddie!" Louisa gasped. That one word propelled *Papi* into the bedroom while Henry, who had entered the kitchen in time to overhear the short conversation, said, "I'll start the fire and boil some water."

"Why?" Louisa demanded as she fumbled through a darkened cabinet in search of a rag.

"I don't know," Henry admitted. "It just seems like someone always needs hot water during a sickness." He paused and then produced a far more practical idea. "I'll run to get *Tante* Joanna."

"Oh, yes!" urged Louisa. "I have no idea what to do!" As Henry ran to the door, Louisa pulled a rag from the cabinet and plunged it under a stream of cold water. Unmindful of the trail of water she left on the floor behind her, she rushed into the hallway where she bumped into Anna and Dorothy.

"What's wrong?" Dorothy asked. "*Papi* sent us—"

"Maddie's sick," interrupted Louisa. "Oh, where is *Tante* Joanna? Take this to *Papi*," she ordered, forcing the rag into Dorothy's hand. Wildly, she turned and ran back into the kitchen. She would have started down the stairs if *Tante* Joanna had not entered at that moment.

"Maddie's sick," Louisa wailed. "Terribly sick. It's worse than before. She's burning up and moaning. I don't know what to do!"

The concern on *Tante* Joanna's face provided no comfort. "Where is your *Papi*?" she asked.

"He's with her," Louisa said.

"Very good. Wait here," *Tante* Joanna instructed.

"She'll know what to do," Henry remarked as *Tante* Joanna rushed to the bedroom.

"Yes, of course," Louisa murmured. She longed to be able to

throw herself into some task that would help Maddie. She could not forget the bloody pillow or the pallor of Maddie's face; Louisa had never seen anyone look so sick. Knowing all too well that childhood disease often ended in death, Louisa sat down at the table and hid her tear-filled eyes in her arms.

Soon *Tante* Joanna entered again. The wise woman sent the other children to the parlor and then wrapped her arms around her niece. She silently rocked Louisa back and forth until the tears began to subside. "Louisa," she whispered, "you must be strong."

"I can't," wailed Louisa. "I'm so afraid. I can't go through another death. First *Oma*, then *Mütti*, now Maddie . . . I'm so afraid!"

"Louisa, you must listen. Maddie is very sick, it's true. But she is still alive, and she may well live until she is old. We can never tell how a sickness will go. Don't kill Maddie in your mind before death comes. Sometimes in such cases it is the child who passes on to eternal life, but often it is the illness that passes. We must hope and pray that Maddie will recover. Your little sister needs you, as do the others. Those who are well are dear to you too."

"I know," moaned Louisa. "I just feel miserable. I don't know what to do. And the blood . . . she must be very sick."

"She had a nosebleed, but it has stopped now. Louisa, we must remember that the Bible says, 'I can do all things through Christ who strengthens me.' What I am asking you to do is impossible on your own; only the Lord can give you the strength." *Tante* Joanna paused and let her words sink in. "Would you like for me to pray with you?"

Louisa nodded with a sniffle.

"Dear Lord," began *Tante* Joanna, "none of us knows what to do. We are fighting an unknown enemy in Maddie's body. You, Lord, You alone, can heal her, if You so choose. Please grant us strength to trust You. Grant us strength to nurse and care for Maddie. Please be with Louisa. Calm her fears. Carry her close to Your heart. In Christ's name we pray, amen."

CHAPTER TWENTY-THREE

The Doctor

Late March 1900

Adhering to a yearly custom, the sky wept often in March of 1900. The rain mirrored the tears that so often collected in Louisa's eyes as Maddie's condition gradually worsened during the last two weeks of that month. Other troubling symptoms joined the little girl's fever and pallor. Early in the sickness, Maddie's elbow became swollen and achy. Although the pain in that joint gradually diminished, the tenderness then moved to her ankles and left wrist. She lay listlessly in bed, unable even to muster enough desire to eat.

Although Louisa longed to remain constantly at Maddie's side, work drew her away each morning. Day after day she waded through ankle-deep mud on her way to the West End. Louisa's irritation at the dirty state of St. Louis became Mr. Hatterly's cook's favorite teasing topic. On Thursday during the last week of March, Louisa walked into the kitchen fretting, "If only all the mud would swallow up all my problems instead of my feet!"

"Why, I don't see any mud on your shoes," Betsy joked.

"Well, of course not!" pouted Louisa. "My street shoes are wallowing in their coat of mud out on the back step! The shoes I'm wearing now may be clean, but I suppose you can at least see the unfashionable brown polka dots that are scattered over the lower half of my dress!"

"I'd have to be blind to miss them," Betsy admitted with a chuckle.

Louisa spent that morning cleaning the parlor windows. As she wiped away a smoky film from one of the lower panes, she glanced outside. A beautiful horse, harnessed to a carriage, waited dutifully before the neighboring house. How that creature reminded Louisa of a snowy evening, only weeks before, when Maddie had been lost in the storm! Louisa had been so relieved to find Maddie that night! During the trip home she had thanked God for His faithfulness and protection.

How quickly her heart forgot such evidence of God's mercy! In place of her joyful praise there was fear, shaking her confidence in the Lord. Would God rescue Maddie from this new trouble attacking her tiny body? The walls of a loving home and all of Louisa's careful care could not protect Maddie this time; God alone could heal her. Louisa wondered if she could ever trust God again if He chose to let Maddie die.

Tears streamed down Louisa's face, and she sank onto the window seat, burying her face in the curtain that hung by her right shoulder. She was never sure how long she stayed that way. A numbing sorrow consumed her, blocking her consciousness until Mr. Hatterly's entrance roused her.

Louisa shot to her feet, her face flushed. Rather than remembering all the times during the past three years that Mr. Hatterly had praised her industry, Louisa instantly recalled the one time he had caught her peeking at a book instead of working. He had shown kindness and understanding then, but certainly he would dismiss her this time!

Undone by Mr. Hatterly's intense gaze, Louisa dropped her eyes to the ground. When she heard him walking toward her, she resolutely raised her head to face the reproach she expected. To her surprise, she found tenderness.

"Louisa, I disturbed you just now," he began, hesitating for a moment. "Forgive me for broaching a topic that might best be left untouched, but I have never seen you so shaken. I am not trying to make you tell me about your troubles, but if there is some way I can be of help . . . Betsy mentioned this morning that your sister has been ill. You need only let me know if there is anything you need."

This display of compassion lured silent tears from Louisa's

eyes. A few minutes passed before Louisa gained enough composure to speak. "Yes, it is my sister," she admitted. "She has been sick
for almost two weeks. She's had a fever the entire time, and she
complains of aching that moves around to different parts of her
body. I'm so scared. My mother died just before I came to work
here, and I'm afraid we will lose little Maddie too. Nothing we have
tried has helped her."

"Has she seen a doctor?" Mr. Hatterly asked, concern deepen-
ing the wrinkles in his forehead.

"No, she has not," Louisa confessed. "All the money we make
goes to pay for our food and rent. We don't know of a doctor we
can afford to pay."

Mr. Hatterly gazed out the window for a moment before reply-
ing. "A friend of mine is a doctor who's well respected in this town.
He has a young assistant in training right now. The lad's just finished medical college and is full of enthusiasm. I'm sure he'd be
willing to come examine your sister just for the experience. He
would know what to do if anyone would; my friend takes only the
best under his supervision. Would you like him to take a look at
your sister?"

"Oh no, sir, I couldn't ask that," Louisa protested, but the hope
that gleamed from her eyes spoke a truer response than her words.

"I will talk to the young doctor for you," Mr. Hatterly countered with gentle firmness. "I expect that he will call late this
afternoon."

"Oh, thank you, sir!" Louisa exclaimed. "But I will understand
if he is too busy."

"Nothing is as pressing as the life and health of a little girl," Mr.
Hatterly declared with finality. "Now, you will need to write down
directions to your home so I can pass them on to the doctor. Who
is staying with your sister now?"

"My aunt . . . Joanna Shumaker. She is the one he will meet at
the door. I am sure she will let him in once she understands he's a
doctor."

"There's no need for concern over that matter," Mr. Hatterly
replied. "You will be there to meet the doctor and hear his
recommendations."

"But, sir, I have a great deal of work to finish before I leave. I cannot be sure I will get home before nightfall, and I doubt the doctor will want to be out visiting at such a late hour. Please just give the doctor my aunt's name."

"Louisa, there is no work here that cannot wait. There's a little girl at home who needs your attention more than dusting and sweeping ever will." Louisa ducked her head to hide her tears. "Poor child," Mr. Hatterly continued, "so young and so sick, and without a mother to comfort her. You must go home at once. And I feel I must quickly seek out this young doctor."

"Thank you, sir," murmured Louisa, her voice overcome with emotion.

Mr. Hatterly acknowledged her gratitude with a slight bow and a compassionate, sad smile. Then with deliberate steps he crossed to a massive mahogany desk from which he withdrew a sheet of paper. "Write the directions here," he instructed. When she had finished, he glanced over the paper a moment before folding it and placing it safely in his coat pocket. "Stay home tomorrow with your sister as well. I shall see you on Monday," he said in farewell as he walked to open the heavy wooden door for Louisa. "I hope then to hear that your little sister is feeling much better."

Once Louisa reached home and relieved *Tante* Joanna, she did not stop pacing between Maddie's bedside and the parlor window until Dorothy walked through the door. "Dorothy!" she exclaimed. "Run down to the side door and wait on the street. A doctor is coming, and someone must be outside to greet him."

"How is Maddie?" Dorothy asked, ignoring the urgency in her sister's voice. A whimper from the corner provided an adequate answer.

"Can't you see she is still horribly sick?" demanded Louisa, glancing toward the bed where little Maddie huddled beneath a load of blankets. "You can help by going downstairs. Now!"

"But how will I know who he is?" Dorothy hesitated.

"How do you think?" Louisa snapped. "A doctor certainly won't be dressed like the grocers and workmen that typically pass our door. And I doubt he'll come on the streetcar or in a rickety wagon. You'll know him. Now go!" Being in no mood to battle with Dorothy's timidity, Louisa punctuated her command with firm hands that piloted her sister out the bedroom door.

Dorothy, however, refused to retreat submissively. "But, Louisa, what will I say to him? He's a stranger!"

"Ask him if he's the doctor sent by Mr. Hatterly," Louisa suggested. "Dorothy, this is not too much to ask! We must have a doctor; it's Maddie's only hope."

Dorothy presented one final plea, "I'll sit up here while you—"

"No!" insisted Louisa. "If you care at all for Maddie, you will go now to meet the doctor!" At that moment a frightful moan called Louisa to Maddie's bed and sent Dorothy scurrying down the stairs on her mission.

Once Maddie had quieted, Louisa impatiently returned to the window. A doctor's phaeton stood before their door, and the owner was speaking to Dorothy. Louisa flew to the door of their flat. As she stood at the threshold waiting, she glanced toward the *Wilkommen* embroidery that still hung where she had placed it just after *Mütti's* death. *Oma's* words, "Never forget to welcome stranger and guest alike," echoed in her mind. How she wished there had not been a need to summon this stranger to their door! Now all her hopes rested on this unknown man.

Louisa heard the creaking of the door at the bottom of the stairs. Her ears traced Dorothy's soft shuffle and the doctor's firm footfall as they climbed the steps. Dorothy came into view first. "He's come," she noted quietly as she let him pass.

Louisa hardly heard this unnecessary announcement. "Oh, I am so glad you are here," she gasped as the doctor finished his ascent. "Our sister is so very sick. She is feverish and achy. You must help us," she pleaded. At that moment the doctor stepped into the kitchen. Even in her desperation, Louisa noted his youth. His sprightly blue eyes and cheerful eyebrows sent a panic rushing through her as though cold water had been poured over her head. Was he too young to help? What if Mr. Hatterly had been mistaken about his skill?

The young doctor seemed unaware of her misgivings. He brushed a steady hand through his rumpled hair and greeted her with a nod. "Hello. I'm Dr. Matthew Burton. Where's the little girl who is ill?" he asked. His calm gaze and steady voice helped lessen Louisa's panic.

"This way," she replied, leading him to the bedroom.

As the doctor slid into a chair near Maddie's bedside, Louisa halted a few steps behind him. Although she could no longer see the doctor's face, an image of this young man remained in her mind. Once before his gentle face had brought her comfort. Once before this young man, this stranger, had come to Maddie's rescue.

He turned back toward Louisa. "What is your sister's name?" he asked.

"Maddie."

"And how old is she?"

"Almost five."

The doctor placed his hand upon Maddie's brow. This roused the sleeping child. With a whimper she opened her eyes. In an instant Louisa noted a sparkle in those eyes that she had not seen since the fever had come.

"Mr. Mattie!" Maddie exclaimed weakly.

The doctor looked inquiringly toward Louisa. "How does she know that name? We have certainly never met."

"In the snow," murmured Louisa. "You picked her up when she fell. I'm sure you don't remember."

"But I do!" Dr. Burton exclaimed. "So you were the ones on the street that day. Fancy meeting you again!" He chuckled a moment before returning to the somber situation at hand.

The examination did not take long. Dr. Burton asked Louisa several questions and seemed especially interested in the fact that Maddie had suffered from a sore throat a few weeks earlier. Maddie willingly let him examine her left knee and elbow since those joints were painful at the time. The areas were so red and tender that Maddie winced when the doctor touched them.

"I'm sorry," he remarked, noting her grimace. "I've seen enough now; we'll cover you back up so you won't get chilled." He quickly pulled the covers up to Maddie's chin. "There. Now I must talk to your sister. Will you stay by yourself for a few minutes?"

Maddie nodded.

"Very good."

Dr. Burton looked up at Louisa for direction, and she led him to the parlor.

"Maddie is a very sick little girl," the doctor began. "She needs more care than you can give her here. I suggest you take her to a hospital."

"We cannot do that. There must be something else you can tell us to do," pleaded Louisa. "I've been warned that hospitals can be dangerous places for children," she added, focusing on her fears rather than admitting that they could not afford the bills.

"Yes, I suppose you have a point," Dr. Burton observed. "Well then, you must get her a nurse. I'm afraid that you cannot properly care for her alone."

"We can't afford a nurse," Louisa whispered, ashamed to voice the truth. "Is there nothing else we can do? I am so afraid!"

Tears clouded Louisa's eyes. The doctor uncomfortably stared toward the window, his hands shoved deeply into his pockets. During the prolonged silence that followed, Louisa struggled to regain her composure. At last Dorothy, whom they had quite forgotten, appeared in the doorway. "Is Maddie really going to die?" she whispered.

Dr. Burton, evidently startled by this intrusion, silently fastened his gaze upon Dorothy. Louisa noticed her sister flatten against the doorframe under the doctor's intense observation. Following several minutes of evident contemplation, Dr. Burton addressed Louisa again. "There is another possibility," he stated cautiously. "Maddie could come to my house for a while. My sister Alice is a volunteer nurse with one of the aid societies in town. Of course, I could not let her come here," he noted, throwing a slightly disdainful glance toward the street. "If Maddie stayed at our house, however, Alice could nurse her, and I could check on her every day. There's a new medicine we can give her that will help lessen her pain."

Louisa's pride revolted against the doctor's perception that the Shumakers' part of town was too low for his sister. She had to stifle her immediate temptation to ask whether a rich girl like Alice would be able to tolerate nursing a poor immigrant's daughter.

Realizing that her feelings must not interfere with Maddie's opportunity for recovery, she wisely voiced her misgivings more mildly. "Surely," she replied, "that would be asking too much of your family. I wouldn't want to put them in danger."

"Maddie's symptoms are not those of diphtheria or some other epidemic disease, and so anyone near Maddie should be quite safe," the doctor explained. "It's likely that she has some type of rheumatism; and if that is true, then Maddie alone is in danger. There's an extra room at my house that the servants don't use these days; Maddie can stay there. She's so little that she'll be no trouble at all!"

"I will have to speak to *Papi*," Louisa replied. "May we give you our answer tomorrow?"

"It will be precious time wasted," replied Dr. Burton.

At that moment the sound of Henry's footsteps on the stairs reached them. "Just a minute!" Louisa exclaimed. She rushed to the kitchen to meet her brother. In a moment she had explained the situation and convinced Henry to rush to *Papi's* workplace. Louisa returned to the parlor. "My brother has gone to ask my father what should be done. He will be back soon. Can you wait?"

The doctor nodded his assent.

Later that evening Louisa knelt beside Maddie's empty bed. No feverish head rested there now; no hand awaited her clasp. Only smooth covers and a lonely pillow remained. *Papi* had decided to send Maddie to Dr. Burton's house. The young doctor had transported Maddie in his phaeton, and Louisa had accompanied them. How difficult it had been to leave Maddie in that large, unfamiliar house! But the doctor had drawn Louisa away from her dear sister's new bedside, urging her to go home for rest. A family servant drove her home, his expression betraying his opinion that one such as her did not deserve such service. The memory of this driver's arrogance roused misgivings within her now. How would Maddie fare in a place where even the servants held her in contempt?

Papi's entrance interrupted Louisa's thoughts. He laid a heavy hand on his daughter's shoulder. "Will they care for her properly?" he asked.

"Yes, *Papi*. She will not want for anything she needs."

Papi sighed. "I do not like my child to be so far away from our home."

"You made the only decision you could have made, *Papi*," Louisa observed comfortingly.

"*Ja*," he nodded, his graying beard brushing against his chest, "but I miss my little girl. I won't rest easily while she is in the hands of strangers."

"Yes, *Papi*, but those strange hands are healing hands," reminded Louisa.

"*Ja*. We must pray that the Lord will use their skill to heal our Maddie."

Dorothy entered at that moment with Anna in her arms, and Henry followed only a few steps behind. "We should pray for Maddie right now," Henry suggested.

"*Ja*," agreed Papi. "Come, children," he continued, motioning for them all to kneel. "Let us bow before our Maker. *Unser Vater im Himmel*, from You comes all healing. We pray that You will heal Maddie and return her to us. Please comfort her while she is alone in that strange place. Let her know that You are there with her. May each of us live as Your servants all the days that You grant us. May we remember that the Lord giveth and the Lord taketh away; blessed be the name of the Lord. Amen."

Soft "amens" echoed through the gathered family as tears were wiped from more than one trembling cheek.

CHAPTER TWENTY-FOUR

Parlor Gossips

April 1900

April 3, 1900

Continuing my work for Mr. Hatterly requires monumental discipline! The past several days I have wanted to devote all my time to caring for Maddie! I know the doctor and Alice are caring for her, and Papi visits her early every morning, but I still worry! I have this dread that one day I'll enter Matthew's house and learn that Maddie has died while I was away. At least when I'm with her, I know she's alive. That comfort makes up for how difficult it is to see her looking so weak and miserable. As long as I'm near her, I feel like I can somehow prevent death from coming. I know that I can't, but whenever I leave the house, I feel like I no longer have any control! If only Mütti were still alive, I somehow feel that everything would be better! I know, though, that if she were here, she would gently remind me to place my trust in God, not man. She loved to recite Psalm 9: "Those who know your name will trust in you, For you, LORD, have never forsaken those who seek you." Those would be her words for me now.

A week after writing those words, Louisa continued to struggle with fears as she rushed toward the Burton house after work. When she reached the back entrance that day, she quietly rapped on the kitchen doorframe. Through the open door she saw Nellie, the family cook. With a bowl held tightly against her waist and her free hand guiding a spoon through the batter, the lively lady spun to greet Louisa. "Come on in!" she encouraged. "I doubt, however, you'll want stay long near this stove."

Louisa entered eagerly. "How's Maddie?" she asked. "Did the doctor leave a message for me?" She knew that neither Dr. Burton nor Alice were likely to be home in the late afternoon.

"Unchanged," Nellie replied. "You go on now. That little girl needs your company! Don't waste time talking to me."

With a thankful nod Louisa crossed the room and mounted the stairs that led to the servants' rooms. To Louisa's relief, Nellie was the only servant who lived there at that time. The less she saw of the other servants, the better. She read disapproval in their eyes every time they met. How unnerving! Only her love for Maddie kept Louisa returning to such an uncomfortable atmosphere.

As she climbed the stairs, Louisa reminded herself that she must feign cheerfulness and optimism. However, since she did not truly have a store of these commodities within herself, it would be nearly impossible to sow them freely in the sickroom.

Maddie's weak greeting rose from the bed the minute Louisa lifted the latch on the door. "Louisa! Finally you're here!"

Louisa forced a smile. The past day had painted no healthy color upon Maddie's cheeks and had sculpted no strength in her limbs. Yet as Louisa slid into a chair by the bed, a smile winked about the little girl's lips, and a soft light shone in her eyes as though attentive nursing had gently stoked the fading embers within her.

Yes, there's life in her yet, a voice murmured within Louisa's head, *but it's perilously near to being snuffed out.*

Before dinner Dr. Burton came and visited with the sisters for a while, as he had each evening during the past two weeks. Long after he left, Maddie fell asleep. Louisa kissed her sister's cheek and silently slipped from the room. She turned down the hallway, wearily descended the stairs, and entered the kitchen. She had expected to find the room empty as usual, but the doctor sat at the table reading. Louisa stopped for a moment, struck by the oddness of his presence in the kitchen. She had never before seen Dr. Burton or his sister in that part of the house. Noticing a glass on the table, she decided that thirst must have drawn him to this room. She began to doubt this theory, however, when the doctor deliberately set down his newspaper and rose with a smile. "Good evening!" he exclaimed. "Is Maddie asleep?"

"Yes," Louisa replied, resuming her walk to the door.

Matthew stepped out from behind the table. "It's much later than you usually leave, I believe?"

"Yes. Maddie was unusually restless tonight."

"I'm sure that your presence comforted her," Dr. Burton replied. "She seemed especially impatient for you to arrive today."

"Yes. I cannot come too early for her!"

"But it is late now. You cannot walk home alone in the dark. I will drive you home."

"No, there is no reason; the streetcar runs near here—" Louisa began.

"Yes, but you will have to switch lines; and besides, there have been several arrests on the streetcars recently for drunkenness and disorderly conduct. It would be reckless to travel alone." When Louisa did not reply, the doctor continued, "It's high time we were on our way."

He had evidently settled the matter, and Louisa felt certain that nothing she could say would change the doctor's mind. He picked up his hat from the table, and Louisa noted that it had obviously been there from the start. Apparently Dr. Burton had planned to escort her home and had waited in the kitchen with that purpose in mind! He opened the door, waited a moment for Louisa to pass, and then exited himself, donning his hat as he entered the cool night air. His horse and phaeton waited behind the house, a second evidence that long before Louisa had come downstairs, he had determined to take her home.

The doctor helped her up to the seat and then climbed up to sit beside her. Louisa glanced toward him as he lifted the reins and was struck by how handsome he looked at that moment. His face seemed relaxed and even kinder than it had before. Perhaps the difference was merely a result of his rounded hat, which was less pretentious than the square top hats he and other wealthy men so often wore around town.

Now that she had begun her ride home, she had to admit that the arrangement delighted her. Since she rarely had the opportunity to ride in a carriage, she argued to herself, unconvincingly, that this is what thrilled her. In truth, however, she knew that a carriage ride with anyone else in the world would not have produced equal excitement. Ironically, her eagerness to secure Dr. Burton's approval marred the moment, causing her to plunge into an unnecessary and antagonistic defense of herself.

As the horse pulled them into the street, the doctor asked, "How many children are there in your family?"

"Henry is my one brother; besides Maddie, I have two other sisters, Dorothy and Anna."

"And you are the oldest?" Dr. Burton prodded.

"Yes, I'm practically like a mother to the youngest ones," Louisa mused.

"Is that why you haven't married yet?" the doctor asked, throwing a sidelong glance toward the young woman. "Do you feel responsible for the younger children your mother left behind?"

"What makes you think I should be married?" Louisa shot back, ignoring the other elements of his question. Even she was startled by her harsh reply. Why had she allowed her tone to turn unkind?

"I never said I thought you should be married . . . although many girls your age are."

"Alice is not married. Neither is Helen, the friend Alice introduced me to yesterday," she retorted. "Why is it that no one thinks a poor immigrant girl should carefully choose a husband?"

"Pardon," the doctor gasped, "I assure you that you have taken my statement beyond any meaning I intended. Had I realized your strong feelings on this topic, I would not have mentioned it. I am sincerely sorry."

Louisa later wished she had accepted this apology, but her worries about Maddie had consumed her lately, wearing away her usual wise caution. "I know that the established citizens of this city have a low opinion of us immigrants. Do you think I don't feel it every day? Even your servants snub me!"

"Miss Shumaker, you must believe me—I meant no judgment," Dr. Burton insisted, his obvious bewilderment finally mollifying Louisa.

She bowed her head in repentant embarrassment. "I'm sorry," she murmured. "I just know too many girls who have foolishly married while young. They marry boys their age—boys who have not grown up. My friend Elsa married a year ago. And now her husband comes home drunk nearly every night. He promises payment of money that they don't have and gambles away what little they do have. She's miserable because she married someone who is still trying to impress the boys." Louisa looked directly into the doctor's eyes and added emphatically, "I will never do that. Never!"

"A wise decision," Dr. Burton observed. "I have no doubt that determination will spare you from heartbreak and will save you for a man who will love you faithfully."

As he finished speaking, they stopped at the Shumakers' home. Dr. Burton jumped down to help her to the ground. "I suppose you will come by to see Maddie tomorrow?" he asked quietly as he released her hand.

"Yes. Good night," she replied, not daring to raise her eyes to meet his.

The next evening Louisa retreated to her bedroom to write. So many thoughts were stirring in her head!

April 11, 1900

I truly feel that every day of the past two weeks has been a repetition of the one before it! I go to work, visit Maddie, eat the dinner I packed in the morning, and then return home. It is always the same!

Of course, I must admit that last night was different. Dr. Burton drove me home. That was kind of him, but somehow I managed to turn the ride into a nightmare! I was so mean! He asked me why I wasn't married, and it seemed like an unbearable question coming from him. How could I marry any of the boys who would marry me—especially when I now know someone like Dr. Burton? I felt I was being taunted! Looking back, I know my response was foolish. This evening the doctor was pleasant toward me. It is more than I dared to hope.

Dr. Burton has been wonderful. He comes every evening and visits with Maddie for part of the time that I'm there. When Maddie

feels well enough, she loves to chatter with him and watch his antics.
I must admit that I also enjoy these times with him.

It is so hard to know what to say to Maddie. I know she is
scared. I sit by her bedside each day and try to be of comfort. I tell
her about her other siblings and how they wish they could visit her.
Dorothy cannot come because she is trying to make up for the cooking and sewing I cannot do, and Henry works nearly every hour that
he is awake. We need every penny we earn just to buy the essen-
tials. At least Papi is able to visit her almost every day before dawn,
but I know she is groggy then. Hopefully the entire family can visit
on Sunday.

It has rained often recently. Even Maddie, who does not have
to walk in the mud and wetness (although I wish she could), grows
more pale and somber (if that is possible) when the clouds come.
With such gray clouds surrounding us, it has been hard to imagine
that Maddie will live. Everything just seems so dismal.

There are a few good things about rainy days (although there is
nothing good about mud!). I actually like being outside on a stormy
day—during the times it is not actually raining! I believe the worst
way to endure an overcast day is to remain cooped up inside. Maybe
this is one reason Maddie is so miserable. When she looks through
her second-story window, all she can see is the gray, cloudy sky. On
dreary days I feel I must eventually escape to the outside. And when
I step outside, the cold, wet breeze awakens my senses. The cold,
wet breeze brushes against my cheeks like one of Anna's soft baby
hands. It is as though the wind is fighting against the general dreari-
ness and is crying, "Wake up, wake up! There is so much to experience—so much to see today!" When I actually do look around me,
I often find that although the sky is gray, the rest of the world is glistening in the wetness. The bark on trees deepens until it's nearly
black, and the grass brightens after receiving a long drink of rain.
Yellow flowers seem all the more bright when the sun is hidden and
no longer competing with them. On these days the rain magnifies
every color. Things I never see on other days suddenly become magnificent. Today I noticed the graceful lean of a tree that I pass each
day. How much it looked like a man who, with arms flung wide
open, is bowing to his dancing partner!

I think I appreciate these little things more when life is difficult.
I notice other things too. Even Maddie's weak smiles are special.
When Maddie wasn't sick, I pushed her aside so often when she
wanted to laugh and play; now I cherish the moments that she has

*enough strength to chuckle. I pray there will be sunny times again
in Maddie's life.*

*The sun did finally come out this afternoon! When I was with
Maddie, I wanted so much to be outside instead. I felt like there was
a lizard within me, scurrying about and crying out with the longing
of my whole being: "Let me out! Let me out!" I wonder if Maddie
felt the same way.*

*It's funny—now that the sun has waltzed back into town, I
seem to have more hope. Maybe Maddie will get better. I certainly
hope she can come home soon. Even though Dr. Burton is friendly,
he makes me nervous. I do like his sister Alice. She's younger than
I (even though Dr. Burton must be several years over twenty). She's
cordial and pleasant, not at all like I had expected a rich girl to be.
I still feel shy around her though, and I'd rather not have to go to
that house anymore. Anyway, Maddie needs to come home! This
is where she belongs!*

The next week brought welcome changes. No clouds amassed to
shield the sun's glory, and Louisa noticed a marked improvement
in Maddie's health. The little girl almost looked like her old self
again!

When Louisa arrived the following Tuesday, Maddie was sitting up in bed. "Look!" she chirped as her sister entered the room.
She pointed to the windowsill, where Louisa saw a lovely bouquet
of roses.

"Where did those come from?"

"Alice!" Maddie announced.

"How nice of her!" Louisa exclaimed. "Did you thank her?"

"Of course," smiled Maddie with satisfaction. "But they're for
you. Happy birthday, Louisa!"

"How ever did you remember?" Louisa asked incredulously.

"*Papi* reminded me, but the flowers were Mr. Mattie's idea,"
Maddie admitted.

"And then you asked Alice to order them," Louisa added.

Maddie nodded, a satisfied smile flickering about her lips.

"Well, thank you very much!" Louisa exclaimed. "I see also
that someone brought you a book. Shall we read it together?"

"Oh please!" Maddie affirmed.

Louisa pulled a worn copy of poems from the night table.

"Alice said she loved this book best when she was little," Maddie whispered. "She said I could keep it."

Louisa nodded as she began to read. Though her eyes read the words and her mouth obediently uttered them, her mind did not attend to the poems. She instead contemplated the gentle compassion and kindness Maddie's nurse had shown.

How cruelly I judged Alice before I had even met her, thought Louisa.

Maddie fell asleep before Dr. Burton came to visit that night. Glad to have an opportunity to go home early, Louisa gathered her belongings and headed downstairs. When she reached the kitchen, she found it tidy and empty. Nellie had evidently already finished cleaning the dinner dishes. Louisa heard laughter in the parlor. "The Burtons must have friends visiting," she mumbled to herself, not unusual for a Friday night. That thought hastened her steps and lessened her carefulness. As she passed the table, Louisa accidentally knocked a cookbook from its precarious position on the edge of the counter. The hollow cellar beneath the floor amplified the noise of the book's landing and announced her presence in clear tones. The laughter in the other room hushed, and Louisa froze. Should she rush up the stairs or out the door? She certainly did not want to be mistaken for a burglar!

Before Louisa could make her choice, the door that led to the dining room swung open, heralding the entrance of a young lady whose striking presence daunted Louisa. Noting the extravagant ornamentation and brilliant blue of her dress, Louisa immediately judged this woman to be boldly arrogant, and a glance at her face confirmed Louisa's worst fears.

"And who might you be?" the young lady questioned with a slight bend of her head and a wry half-smile. "I was not aware there was a new servant in the house."

Louisa's words stumbled over her lips. "I . . . I am here to see my sister . . . Maddie . . . who's sick."

"Oh, you're the sister!" exclaimed the elegant lady, her eyes shining with an enlightenment that did not put Louisa at ease.

"Why then, you can explain something for us. We've been puzzling over it for quite the past quarter of an hour. Come this way," she commanded with a flourish of her hand.

"No, I'd really rather not. I mean . . ." Louisa searched for the right words.

"Oh, nonsense. It really shall be quite amusing!" And with absolutely no doubt about being obeyed, the young lady swirled about and began parading toward the parlor.

Louisa fumed silently, knowing she would end up being an amusement for the ladies while enduring embarrassment herself. However, she felt that fleeing would provide the ladies with additional reason to mock her. She set her flowers on the table and followed the haughty lady.

The nature of the carefree conversation that had resumed in the parlor gradually became discernible. "I really think we should go to the Olympic Theater tomorrow night," one voice declared. "I hear the latest show there is quite entrancing."

"No, no!" insisted another. "Castle Square Opera Company's production is not to be missed. My brother says the lead singer is spectacular."

No one replied, for at that moment Louisa and her escort filed into the room. In the brief silence that followed, Louisa quickly surveyed the scene. Five young ladies adorned the lavish parlor. Louisa only recognized Helen; neither Alice nor Dr. Burton were present. A dizzying array of exotic decorations surrounded the party— draperies, plants, oriental ceramics, tassels, and lace. The ladies perched on imposing Turkish ottomans and easy chairs that were covered with velvets and tapestries. The young women's fringed and tailored dresses added to the opulence, making it sometimes difficult to ascertain where a dress ended and a chair began. The room provided a playing field for more colors and patterns than Louisa could possibly take in during her cursory glance. She vaguely wondered whether she should be impressed or amused. The young ladies, however, did not allow Louisa any time to formulate an opinion one way or the other.

"Well, Ethel?" inquired a young woman who held her chin

high above her shoulder as she turned to survey Louisa. "What have we here?"

"I have discovered our feared burglar. She is the sister of Matthew's little invalid," Ethel announced triumphantly. "I thought maybe she could help explain the situation to us."

Louisa shuddered. She knew a daintily brutal inquisition would follow.

"Oh yes, do tell!" said a lady in a fine yellow dress edged with fringe. "What illness does your sister have? I certainly hope it isn't catching!"

"Oh no, surely not!" Ethel gasped in mock horror. "It wouldn't do at all to put Matthew and Alice in danger. I know of quite a few in this room who would be perfectly devastated to learn that Matthew was in danger of catching any disease!" Ethel cast knowing looks at several of her friends, causing them to giggle nervously. Louisa stiffened as she realized that Ethel had just exposed their admiration for the doctor. Even in the midst of this unnerving situation, Louisa felt displeasure at their esteem for him. The hint of jealousy in her heart surprised her and heightened the confusion of the moment.

Soon Ethel, sensing the fading impact of her last words, wove another strand into the conversation that had already nearly smothered Louisa. "I suspect that Matthew's parents would be most displeased with these goings on. They're away on a European tour, you know. I wonder if they know. To think that a common immigrant is staying in this house!" She peered contemptuously at Louisa. "Why, it really is disgraceful if one thinks about it. Such a pity that Matthew and Alice didn't have more sense."

"Well, I think it's perfectly dear," countered one of the girls who had blushed at Ethel's earlier insinuation. "What kindness and charity he has shown! How noble to care for those who are less fortunate than ourselves." She cast a patronizing glance toward Louisa.

"But to bring them into one's own home!" another lady added hastily as she set aside a stereoscope she had ceased using when

Louisa entered. "Why, I've never heard of such a thing being done. My parents certainly wouldn't allow it!"

"Do you think Alice's father is going to allow it?" questioned the lady in pink. "Not for a minute. When word of all this madness gets back to him, he will not be pleased!"

An abrupt cease-fire occurred when a short gasp from one of the ladies directed everyone's eyes toward the hallway. Alice stood just beyond the parlor door, her horrified expression declaring the betrayal she certainly felt. Dr. Burton stood at her side, observing the scene before him with a grave countenance. After a moment his eyes fixed on Louisa. Certain that her presence among this group displeased him, she bowed her head in shame. Incapable of executing a respectable retreat, she focused on holding back the tears that fought to escape from her eyes.

Suddenly Louisa sensed that the doctor stood before her. She cautiously raised her eyes and found in his expression gentle compassion that dissolved her fears. He held out his arm to her. "Come, Louisa," he said softly. For an instant she feared he might be mocking her, but the warmth in his eyes communicated only sincerity and confidence. She slipped her hand through his arm. With a slight smile acknowledging her acceptance, Dr. Burton turned and led her from the strained silence of the parlor.

As they passed into the hall, Alice smiled quickly at Louisa, then leaned toward her brother with relieved admiration. "Thank you," she mouthed.

Once removed from the presence of her aggressors, Louisa could no longer hold back her tears. The knowledge that Ethel felt no remorse for her cruelty heightened Louisa's bitter embarrassment. From the parlor came the sound of the lady's carefree dismissal of the recent mischief. "Why, Alice, we were just discussing our opinions of the current shows at the theaters. Which one shall receive your vote of favor?"

Dr. Burton guided Louisa into the kitchen and shut the door. He indicated that Louisa should sit in a chair at the table and handed her his handkerchief. Then he walked to the window and gazed steadily out toward the garden while she wiped her tears and sought to regain control. How foolish she felt!

"I'm sorry," she whispered after conquering the last sign of emotion.

Dr. Burton sighed as he returned to her side. "Their behavior is inexcusable. I'm ashamed that you have endured such ill-treatment within my own house. Not a very happy birthday present," he observed with a wry smile as he picked up Louisa's bouquet from the table.

CHAPTER TWENTY-FIVE

Maddie's Return

When Louisa arrived home that night, she found *Papi* sitting at the kitchen table browsing through an old catalogue from a local hardware company. He glanced up as she entered. "It's good to see you, *mein Kind*. You're a little early tonight. Is Maddie all right?"

"*Ja, Papi.* She is doing better, and I think she is actually beginning to feel penned up in that room they've given her. When I see her, I think of those old cows *Oma* Schuhmacher used to have in Germany." She chuckled as she continued, "Remember how they always wandered out to pasture when someone left the gate open?"

"*Ja!* How I miss those old cows! And how I miss the wonderful treats your mother used to make from their milk," he remarked, his voice trailing off into a sigh. Louisa understood that this mention of *Mütti* had hurt *Papi.* "*Ach!* I miss her so much," he murmured. "We had such dreams of what life in America would be like. Things have turned out so differently than we had planned. I often regret the two years we spent apart. If I had only known how short our time together would be . . ." He ended with a sigh and closed his eyes for a moment as though to shut out the pain. "Perhaps I made the wrong decision. Perhaps it was selfish of me to bring my family to America." He shook his head and stared blankly toward the wall before him.

Louisa rushed to *Papi's* side and threw her arms around his neck. "*Papi*, please don't say such things! You did what seemed best, and you have always provided for your family. You are the most wonderful father any daughter could ever hope to have. Remember when you told me so many years ago that you would not forsake us? Well, you have been true to your word. Other fathers deserted their children. Do you remember my friend Frederike in Germany? Her father never sent back for his family. They waited through years of silence and finally gave up hope of ever hearing from him. I know you will never abandon us."

"Louisa, don't you see that what you say is not true? That's what is torturing me. Maddie, my little daughter, is sick; and surely she must feel I have forsaken her. I have allowed her to be taken into a stranger's house, and I can only visit her for a short time early each morning!"

"Oh, *Papi*!" Louisa gasped, unable to think of a better response.

Papi turned toward her and stretched his strong arms around her. "I have uttered misgivings that I should have silenced. What a blessing you are to me, Louisa. How hard you work to care for us all!" He paused a moment before continuing. "I have spent the day thinking about Maddie, and I am displeased with how I have responded to her sickness. I made the decision to send her to the doctor's house in a moment of desperation. I feared for her life, and I did not have time to think clearly. Now that Maddie is doing better, we must bring her home. She belongs with her family, and we must care for her. No one else can show her the love she needs. I cannot allow our family to continue to be split apart for a second time unless it is absolutely necessary."

"Yes, *Papi*," Louisa agreed wearily. She knew she must accept his decision, although she wondered whether they could really give Maddie the care she needed.

"Tomorrow we will go together to bring her here," *Papi* continued.

Louisa nodded. Her days would be less complicated without the visits to the Burton house, and yet she did not rejoice when she heard she would no longer have reason to go there.

When Louisa and *Papi* left the flat the next morning, a hint of coolness still laced the air. Neither the sun nor the masses had yet brought their heat to bear upon the pre-dawn scene. Everything appeared still and peaceful as Louisa viewed block after block through the streetcar window. How the city's serenity contrasted with the turbulent blood that her pounding heart pushed through her body! As they neared the West End, Louisa voiced her fears. "*Papi*, what exactly are we going to do when we get there? We can't just force our way into the house."

"The cook will be there," *Papi* replied. "She lets me in every morning."

"Yes, but we can't just go in and take Maddie. We'll have to explain our action to Dr. Burton. What if he's not awake?"

"Any respectable human being who works for his bread and butter will be up," grunted *Papi*.

Louisa wrinkled her lips in frustration. How she wished *Papi* spoke enough English to explain their actions himself! If only she did not have to do the talking! Moreover, she thought it possible that the doctor would still be sleeping; not everyone had to work on Saturday like *Papi* and Henry did! She unconsciously allowed a puff of air to escape from her lips despite her resolve to honor her father's wishes without further audible protest.

When they reached the Burton house, the awkwardness of the situation increased. Louisa's early arrival at the kitchen door produced an obvious show of surprise from Nellie. After greeting the cook with forced cheerfulness, Louisa dismissed any thoughts of explaining the situation to her and quickly led *Papi* up the stairs.

As she gently pushed open the door to Maddie's room, a sound reached Louisa's ears that at once thrilled and froze her heart. In a moment her eyes confirmed what her ears had suspected. Dr. Burton, book in hand, sat beside Maddie's bed. With great animation, he delighted her with a story about forest animals. The creak of the door caused both of them to glance toward their visitors.

"*Papi*!" shouted Maddie with glee when she saw his familiar husky frame in the doorway. Briefly ignoring the tension of their visit, *Papi* rushed to the bedside and knelt to wrap his strong arms around his little daughter. When he finally released Maddie, a healthy flush that Louisa had not seen for weeks had returned to her cheeks. This improvement gave Louisa the courage to advance to the task before her. Clearing her throat, she began, "Dr. Burton,

I need to speak with you please." Her trembling voice betrayed her distress and instantly drew the doctor's full attention.

When Louisa did not speak during the silence that followed, Dr. Burton stepped forward to ask in a low voice, "Shall we leave Maddie alone with your father for a while? We can talk in the hallway." Louisa nodded with gratitude for his sensible suggestion.

Once they reached the hall, Louisa quickly explained the reason for their early-morning visit.

"I don't understand," Dr. Burton responded in obvious frustration. "Maddie has just begun to improve. She might even have a chance at getting completely better. If you take her home, she may worsen even to the point of death!"

"We will care for her," Louisa insisted emotionally. "I have watched what both you and Alice do. We can do the same things." She leaned back against the wall for support and added, "Most of them anyway."

The doctor bowed his head, evidently searching for words to dissuade her. Louisa took advantage of his silence to bolster her argument. "Maddie needs to be home with her family. She's too young to be away from us for so long."

"She's not well enough yet!" Dr. Burton protested. "The rheumatic fever may yet harm her heart and prove fatal!"

At that moment *Papi* appeared at the door, evidently beckoned by the stormy sounds from the hallway. In desperation Dr. Burton shifted his appeal to the father. "Is death what you want? A daughter buried at a young age? Surely as a father, you want what is best for your daughter!"

"You forget, Dr. Burton," Louisa observed sourly, "he cannot answer your English words, although I'm afraid he understands your meaning all too well! Your opinion of our desire is written clearly across your face!" She paused, her control of her emotions beginning to waver. Her eyes pled with the doctor, asking him to accept *Papi's* resolve without dragging her further into a battle of words. "You must see that my father wants only what any father would want for his daughter. The best thing for Maddie is to be with her family. She's not quite five years old! We had cared for her since her birth until we allowed her to come here. Now we realize that we made a mistake." Although the doctor winced at her words, Louisa continued, "Maddie must come home. Do not ask us to relinquish the joy of being with her or the privilege of caring for her."

While Dr. Burton's somber face clearly expressed his continued opposition to the Shumakers' plan, he voiced only civil resignation, "All right, I give up."

Louisa continued, "She is not dead yet. She is better and may recover."

"But if she does die—" Dr. Burton began.

"Then we shall not blame you," Louisa interrupted.

After a few minutes of awkward silence, the doctor stated, "I insist at least that you let me drive her home in my carriage. It would kill her to be carried through the streets and then crammed into a streetcar."

Even in her frustration, Louisa saw the wisdom of the doctor's plan and quickly consented.

In silence the plan was carried out. Maddie, evidently sensing the tension among the others, offered no protest. When they finally reached home, *Papi* quickly scooped Maddie from the seat and carried her into the building. Louisa noticed the sad and frightened smile that Maddie bestowed on Dr. Burton at their farewell and then realized the little girl had guessed that dark words had passed between this friend and her family. The little one seemed afraid that any greater show of emotion would bring offense from some corner.

After *Papi* and Maddie disappeared, Dr. Burton silently handed several pieces of baggage to Louisa. "Well, I sincerely hope Maddie does get well. She has improved greatly during the past week," he noted. Then, as he stared down the street, his face hardened, and he offered uncharacteristic sarcasm. "At any rate I'll be spared a fight with my father. He is at this moment rushing home from Europe to evict your sister from our house!" At the doctor's signal, the driver urged the horses forward. Over the rumble of the wheels, Louisa heard the doctor's cold farewell. "Good-bye, Miss Shumaker."

"Good-bye," she whispered. She stood motionless in the street as he drove away. How his parting comments had wounded her! "I am glad to be done with him!" she muttered in an effort to throw off the pain she felt. By nightfall, however, kinder thoughts crept unbidden into her mind. Vainly did she try to beat them back, for her heart kept presenting noble pictures of Dr. Burton—a friendly doctor reading stories to Maddie at dawn, and a polished gentleman rescuing Louisa from the parlor gossips.

At last she felt driven to her journal, hoping that through writing she might sort out the muddled thoughts battling within her.

April 21, 1900

I had not planned to argue so vehemently when I went to get Maddie today. I should not have said that we made a mistake in letting Maddie go there. What must Dr. Burton think? After all he's done for Maddie, he certainly deserves more appreciation than I granted him! He surely must see how foolish I have acted! If only his opinion didn't matter to me. If only I could just forget him and go on with my life. But I cannot. His statements irritate me at times, and yet I am crushed when I sense his disapproval. My feelings just don't make sense!

It's just that Dr. Burton is so different from every other young man I know. He's obviously richer, but it's something deeper that has drawn my notice. Although some things he says seem arrogant, I believe he sincerely cares about others—even poor immigrants like Maddie. That trait certainly is a rarity among young men—wealthy and poor alike! But even this is not enough to account for the opinion I have of the doctor. I can't explain the way I feel. I only know that it frightens me because the more I try to stop wanting to see him and please him, the more my admiration for him increases. The worst of it is that I know this is all foolishness. A poor, sick child may stir compassion in Dr. Burton's heart, but the twenty-three-year-old sister can hold no hope of stirring anything other than contempt, especially if she acts as I have!

I have tried so hard to follow the advice Mütti gave me before she died. She told me never to try to make myself love someone just so I could get married. I wonder if she ever guessed I'd battle with the opposite problem. How do I squelch admiration that will not die? How do I keep myself from loving someone whom I know I can never marry?

Oh, how I miss Mütti!

CHAPTER TWENTY-SIX

A Day in the Park

May 1900

Although Louisa did not voice the thought even in her journal, she secretly hoped Matthew would contact her family in some way. For over two weeks she awoke daily with a fragile sense of anticipation until repeated disappointments at last created within her an attitude of realistic resignation. Consequently, when a letter arrived at the Shumaker flat over two weeks after Maddie's return, the unfamiliar handwriting caused Louisa first to wonder, then to tremble as her hopes suddenly blazed anew. Typically the Shumakers' mail bore characteristic German lettering and foreign postmarks. Might this local correspondence be from Matthew? With shaking hands, she broke the envelope's seal and read the contents.

May 7, 1900

Miss Louisa Shumaker:

I hope that all in your family are doing well and that Maddie has continued to grow stronger. She has remained in my prayers. I have often regretted my rudeness at our last parting. I beg your forgiveness, as well as that of your father.

The weather has been so lovely. I thought Maddie might like a picnic in Forest Park if she is doing well. Would you and she join me on Saturday for a drive through the park? I recently visited the bear pits with my cousin Theodore, who is Maddie's age. He enjoyed the outing, so I thought Maddie might as well. I think the trip outdoors in the fresh air might do her some good, and I would so much like to see her again. If it is convenient, I will call for you at 9 in the morning. I will await your answer.

Yours, Most Respectfully,
Matthew Burton

That evening Louisa shared the letter with *Papi*. "This letter concerns you as much as it does me," she explained. "What should we do?"

After *Papi* had listened to Louisa's translation of the letter, his first words surprised her. "It is a rare young man who will humble himself in this way. I will forgive him. Will you, Louisa?"

"Yes," she murmured. "I have already."

"Good. Now, about the invitation, I think the time outdoors would be good for Maddie; she's been feeling so much better. I also think the excursion would be fun for you."

"Please don't make me go, *Papi*," Louisa begged, suddenly fearful of such a casual encounter with Dr. Burton. "I'm sure Maddie will be fine by herself."

"Louisa," *Papi* observed, "I believe that deep down you really want to go. And there's something else you need to realize—I think this young man wants to see you again, just as much as he wants to see Maddie." Louisa began to protest, but *Papi* continued, presenting his case from a different angle. "You must go, Louisa. Maddie is too young and still too fragile to go alone. Remember why we brought her home? She is a part of our family, and we must always care for her. I know this will be hard for you, but I'm asking you to do it for Maddie's sake. She has not had much sunshine in her life recently."

"Yes, *Papi*," answered Louisa obediently as she moved to the table to compose a reply.

May 8, 1900

Dr. Matthew Burton,
Dear Sir:

Papi and I believe that the outing you propose would be an excellent opportunity for Maddie to get out in the fresh air. We both thank you for the invitation and look forward to your arrival on Saturday at 9.

Most Sincerely,
Louisa Shumaker

On Saturday morning Louisa waited outside for Dr. Burton. As soon as his carriage came around the corner, he called out, "Hello! Isn't this a grand day?"

"Yes, of course," replied Louisa, noticing with slight embarrassment that he had chosen his family's carriage for their outing instead of the phaeton. The driver wore a sour expression that caused Louisa to wonder whether she should have accepted the doctor's invitation. She questioned her own ability to spend a day in the company of a servant who so openly displayed his contempt of her. However, Dr. Burton's exuberance provided an adequate balance to the driver's snobbishness. Even his clothes showed that he had exerted effort to ensure she would feel at ease. Louisa had never seen him so simply dressed. She conceded inwardly that he had provided no grounds for her to accuse him of arrogance on this day. Despite his common dress, however, Louisa still noted a fineness in his bearing that she had to admit delighted her!

"Shall we go get Maddie?" the doctor asked as he strode to the door.

"Yes, she is waiting for you, Dr. Burton," Louisa affirmed.

He turned to face her. "I do not come as a doctor today, but as a friend," he explained. "Please call me Matthew."

Lousia shyly nodded her agreement, and Matthew pushed open the door and allowed her to pass. When they entered the Shumakers' flat, Louisa shouted, "Maddie! There's someone here to see you!"

"Mr. Mattie!" Maddie exclaimed from her bed.

Matthew strode into the bedroom to greet his friend. "How are you, little one? Better, I hope!"

In her excitement Maddie ignored his question. "I'm so excited! Henry said it might rain, but it didn't! I'm so happy!"

"You are definitely better!" Matthew remarked with a laugh as he bent down to hug the little girl. "Are you ready to go?" When Maddie nodded, Matthew slid his arms beneath her, raised her from the bed, and announced, "We're off!"

They soon reached the street. "You brought Lady!" Maddie exclaimed as soon as she saw the horses.

"Of course," Matthew replied as he gently placed Maddie in

the carriage. "I know she's your favorite!" He helped Louisa climb up beside her sister, sat down facing the two sisters, and instructed the driver to head for Forest Park.

Matthew devoted his full attention to Maddie's constant chatter. Louisa, relieved to see her sister's conversation directed toward someone else, allowed herself to relax and enjoy the city sights. The carriage gradually emerged from the city's foul cocoon of smog, stone, and grime into a world of cleaner streets, bluer skies, and abundant trees. What a wonderful change! When they entered Forest Park, the natural landscape surrounding them caused Louisa to yearn for the country village of her childhood.

They first stopped at the bear pits. Matthew carried Maddie to a spot where she could get a good view of the pacing bears. Although Maddie kept her cheerful smile, Louisa noticed that she clung to Matthew's neck more tightly than usual. "Very big bears!" she remarked.

"Yes," Matthew laughed. "I wouldn't want to meet one in the woods!"

Matthew soon suggested that they return to the carriage and look for a picnic spot. "It's a little early for lunch," he admitted, "but I'm feeling hungry already. I propose that we eat now. How does that sound to you two?" Both girls cheered Matthew's plan; and when they were settled in the carriage once again, Matthew instructed the driver to take them to the other side of the River Des Peres.

As they crossed a bridge over the small river, Louisa noticed that its pleasant appearance was deceptive; a rank smell rose from the waters. "We'll want to eat some distance from here," she commented.

"Certainly," Matthew agreed.

"Oh!" Maddie squealed a few minutes later as she pointed eagerly. "Let's eat there! Under that tree. How I wish I could climb it!"

"I suppose that eating beneath it will be nearly as fun," said Matthew with a smile. "We'll stop over by that tree," he called to the driver.

When Matthew first opened the picnic basket's lid, Louisa's

eyes fell on a bowl of strawberries. "These are some of the best of
the season so far," Matthew commented as he placed them on the
blanket. "I think I remember you saying, Louisa, that you have a
special love for strawberries?"

When Matthew glanced toward her with a smile, Louisa murmured in surprise, "Oh, yes! *Papi* bought some for *Mütti* the summer before Anna was born. She shared one with me, but that's the
only time I've tasted a strawberry."

"Well, today you can eat your fill!" Matthew announced.

Louisa had never before enjoyed such a wonderful picnic.
Nellie had outdone herself in the preparations. Perhaps the dessert
finale was the best of all. Maddie squealed when she saw the plate
of chocolate cookies Matthew had kept hidden away until they had
eaten everything else. Maddie had a passion for chocolate, and
Louisa thought it likely that the little girl had informed Matthew
of this during her stay at his house. After Maddie had enjoyed more
chocolate than she had probably consumed in her entire life,
Matthew indicated that they must pack up and continue their
excursion.

The carriage path wound beneath a cool overhang of dense
trees. They passed several other carriages and many bicycle riders.
"That looks like fun!" Maddie exclaimed, observing a group of
cyclists.

"Yes," Matthew agreed, "it's becoming quite popular these
days."

A moment later Maddie sighted something even more exciting. "Look! Boats!" she exclaimed, pointing toward a lake.
Although the little girl did not fully voice her desire, Louisa
noticed a longing in her sister's eyes.

Matthew obviously read the same meaning in Maddie's expression, for he looked at Louisa, and his eyes questioned, *Is it all right?
I'm game for a boat ride if you'll consent.*

The moment Louisa nodded her agreement, Matthew
declared, "It's a perfect day for boating. Don't you think so,
Maddie?"

The little girl gasped and whispered, "Oh, yes!"

Matthew directed the driver to stop, then jumped down to the ground. "If you ladies will wait here, I'll go rent one of those fine rowboats! I'll be right back," he called out as he strode toward the boathouse.

Matthew returned in a minute with the news that he had secured the one boat still at the edge of the water. Maddie nearly jumped from the carriage, but Matthew gently stopped her. "You must still be careful, Maddie. You're not completely well yet." He lifted her down and, with Maddie's arms about his neck, carried her to the water. Maddie rested her head against Matthew's shoulder, causing Louisa to fret inwardly. *She's tired and has been trying to hide it*, she thought. *I hope this is not a mistake*. Yet Louisa knew Matthew would not do anything that might harm Maddie. Throughout that day she had marveled at how this young man's attitude toward her little sister displayed the tenderness of an older brother.

When they reached the boat, Matthew asked, "Where do you want to sit, Maddie?"

"I want to go backwards! That's fun!" she decided.

"Okay. You go in first then." Matthew steadied Maddie as she crawled to her seat. "Be careful; don't stand up," he warned.

As soon as she was seated, Matthew turned to Louisa. "Are you ready?" he asked. She nodded. He steadied the boat, offered his free hand to her, and then suddenly straightened himself and glanced toward her with an amused smile. "Here come some friends of mine," he remarked. Louisa looked in the direction he indicated, then turned back toward the boat and attempted to climb in quickly. Matthew put a gentle hand on her arm to stop her. "We must be civil," he whispered. "They have certainly seen us. We can't just shove off."

Louisa reddened. She knew he was right, but that did not lessen her mortification. Before she had time to consider what she might say, the couple joined them.

"Why, Matthew, we didn't expect to see you here!" the young lady exclaimed.

"It seems impossible to come to the park on such a beautiful day as today and not meet a friend," Matthew replied cheerfully.

"I don't believe we have met this young lady," said the man, regarding Louisa with evident curiosity.

"No?" answered Matthew. "I want to introduce you. Louisa, this is Blanche and her brother James. James and Blanche, this is Louisa. Maddie, Louisa's sister, is in the boat already." Matthew stepped aside to let them see the younger Shumaker. "Maddie, these are some friends of mine," he explained.

The little girl waved and smiled with an open friendliness that Louisa envied. "I'm pleased to meet you," she stated, just as Alice had taught her.

"You may remember that Maddie stayed at our house for a while," Matthew remarked.

"Oh, yes, the poor little sick girl. I thought she had gone home several weeks ago," Blanche remarked, placing disdainful emphasis on "poor."

"Her health has improved, and she is now back with her family where she belongs," Matthew explained. "I invited Louisa and Maddie to come for an afternoon in the park. It is such a lovely place."

"Yes," agreed James. "Well, we must be going. We're meeting Sidney and Harriet for an early dinner tonight. We'll catch the show at the Olympic Theater afterwards. Too bad you can't come along, Matthew," he added.

"On a day like today, I much prefer enjoying the perfect weather," laughed Matthew. "There will be other great shows at the Olympic."

"Well, good-bye, Matthew," said James as he turned to leave. Blanche echoed his farewell with cool civility.

"Good-bye, James. Farewell, Blanche," Matthew called. He stood still for a moment, gazing reflectively after his friends. Then he turned to Louisa and held out his hand. "I was wondering if they were ever going to honor us with their departure," he remarked with a wry smile as he steadied her entry into the boat.

As Louisa sat down, Matthew called to the boat owner, indicating their need of the burly man's assistance. Matthew climbed into the center of the boat, carefully turned to face Louisa, and lowered himself into the oarsman's seat. "We're ready," he cried. With one hearty heave, the man sent them on their way. Matthew propelled the boat into the center of the lake.

"Don't run into anyone," Maddie called out.

"Didn't I tell you, Maddie?" Matthew asked over his shoulder. "I need your help. You have to keep looking behind you so you can tell me if I am about to hit another boat. Will you do that?"

"Of course!"

"I was sure I could count on you, Maddie," Matthew declared.

They only stayed on the water for fifteen minutes since Maddie's weariness became increasingly evident. Surprisingly, Maddie did not protest when Matthew headed for the shore. Five minutes after the carriage began to roll toward the park's exit, the little girl's eyes closed, and her breathing became heavy with sleep.

Louisa soon wished Maddie was still awake, for silence had replaced her sister's prattling. Matthew finally spoke first. "So, did you enjoy yourself today, Louisa?"

"Yes," she answered. "It's not often that we take even a half-day holiday."

"Why don't you come to the park more often?" pressed Matthew. "It's free, and the trolley cars run here."

"That may be true, but most of our hours are spent working for the little money we have. And anyway, you don't see many of our type here."

"And what exactly is your type?" Matthew inquired impulsively. "I didn't think you looked out of place today. You seem to see things that others don't."

"James and Blanche seemed to share my assessment," Louisa countered with a tinge of bitterness.

"Is their opinion the measure that the rest of us should live by?" Matthew questioned. "I might have agreed with them a few months ago, but I hope I've learned better. It's all a silly game, Louisa. You feel outcast from the society of West End, but has it ever occurred to you that I feel the same way on your street?" Louisa started at this revelation. "Don't you see, Louisa? Your world is just as inaccessible to an outsider as mine is. It's just not as obvious because few people from my neighborhood are trying to rent a flat in your part of town. But the same cold shoulder is there. I get suspicious, slanted looks from man and boy alike when I enter your neighborhood. I'm not an immigrant, and I'm wealthy. According to your neighbors those are two sins that I can never overcome." Louisa looked at the floor as the truth in his words pricked her heart. "Louisa, don't hang your head," Matthew implored. "I don't say these things to hurt you. I know that *you* do not feel that way."

Louisa sensed that this last statement expressed what Matthew hoped about her opinion rather than what he believed with certainty. In her heart she acknowledged that he had reason to doubt her ability to embrace the inhabitants of the West End. Rather than admit this, however, she voiced a defense of her neighbors. "Many people on my street are proud of their homelands but have been hurt by disillusionment. We came to America believing the promise of a prosperous life. Stories of gold in the streets lured people who should have known there are no such places on earth."

"I don't blame immigrants for their bitterness; I would feel the same way."

"But," Louisa conceded, "we are not completely in the right. Disappointment is no justification for hate. I sometimes envy Maddie's outlook; she is truly content. She loves our family and trusts God to care for her. That is enough wealth for her. She is not bitter even though there has been little sweetness in our lives since her birth."

She finished speaking as the carriage halted beside *Onkel* August's building. Louisa noticed Henry leaning against the brick wall near their door. He glared at Matthew, his eyes filled with suspicion. With dread Louisa realized that in their recent conversation Matthew had unknowingly described her own brother's prejudice.

Louisa gently shook Maddie, and the little girl blinked rapidly in the bright sunlight. "We're home already?" she mumbled.

"Yes, sleepyhead," Matthew laughed, leaning forward to tousle her hair.

"I had fun," Maddie said with a smile.

"Yes," Louisa added softly. "Thank you, Matthew."

"I'm so glad you could come," Matthew declared, lifting Maddie from the carriage.

Before Matthew could step forward, Henry sauntered up. "I'll carry her upstairs," he commanded gruffly.

After a moment's pause, Matthew nodded, saying, "Very well then." He handed Maddie over to her brother, adding quietly, "Good-bye, Maddie. I enjoyed spending the afternoon with you."

"Thank you! I had so much fun!" Maddie called out as Henry quickly carried her through the doorway and up the stairs.

Louisa remained on the street a minute longer. "I'm sorry," she murmured, raising her eyes to meet Matthew's gaze. "Henry—"

"No," Matthew interrupted, "don't apologize. My only memory of today will be of the pleasant company I enjoyed in the park." He glanced toward the door as though contemplating whether to say more. When he looked back at Louisa, his only words were, "Good-bye, Louisa . . . and thank you."

As she whispered her echo of this farewell, Matthew jumped up into the carriage. The driver immediately urged the horses forward, leaving Louisa standing alone in the street.

When Louisa entered the kitchen, Henry sat at the table waiting for her. Louisa, having no doubt that he meant to confront her, pulled the door shut and stood in silent expectation.

Henry wasted no time. "So, Louisa, you had a nice time today, didn't you?" he observed.

"Yes. I would say that everything went well," she replied, tempering her enthusiasm.

"I thought we had seen the last of that fellow when Maddie came home," Henry growled. "No doubt you enjoyed his company today a bit more than you should have. There's a flush on your cheeks that you can't control as handily as you've mastered your voice!"

Louisa sought composure beyond what she felt, but she could not contain the rebuttal rising within her. "Why are you suddenly so concerned about the color of my cheeks? Did you so much as glance at Maddie's cheeks? They're bright and rosy. Healthy almost. The ride did her good, Henry. That is what matters to me."

"You don't fool me one bit, Louisa," Henry insisted, donning a smirk as he continued. "And neither does that fine, rich doctor. Did he really want to spend an entire afternoon with a sick four-year-old girl, or was that a plan to hide his real purpose?" Louisa attempted to protest, but Henry forged ahead. "I don't trust him, Louisa. I don't trust his intentions. Why would he show favor to a poor girl like yourself? Even you must question his motives."

"Well, thank you, Henry, for such brotherly advice!" Louisa replied sarcastically. "It's amazing . . . to hear this from the one who has urged me to be more friendly to young men! Can I help it if I don't like any of your friends? I haven't noticed any of them making even a slight effort to help Maddie."

"You miss my point, Louisa," Henry countered. "Dr. Burton is rich and arrogant. One thing I have learned in America is that wealth and poverty do not mix. Certainly it is possible that a poor man might become rich; but until he does, no rich man will risk his reputation by associating with that working man's daughter. Dr. Burton cannot entertain even the remotest thought of marrying you. Be reasonable, Louisa."

"Henry, are you out of your mind?" Louisa snapped. "Where did this idea of marriage come from? Maddie and I went on a picnic with Maddie's doctor. What's the crime in that? *Papi* even told me to go!" She rushed to the parlor, slamming the door behind her. In truth, she could not tolerate hearing Henry put into words the fears that her own heart had already whispered.

CHAPTER TWENTY-SEVEN

A Returned Enemy

Louisa was disappointed when Matthew did not attempt to communicate with the Shumakers during the week that followed. With fierce determination fueled by pride, she shoved emotion aside and forced herself to adopt an indifferent attitude toward the matter. Maddie, however, did not disguise her impatience as she waited for her friend and physician to reappear. Despite her growing desire to see him, her need of his care waned. Thankful praise to God stirred in Louisa's heart as she watched Maddie regain strength. For the first time in weeks, she began to believe that her little sister would completely recover.

On May 28, Maddie's fifth birthday, Louisa rushed home from Mr. Hatterly's to prepare a special dinner. An annoying spray of water ambushed her when she rounded a corner and stepped onto her family's street. "Oh no!" she exclaimed. "The sanitation man is spraying out the gutters, and I'm sure to get wet!"

Children, not sharing Louisa's sentiments, filled the street. They frolicked joyfully in the water as Louisa frowned in disgust. "The streets are dirty, and the weather is still a bit cool," she muttered. "Any mother with sense would lock her children up rather than let them out today!" Her scowl deepened as she lifted her skirts and carefully picked her steps toward home.

Soon, however, all thoughts of mud were forsaken. Louisa had spotted her sick sister standing in a puddle.

"Maddie!" she yelled. "Come here this instant!" The incredulous sternness that covered her face quickly spoiled the glee that had shone in Maddie's eyes.

"What are you doing out in this mess?" demanded Louisa.

"Playing," Maddie stated.

"And where is *Tante* Joanna? Did she let you come outside?"

"No," answered Maddie as she cautiously shook her head.

"Why are you here then?"

"*Tante* Joanna left us with Rudi. He said I could play."

"Where is he now? And where is Anna?" Louisa demanded.

"Anna's at home, I think," whispered Maddie, intimidated by Louisa's anger. As she spoke, Louisa spotted Rudi darting into the side door of *Onkel* August's building. Grabbing Maddie and hoisting the child awkwardly into her arms, Louisa set off after her cousin.

A moment later she stormed into *Tante* Joanna and *Onkel* August's flat, where she discovered Rudi lounging at the table. "Are you crazy?" she demanded, setting Maddie on the floor and racing toward Rudi. "To take Maddie out onto the streets . . . to allow her to get wet—are you insane? She has hardly been out of bed more than a few days since she's been sick. Think about it, Rudi! She was getting better, but now who knows what will happen!"

"Okay, okay," Rudi muttered. "I'm sorry."

Louisa hardly heard him. "I must get Maddie into dry clothes immediately. Anna?" she shouted. The three-year-old cautiously peered around a corner. "Come with me," Louisa commanded. "We are going home. Rudi, don't even think about showing your face in our flat anytime soon. I can't bear the sight of you!"

In a matter of minutes Louisa had her little sister dry and warmly dressed. "Do you feel well, Maddie?" Louisa asked anxiously.

"Pretty well," Maddie answered.

Louisa's heart longed to believe her.

By the next morning, Louisa's fears had proved justified—Maddie's fever had returned. She whimpered in pain; and her arms, swollen and red at the joints, occasionally twitched although she willed them to stay still. "Please, Louisa, please don't leave," she begged, her frightened eyes trained on Louisa as her older sister wiped her forehead. *Papi*, overhearing her pleas, sent Henry to Mr. Hatterly's to explain that Louisa would not be able to come that day.

Despite Louisa's best efforts at nursing, Maddie's misery continued throughout the day. By early afternoon Louisa had used all the ice that had been stored in either of the building's two iceboxes. She grew desperately anxious for the arrival of the ice wagon and posted little Anna at the window to keep watch.

"We cannot miss him," Louisa muttered. "Not today—not today!"

At last a rumble in the street sent Anna barreling through the flat and down the stairs. She would first summon Henry from the shop and then hold a place in line until he joined her.

"Finally!" murmured Louisa, watching her go. "The iceman certainly took his time today!" She turned back toward the bed. "Henry and Anna will be back soon with ice, Maddie," Louisa promised. Maddie nodded and gulped hard in pain. Only a year ago the five-year-old would have led Anna in the race down the stairs.

Louisa strode to the window and scrutinized the street below. Anna, along with several other children, had reached her destination and stood beside the ice wagon. "Good for you, Anna," Louisa whispered, noting her sister's position in front of the other children. "You got there first!"

The iceman heaved a glassy block of ice from the wagon. His muscles bulged with strength beneath his rolled-up sleeves, dampened by hot sweat and cool, melting ice. He set the frozen block onto the pavement with surprising gentleness considering the heaviness of his burden. With a quick motion he lunged toward his wagon and deftly grabbed his saw from its resting spot. The gathered children, anticipating his next action, jumped clear of the alligator-toothed edge, laughing as they jostled against one another.

The iceman appeared oblivious to the children's excitement. Grimly he bent his head and began sawing the blocks into chunks. Small pieces of the ice cracked from the large block and tumbled to the ground. One girl boldly grabbed one of the larger chips and stuffed it into her mouth. Louisa noticed sympathetically that she wore thick black woolen leggings. "No wonder she wants ice,"

Louisa muttered. "Who would put a child of six or seven in stockings on this warm day?" Anna's outfit looked reasonable in comparison—a loosely fitting dress and socks that reached no higher than the tops of her boots.

Finally the ice man separated the first chunk of ice from his block. Louisa saw with relief that Anna thrust her coin forward and was rewarded with the first piece just as Henry joined her on the street. The iceman set their portion onto a cloth wrap that Anna provided, and Henry lifted the ice to his shoulder.

A kick at the door indicated that Henry and Anna had completed their ascent. Henry deposited the ice in the sink. Then, using a chisel and a hammer, he chipped off the small pieces that Louisa needed to cool Maddie's feverish forehead.

As Anna watched in silent solemnity, Louisa admitted to herself, "This is too much to expect her to endure." She walked over to tousle her sister's bangs. "Anna, why don't you go downstairs and play at *Tante* Joanna's?" she suggested. Anna eagerly put Louisa's idea into action, lingering only long enough to grab her dolly from the parlor.

After she had left, Henry said, "Maddie is very sick this time, isn't she?"

"Yes, very sick," Louisa answered with tears in her eyes. "I don't know what to do."

After a long silence Henry offered a remarkable suggestion, considering his earlier attitude. "I think we should ask the doctor to come."

Louisa did not attempt to hide her amazement. "Matthew?" she gasped.

"Of course. Who else would we call? All that matters now is that Maddie gets the care she needs. Tell me where he lives and I'll go for him."

Nearly an hour passed before the open bedroom window admitted the voices Louisa had longed to hear. "I'll wait with the horse," Henry said. "Go in through the shop—my uncle, August Shumaker, will show you the way upstairs."

"Very good," Matthew replied.

A few minutes later *Onkel* August and Matthew reached the top of the stairs where Louisa waited. Before leaving, *Onkel* August stated, "I think your *Papi* would like to be here. I'll close the shop and go get him." Louisa began a feeble protest, but to her relief her determined uncle started down the stairs to enact his plan.

As Matthew entered, he laid his hand on Louisa's shoulder. "Henry explained everything," he said. "Take me to her quickly."

Maddie managed a weak smile when Matthew walked into the room. He felt Maddie's head and looked up at Louisa. "You've kept ice on her all day?"

"Except when we ran out," Louisa moaned. "I've tried everything I know."

"I'm sure you've done quite well," Matthew replied softly. "You were right to call me."

"It was Henry's idea," Louisa admitted. Matthew glanced toward her with momentary surprise before silently beginning his examination of Maddie.

Soon *Papi* walked into the room. "Good day," he said, making use of his limited knowledge of English. "*Was haben der Doktor gesagt?*"

Louisa turned questioning eyes toward Matthew.

Matthew set down his stethoscope and somberly explained, "I'm afraid that the earlier bout with the fever damaged her heart. It will be hard for her body to fight the return of the sickness."

As soon as Louisa had translated Matthew's words, *Papi* strode forward and grasped the doctor's arm. "Tell us what we must do!" *Papi* entreated in German.

Matthew quickly responded to Louisa's translation. "She must always have someone with her. She must get nourishment even though her stomach is weak." He continued with recommendations until Louisa sank to her knees in despair.

"We cannot possibly give her the care she needs," she moaned. *Papi* slid down beside Louisa to comfort her. At his urging, she reluctantly related the impossible treatment Matthew had prescribed and her own frustrations and fears. As he listened, *Papi's* eyes filled with tears. At last he rose and walked to Maddie's bed.

There he knelt in silence, his hand smoothing the sleeve of Maddie's nightie against her arm.

He's praying, Louisa thought. *I have forgotten to pray; I have been so busy . . .*

When *Papi* turned back to face Louisa, she knew from his expression that he had made a decision. "Louisa," he instructed in a low voice, "ask the doctor if he will take Maddie back, if he will care for her in his home. This is Maddie's only hope. We cannot ask her to die because we are too proud."

If this message astonished Matthew, he showed no evidence of surprise. He only said, "Very well. I will do all I can for her."

"But your father . . ." Louisa protested.

"He will not mind," Matthew insisted. "The person who wrote to him gave an exaggerated description of Maddie's stay. Once I explained everything to Father, he agreed that I had made the right choice. He is now traveling again, and he will not object to our current plans. Now, we must hurry. Will you gather the things she will need?"

"Yes," Louisa murmured.

Matthew moved back to the bed. "Maddie, dear, you are going to be my guest once again," he said softly. "Once you're at my home, we will do all we can to help you feel better." Maddie smiled with simple trust. Apparently she did not notice the absence of Matthew's usual optimistic exuberance. Louisa's observations, however, convinced her that Maddie's condition concerned the doctor.

"Come, Maddie," he directed. "I will take you gently now. We are going in my carriage."

Maddie's eyes brightened as her friend slipped his arms under her frail frame and lifted her from the bed. "Did you bring the prettiest horse?" she murmured feebly, a faint smile whispering about her mouth.

"I don't know, honey," Matthew admitted. "I just took the nearest one—I was in such a hurry to get here." Matthew cast a distracted, questioning glance toward Louisa who stood by the window. "Is it Lady?" he asked.

She glanced toward the street. "Yes, Maddie, I see Lady, your favorite," she said as she stuffed a few final items into the bag she had been packing.

Matthew carried Maddie from the room. A few minutes later Louisa crowded into the phaeton with them, and Matthew began the drive toward his home.

A few hours later two sleeping sisters occupied the small upstairs room at Matthew's house. Maddie's fitful frame stretched across the bed, and Louisa sat in a chair, slumped forward so that her head rested on the bed. A creak of the door awakened Louisa, and lifting her head, she saw Matthew standing in the doorway.

"Come, you are worn out," he whispered. Louisa nodded groggily and allowed herself to be led from the room. At the bottom of the stairs Matthew said, "I know it's time for you to go home and that you desperately need sleep, but I must talk to you first. Will you stay for a few minutes? I will drive you back afterwards."

"Of course," murmured Louisa.

Matthew led her into the parlor where Ethel and her friends had interrogated Louisa over a month before. How different the room looked now—an empty and somber setting. The weak light of a lone Tiffany lamp created deep shadows that hid the brilliant patterns and colors of the tapestry fabrics. The poshness of the room remained, however, as Louisa realized when she sank into the soft cushion of a chair.

After an unpleasant pause Matthew began, "I must be completely honest with you, Louisa. It is very unlikely that Maddie will live. I had new hope after our trip to Forest Park, but today everything has changed. It is not uncommon for an illness such as Maddie's to return, and the second bout is often much worse than the first. When I brought her here several months ago, I thought I could save her. I hoped the disease would not damage her heart. Now I must admit that I had too much confidence in my own abilities. Since then I have been reminded that God is the sole provider of life and that He numbers each person's days. I have also realized all too clearly that I have been too proud in many ways, and I'm afraid that my arrogance has hurt you at times. I am sorry for those times, and I am also sorry if I have given you false hope during these past months. I beg your forgiveness."

"No—please—you have no reason for such apologies," Louisa protested. "If you have not been able to save Maddie from death, you have at least spared her from misery. I know she has been happy when you have cared for her. Matthew, she adores you. You treat her like a princess, and that is not a small thing to a poor girl like Maddie. As for me, I think I have always known that death has been just around the corner for Maddie. The fear has never really left me. Or actually it had only just begun to leave. And then . . ." Louisa broke into tears before struggling to continue. "She was doing so well, I thought the worst was over." She looked up at Matthew, searching for words of comfort.

"I know, I know," he whispered. "I had hoped the same." Matthew pulled a handkerchief from his pocket and offered it to Louisa. "I've kept you too long, but I had to tell you the truth. I will take you home now so you can sleep."

"Yes, of course," Louisa murmured. "Thank you."

While driving home, Matthew came to a sudden stop in the middle of an intersection a few blocks from Louisa's home. "Look!" he exclaimed, pointing down the street that crossed the one they were traversing. "Fire!" A block away black smoke poured from the windows of a small warehouse. In sharp contrast, bright, menacing flames glowed from within the building. Matthew jumped to the street and ran toward a fire alarm box that stood at the corner. The contraption looked like a ludicrous birdhouse with red walls and a pointed roof. But Louisa knew that as Matthew frantically twisted the gold knob screwed to the front, a telegraph message raced to the nearest fire station. Finally Matthew stopped his effort. "I hope the signal got through," he muttered, glancing back toward the building.

At that moment Louisa noticed a man in one of the building's second-story windows. "There are people inside," she screamed, jumping from the carriage and racing toward the building. Matthew hurried after her and caught her arm just as she reached a group of onlookers. Louisa spun to face him.

"Aren't you going to do anything?" she demanded.

"I did. I called for the firemen, the ones who can help."

"But they are not here now," Louisa insisted.

"No one can go in there, Louisa," Matthew countered. "It would mean certain death and would not achieve rescue."

"But someone must help them," Louisa persisted. "The people inside will die!"

"You can do nothing, Louisa," Matthew replied. "The man you saw has jumped to safety. He will know whether anyone else is inside, and those who can help will."

The din of a team of horses pulling a fire engine down the granite-paved street checked the protest that rose in Louisa's throat. As the horses slowed to a stop, Louisa noticed for the first time that the crowd had formed a bucket line from a nearby store. The effort had not been very effective, and the people now raised their voices to cheer on the firemen as they went to work.

Louisa sank to the ground in exhaustion. Matthew's words "You can do nothing" echoed in her mind. Tears streamed down her face as she contemplated the truth in his statement. She had listened to similar words from Matthew in the parlor a half hour before, but the drama of the fire had intensified the reality of her own inability to halt Maddie's decline. She could no more heal Maddie than she could rescue a man from a burning building!

CHAPTER TWENTY-EIGHT

Henry's Change of Heart

June 1900

A few days later Maddie asked, "Louisa, am I going to die?"

Louisa knew she could not dodge this straightforward question, but she chose to focus on the small bit of hope she still possessed. "Maddie, my deepest prayer is that the Lord will allow you to stay with us. But you are very sick, and we don't know for certain that you will get well."

"Will you miss me . . . if I die?" Maddie whispered with a trembling lip.

Louisa took a deep breath. "Maddie, I miss you even now. Our home is empty without your smile."

Maddie's face brightened for a minute before clouding again. "I miss you too, Louisa. I don't want to die," she stated hoarsely.

"Oh, Maddie!" Louisa exclaimed, throwing her arms around her little sister. "Whether you die tomorrow or in seventy years, you can be certain you will go to heaven to be with Jesus because you know Him as your Savior. No one will be lonely or sad or sick in heaven."

"That's what *Papi* said this morning," Maddie commented.

"You know, remembering that *Mütti* is in heaven has helped me many times when I have missed her. Maddie, we will see her again! And we can know that even if you die we will be together in heaven someday."

"I still don't want to die. I don't want to leave everyone," Maddie admitted.

"Maddie," Louisa replied, "before you were born, *Mütti*, Henry, Dorothy, and I left Germany to come to America. I was afraid and sad. I had to leave almost everything behind. Even worse, I had to leave people I loved dearly. When I said good-bye to *Oma*, I thought I would never stop crying. The one thing that made it possible for me to endure the separation was knowing that *Papi* was waiting for us in America. Germany had stopped being home because I missed him so much. When we arrived in St. Louis, it was absolutely wonderful to be with him again. Although I didn't like St. Louis then, I felt like I was home. That is how heaven will be because our heavenly Father is waiting there for us in our true home."

"I'll still miss you," Maddie insisted. In her eyes, however, Louisa saw a new peacefulness.

An hour later a soft knock at the door gave notice of Matthew's arrival. "Excuse me," he stated. "Maddie, it's time for bed, and Louisa needs to head home." Louisa sensed that something was wrong. Matthew appeared agitated, and his comments were uncharacteristically abrupt. After he withdrew into the hall, Louisa said a quick good-bye to Maddie and hurried to join him.

Matthew waited only until she had shut the door, and then he began explaining. "Rudi has been here."

Louisa fixed her eyes on him in surprise and fear. "Rudi?" she repeated. "Whatever did he want?"

"It's Henry," Matthew continued as he rushed her down the stairs. "He's been hurt. Apparently some men brought him home. As best I could make out from Rudi's hasty message, it's somehow tied up with the streetcar violence. You know, of course, that the drivers have gone on strike?"

"Oh!" Louisa gasped, stumbling down the last step in numb shock. "I've read about shootings in the paper. Was he shot? Didn't Rudi tell you anything else?"

"Nothing. Rudi looked badly shaken—" Matthew began.

"Oh, we must hurry," Louisa moaned. "Rudi takes pride in being unshakable! I could not stand to lose Henry as well as Maddie!"

"Louisa," Matthew said with a note of authority, "don't leap to such horrible conclusions. At least wait until we get to your home and find out the truth!"

Matthew steered her out the kitchen door and toward his waiting phaeton. Once they had climbed up, Matthew hastily urged the horses forward. Though they traveled at a swift pace, Louisa had nearly reached the end of her patience by the time the phaeton halted at her doorstep.

Matthew jumped from the phaeton and turned to steady Louisa's descent. For the first time Louisa realized, with relief, that Matthew planned to enter with her. Yet her surprise heightened as she observed the doctor pull his medical bag from beneath the seat in readiness to care for one who despised him!

They rushed upstairs, threw open the door, and nearly collided with a group of young men loitering in the kitchen area. The tallest man solemnly directed Louisa to the girls' bedroom where they had laid Henry. Matthew suggested that he wait for a moment in the kitchen, and Louisa nodded her agreement. She raced to the bedroom door where she stopped abruptly, startled by the pale, gaunt face that lay sunken on the pillow. The spark that had always flashed in Henry's pale blue eyes burned dangerously low.

"How did you get here so quickly?" he gasped, attempting a feeble smile.

Louisa hesitated before admitting the truth. Despite the fact that Henry had suggested they call Matthew to help Maddie, Louisa still feared that her brother harbored animosity toward her friend. At last she whispered, "Matthew brought me."

"Matthew?" Henry echoed, gritting his teeth in an apparent effort to fight a wave of pain. Louisa prepared for the anger that she assumed would rise as soon as his suffering eased. Instead, tears came to Henry's eyes. "Louisa, I have been unfair. He did not deserve my cruel words. He has shown only kindness to you and Maddie."

"Don't worry about that now," Louisa insisted. "You must get better first. Anyway, he does not know you have hated him so. Tell me quickly what happened."

"I was riding the streetcar and had nearly reached home when a mob formed. So many people are angry at the streetcar owners, you know. Several passengers were pulled from my car. Their clothes were torn, nearly stripped from them. Two men grabbed me and threw me to the ground. They continued to hit me, and then I fainted. One of my friends finally recognized me, and he and some others brought me home. I just woke up a few minutes ago. Louisa, I'm so scared," he admitted "I know I've been awful toward him, but do you think Matthew would help me? I would trust him."

Louisa stared in amazement. "You are sure you want Matthew to care for you?"

"Yes," Henry replied with a look that told Louisa he did not wish to waste the energy of words over this point any longer.

"Very well. He is in the next room. I will go for him," she said as she rose to leave. Turning back she cautioned, "You will be civil to him, won't you?"

"Of course," he replied with a weak smile. With that encouragement, Louisa headed toward the kitchen.

She found Matthew sitting calmly at the table. The four men remained, propped against the same spot as they had been when Louisa first arrived. They all eyed Matthew with unabashed suspicion.

Louisa darted to the chair nearest Matthew. In hushed tones she quickly explained Henry's request. "Will you help him?" she pleaded.

"Of course," he assured her. "I will do all I can for him. I came prepared in case he would agree to allow me to do so." Matthew began to rise, but Louisa suddenly grasped his arm and drew his ear to her mouth.

"Please," she begged quietly, her eyes scanning the faces that surrounded them, "will you ask these men to leave? I don't want them here now." Matthew's eyes followed hers, and he nodded.

Righting himself, Matthew quietly addressed the onlookers. "You have done well in bringing Henry home. Perhaps you have even saved his life. There is nothing more you can do now, and it would be a comfort to Louisa to be alone with her brother at this time. If you care to stop by later, I'm sure Henry will be more up to having visitors then."

Matthew spoke humbly. With begrudging respect, the men nodded their agreement and headed out the door. Louisa dropped her head to the table in a mixture of relief and exhaustion. Matthew laid a reassuring hand upon her shoulder and hurried toward the room where Henry lay.

The peace in Matthew's face when he emerged from the room instantly comforted Louisa. Even so, she prodded, "Will he live?"

"Yes," Matthew declared with a weary smile. "His life is not in danger. He was badly beaten and has several gashes, but no bones are broken. He's weak and will need to stay in bed for several days, but he'll recover without any permanent damage. I have cleaned and bandaged his wounds and given him some medicine that should cause him to sleep soundly and forget his pain."

Louisa nodded in relief. "Praise God!" she murmured. "I could not bear to lose them both." Once again her head sank to rest upon her arms.

During the following week, Matthew cared daily for Henry after bringing Louisa home from her visits with Maddie. An unlikely friendship formed between the two young men, and Louisa was thrilled to see the respect that shone in Henry's eyes whenever Matthew entered the room.

Each day Matthew brought news of the continuing streetcar strike. "Riding a streetcar has become too dangerous to risk," Matthew stated grimly one evening. "I think some citizens have lost all sanity. Attackers even keep swaths of ripped clothing as trophies of their savagery. It's out of control! Tracks have been dynamited and countless people injured!"

"The violence cannot help the drivers' cause," Henry stated. "Most of the people in the mobs don't even work for the streetcar companies. This is just their chance to display all the resentment they have felt for years toward the rich folks who they see siding against the working man. They're using this one strike to vent all their anger." Henry fell silent for a moment. Then he added, "Take care, Matthew, when you come to visit. I fear for you in this part of town now. Angry people can't always pick out a kind man when he's dressed in fine clothes."

CHAPTER TWENTY-NINE

A View from the Bridge

Toward the end of the week, Matthew encouraged Henry to visit Maddie. "Her father comes every morning, and Louisa's there every night, but I know she'd like to see her big brother. I could pick you up at four o'clock on Saturday, and you two could have an early dinner together."

Henry readily accepted the invitation, admitting, "I never before understood how difficult it is to be confined to bed. Now I know! Only four days inside has nearly made me crazy!"

Since most of the streetcar lines were now closed because of the strike, Matthew picked Louisa up Saturday morning and then went back for Henry later in the day. Maddie squealed with delight when she saw her brother. During the following hour, the visitor drew soft giggles from the invalid with his teasing cheerfulness. Louisa, witnessing Henry's wholehearted effort to please Maddie, realized just how much she loved her younger brother.

The silliness ended when Matthew carried up a cold dinner Nellie had prepared earlier. Louisa could tell that Henry thoroughly enjoyed the meal, which went well beyond the basic staples that typically appeared on the Shumakers' table.

As soon as everyone had finished, Matthew ordered Maddie to rest. "It's been a long day with lots of excitement, so bedtime is early tonight," he explained. "Alice will come check on you after it gets dark."

Reluctantly, the little girl hugged Henry, begging him to promise to return soon.

"Of course," he agreed. "I'll make time somehow. I love you so much, Maddie!"

Maddie snuggled down under the covers as her guests departed. After shutting the door, Matthew turned to Louisa with mischievous, sparkling eyes. "And now," he announced, "Henry and I have a surprise for you—that is, if you will grant us the honor of your company this evening."

Louisa threw a questioning glance toward her brother, but he only smiled conspiratorially. "What sort of surprise?" Louisa asked Matthew.

"An outing. Have you ever been across Eads Bridge?"

"Just once," Louisa replied. "When we first came to St. Louis on the train."

"But you have never been there at night?" Matthew pressed.

"No," Louisa agreed.

"Well then, I propose a trip to Eads Bridge. Henry has already consented. It promises to be a wonderfully cool evening; and when darkness comes, the stars will certainly be bright."

"The bridge is a sight I'd like to see again," Henry remarked. "I've never forgotten entering St. Louis the first time, and I've never again crossed that bridge."

"Well, I certainly wouldn't deny you such a treat," Louisa said with a laugh. "Let's go!" She moved toward the kitchen door, but Matthew gently grasped her elbow and guided her toward the main hall.

"The carriage is waiting out front," he explained. "I do not make a practice of using the back door when I am spending an evening with friends."

Louisa glanced back at Henry, wondering what he would think of Matthew's tenderness. The expression of unrestrained amusement that danced about her brother's lips took her by surprise and brought a blush to her cheeks.

When the trio reached the front door, they disturbed an aged butler who prided himself in his stone solemnity. That night the ancient scaffolding that had held his face in the same posture for so many years failed him, and his scorn of the company that Matthew had chosen shone clearly in his smirk.

Matthew ignored the butler's indignation. "Good-bye, Joseph," he called out cheerfully as the stately man opened the door. At the head of the stairs, he offered his arm to Louisa and, with Henry following, escorted her to the waiting carriage.

They made quick progress through town. The streetcar strike proved to be a surprising blessing for them; although the streets were more crowded with wagons and carts than usual, there were no streetcars to dodge.

"I've seen some sorry-looking horses today," Henry noted.

"Yes," laughed Matthew. "I heard that some of the stables in town are renting out horses that are nearly dead. Everyone's desperate for transportation. And look at that cart over there. I bet it hasn't been used since 1880; the wood looks like it's ready to splinter into pieces!"

"Look!" Louisa shouted when Matthew stopped talking. "Some strike sympathizers have been at work here." In the air above them, pots, ropes, tin cans, rags, and other castoffs dangled from the streetcar lines. As the weighted wires swung in the breeze, the giant wind chime voiced the working man's discontent.

"It will take a while to get all that cleaned up," Henry noted. "What a lot of junk!"

A few minutes later he exclaimed, "Look, Louisa!" He pointed to a spot where smoke spewed from a hole in the street. "That's from the tunnel the train runs through. Do you remember?"

"Of course," she replied. "What a horrid place!"

Soon they reached the levee. Matthew suggested that they take a ferry across the river. "The driver can meet us on the other side; then we'll ride back into town," he explained. Henry and Louisa agreed to this plan, and they all stepped down onto the street.

"You must stay close to me now," Matthew instructed Louisa, tucking her hand safely under his arm, "I would not want to lose you down here." He glanced toward Henry and asked, "Are you feeling all right?" Henry gave a firm nod. Louisa guessed he was enjoying the excitement of the levee.

Matthew artfully led Louisa and Henry through the maze of materials, men, and horses that crowded the riverfront. Cotton bales were stacked as high as a man's shoulder, forming hallways leading to the water. Above these temporary walls rose the tall, crowned smokestacks of the queens of the river. Louisa noticed that the beauty of these steamboats dimmed as she drew nearer to them. Their heyday had ended, and the few that endured on the levee that day had grown weary. When Louisa emerged from the cotton bales, she saw that flat barges filled many of the gaps she had noticed earlier between the steamboat smokestacks.

Water gently lapped a wide cobblestone street that slanted down into the mighty Mississippi River. Wagons clattered and bumped along the unevenness of the street, which bore the scars of an existence shared with the river. Often during spring and summer rains, parts of the street would flood, requiring repairs when the river retreated. With the city's care, the road had always weathered such floods, and Louisa was thankful for the stones that kept the dust at bay on that dry day. "I think this must be one of the most interesting parts of St. Louis," Louisa commented as they reached the ferryboat company's office.

Matthew paid the fare, and they boarded the ferry just before the captain began to edge the boat away from the dock. "The last time we were on a ferry, Henry, was at Ellis Island," Louisa mused. "Do you remember?"

"How could I forget!" Henry exclaimed. "I have never been so nervous in my entire life! This is much better."

The view from the river was marvelous. "I'm glad the wind has recently blown the smoke away from the city," Matthew commented.

"I wish I could see what the shore looked like before St. Louis was built," Louisa said.

"I have an ancestor who would be able to give you a pretty good description if he were still alive," Matthew replied. "He immigrated as a fur trader in the 1700s."

"Did he fight in the Revolutionary War?" Louisa asked.

"No. He was a Frenchman, and this area belonged to France. My Grandpa Milton, however, fought in the Civil War."

"Really!" gasped Louisa. "What side did he fight for?"

"Grandpa and his brother Joseph fought for the North; but

their brother James fought for the South. The people of St. Louis were split during the war. Missouri was a slave state, but many citizens supported the Union."

"Sometimes," Louisa reflected, "I don't feel like I can ever be as truly an American as someone whose family has lived here for several generations."

"You are wrong, Louisa," Matthew offered. "During the early days of our country, Americans were characterized by their bravery, their perseverance in spite of hardship, their devotion to God, and their desire for freedom. Certainly, Louisa, those traits describe you and all in your family."

The end of the ferry trip concluded the conversation. In the twilight they could just discern the outline of Matthew's carriage waiting for them. Soon they were perched upon its cushioned seats once again.

When they reached the bridge, Matthew paid the toll, and they began their drive across the mighty, muddy Mississippi. "Just think," Matthew commented, "until twenty-five years ago people couldn't walk or ride across the Mississippi; the ferry was the only way to cross. They say there was a huge celebration on the bridge when it opened. My parents remember that day."

"The city is so beautiful," Louisa exclaimed. "I wish we were not traveling so quickly. I want time to enjoy it all."

"We could walk the rest of the way," Matthew suggested. Louisa's eyes gleamed. "What about it, Henry?" Matthew asked. "Are you up for a walk?"

"No. I'm enjoying the ride. This is a rare treat for me!" he said with a laugh. "You two can walk though, and I'll wait for you at the other end."

Matthew and Louisa climbed down from the carriage and strolled to the edge of the bridge. The stars were beginning to shine, and the streetlights were burning brightly.

"I clearly remember getting my first look at my new home when our train came across this bridge," Louisa remarked as they leaned against the railing. "I was thrilled to find that St. Louis is situated on a river because I loved the rivers we traveled on in Germany." After a pause she added reflectively, "It was more beautiful there though. Sometimes I still miss my first home in Germany."

"It must have been very hard to leave everything behind never to return," Matthew commented as they began to walk.

"Well, I came with my closest family members, and as my grandmother said, that's what's most important. I also knew then, as I know now, that God is always with me. My father told me when I was a very little girl that I must never forget that God does not forsake His children. That has strengthened me through many a tough time."

"This past year with Maddie, for example?" Matthew questioned.

"Yes," Louisa admitted with a sigh. "The words of both my grandmother and my parents have come to mind many times."

"What wonderful wisdom runs in your family—the wisdom of fearing the Lord and following His ways!" Matthew said thoughtfully.

At that moment, without warning, a train rushed beneath them. The suddenness of its coming roused Louisa from her thoughts and reminded her to gaze once again at the city. Its lights glittered in competition with the stars that jeweled the sky. "Oh!" exclaimed Louisa, sucking in her breath at the sight. "How beautiful it is!"

"This is what I wanted most for you to see," whispered Matthew, stopping again at the rail to enjoy the view.

"How Maddie would love it!" Louisa remarked. "I wish she could have come."

"But you, Louisa, are the one I wanted to bring here," Matthew confessed.

Louisa, confused by the rush of blood to her cheeks, hesitated, trying to decide how to respond. She chose to change the subject. "The city looks so perfectly beautiful from here that I could almost believe everything is happy and serene there . . . that around each glowing lamp, family and friends have gathered in joy and health. The bright and hopeful lights speak of such scenes," said Louisa, "but they lie. I know because I live among those people, and I know that sorrow and pain dwell in that city." She spoke her final thought in a whisper. "I almost wish I could stay here and believe the wonderful dream of a happy city."

She fell silent, for she did not trust herself to continue. It occurred to her that her true wish was to remain always at Matthew's side. For when she was with this gentle, noble man, the whole world seemed to sing with joy. At that moment she dared not look at him for fear that her eyes would speak that which her mouth must yet guard. What immense respect she had for him! True, there were feelings that lay even deeper than admiration, but she did not trust herself to face those. Not at this time or at this place.

Suddenly the wind began to blow, grasping the river's chill and tossing it up toward the top of the bridge. An unbidden shiver moved through Louisa and made her teeth chatter. She rubbed her arms in an effort to warm herself.

"You are cold!" Matthew observed. "I should not have kept you here so long." With one sweeping motion he removed his jacket and gently laid it across Louisa's back. His hands rested on her shoulders for a moment as the garment settled about her. Then he offered her his arm and led her back to the real St. Louis—a city whose pulse at times rose with the anger of a streetcar strike and sometimes lulled with exhaustion in the hot humidity of a summer afternoon; a city that Louisa feared would not approve of a bond between a wealthy young man and the daughter of a poor German immigrant. But why contemplate society's opinion? It remained unlikely that Matthew himself would engage in such a courtship. This thought consumed her mind as they reached the end of the bridge and rejoined Henry in the carriage.

CHAPTER THIRTY

Words of Love

On June 14, 1900, a knock at the door startled Louisa during her breakfast preparations. Never had they received a visitor at such an early hour! Dorothy rose, but with fearful premonitions Louisa shook her head and stepped forward to open the door herself.

A darkly clad figure waited in the stairwell, his garments blending with the blackness of the surroundings. Despite the dim lighting, Louisa instantly recognized Matthew and discerned the concern in his expression. Matthew grasped Louisa's hand and pulled her into the stairwell.

"What is it, Matthew?" she gasped.

"You can surely guess," he whispered mournfully. "I do not think Maddie will last much longer. You and your family must come with me at once." Louisa lunged forward with a choking cry, and Matthew caught her and held her closely. "How I wish I could bring you happy news!" he murmured. "You must be strong, relying on God to sustain you! No time can be wasted here—we must go!" Louisa stepped back and nodded, gulping back tears. Matthew wiped the dampness from her face and counseled, "Come, we must tell the others."

"Of course," Louisa whispered. "Everyone is here except *Papi*. He is already on his way to visit Maddie."

A quick explanation spurred both Dorothy and Henry into action. The former ran downstairs to explain the situation to *Tante* Joanna, and the latter scooped up Anna to carry her to the carriage Matthew had waiting.

When they arrived at Matthew's house at dawn, Nellie informed them that *Papi* was already with Maddie. Louisa motioned to the others to wait in the kitchen, and she turned to climb the stairs alone. Her feet, nearly paralyzed by dread, moved as though she were treading through the ankle-deep mud of a rain-drenched street. As on the day of *Mütti's* death, her heart whispered that if she did not enter the room, the inevitable would not have to happen. But she knew she had to go on. She had to live through that day though it would most likely prove to be one that would change her life forever. Because she had no choice, she walked to the door and turned the knob.

Papi's voice, soft yet strong, controlled the room, filling it with love and comfort. Although the words he spoke were for Maddie, they were a balm to his oldest daughter as well. "I love you, Maddie, my precious child. What a gift from God you have been to your family! I know that God will take care of you, Maddie. He will love you even now as you are taken from all of us who love you so much."

Louisa could see the tears begin to stream down his face, and yet his eyes remained riveted on the pale, jerking form that lay before him. Unaware of Louisa's presence, he passed a gentle hand across Maddie's brow and returned the wan smile that dawned on her face in response to his tenderness. "Oh, Maddie," he sighed, "my dear daughter. How I wished when you were born that your *Oma* could have met you. We named you for her because she was a godly woman without equal. Now you shall join her in heaven. I never thought you would meet her before I saw her again." *Papi* choked and bent forward in grief. Maddie shifted apprehensive eyes toward the door and sighted her sister.

Louisa rushed forward to kneel beside *Papi*. She threw one arm around his shoulders and reached toward Maddie with the other, laying her hand upon her sister's feverish cheek. "Good morning, Maddie," she whispered. "I love you."

"Yes," murmured Maddie as she gasped for breath. "I hoped . . . you would come. I told *Papi* . . ."

"I'm here, Maddie. I won't leave." Louisa cried as the image of her sister blurred with her tears."

"Where's Henry?" Maddie asked in a barely audible voice. "And Mr. Mattie?"

"They are here," Louisa assured her. "Dorothy and Anna too. Shall I get them?"

Maddie nodded weakly, and Louisa rushed to bring them.

The kitchen was silent and somber. "She is not well," Louisa whispered from the doorway, "but she wants to see all of you." Anna began to cry, frightened no doubt by the sadness of those around her. Louisa, summoning strength, strode to where Henry still sat and took her littlest sister from his lap. "Come," she said, her eyes pleading with Henry, "we must all go."

"Of course," agreed Henry, his resolve strengthened by her appeal. He headed toward the stairs, followed by his three sisters.

Louisa looked back at the remaining figure. "Matthew, Maddie asked for you too," she insisted.

"No. It is right for your family to be with her. I have said my good-bye."

Henry stood aside at the door to let his sisters pass. As Louisa climbed the first step, she heard him echo her entreaty. "Maddie wants you to be there with us, Matthew. That is what we all want." By the time Louisa reached the last step, two sets of heavy footsteps were audible behind her.

Peace flooded Maddie's countenance as the room filled with those she loved. Her eyes roved from face to face, and Louisa wondered, *How can she find comfort in faces filled with such sadness, in eyes clouded by so many tears? She is stronger than any of us, even though she is the one who is near death.*

Louisa set Anna down on the floor. The little girl cautiously stepped to the bed and gripped the sheets with her tiny hands. Her gaze moved searchingly from Maddie, to *Papi*, to Louisa. Then she stretched out a hand to grasp Maddie's arm that lay so near her. Despite the unannounced jerks that flared through the arm, Anna kept her grip as she murmured through tears, "I love Maddie. Anna love Maddie always!" With these simple words, three-year-old Anna dispelled the awkwardness of the moment, and her siblings all followed her to the bedside. Dorothy knelt beside Anna and slid an arm around the little girl. With her free hand, she reached forward to stroke Maddie's hand. Henry moved to the other side of the bed, perched near Maddie's pillow, and smoothed her damp hair. Louisa chose a spot behind *Papi* and encircled him with a hug.

Once his children had gathered around, *Papi* spoke. "We have always prayed together, both in times of rejoicing and in times of fear. Let us do so now." His children bowed their heads as he began. "*Unser Vater im Himmel*, how great is Thy love for Thy children. We praise Thee, for You have blessed our family. For five years You have given us the joy of knowing and loving Maddie. Father, thank You for making each one of us a part of this family. Thank You that we are together now. We commit Maddie to Thy care, for our hands can do nothing to save her life. Our hearts cry out for Thy mercy, praying that You would spare her life. But if this be not Thy will, we pray that You will give us courage and faith that we may be steadfast. May Thy will be done. Amen."

When the prayer ended, all eyes opened except Maddie's. The room was absolutely silent, and Louisa suddenly realized that Maddie no longer gasped for breath. With a sinking heart, she glanced about and saw that this fact had not escaped anyone's notice. Anna and Dorothy withdrew their hands from the arms that no longer jerked. Henry straightened himself and looked pointedly at Matthew, his eyes begging the young doctor to attend to his patient. Matthew sprang forward as Henry moved to make room for him at the bedside.

The entire family waited as Matthew clutched Maddie's wrist and put his cheek to her lips. Did he feel her breath? Louisa felt certain he did not. In fact, in that silent moment Louisa sensed the suspension of all breath in that room. The intense stillness was such that Matthew's voice startled Louisa although she had been waiting to hear his verdict. "Her life has ended," he murmured. "She will suffer no more."

On Saturday the Shumakers buried Maddie beside *Mütti*. The family drove in Matthew's carriage to the cemetery, where *Tante* Joanna and *Onkel* August met them at the graveside. Even Rudi made an appearance, and he looked genuinely somber. Matthew, a rod of strength, stood beside Louisa with a comforting arm around her shoulders. To Louisa's relief, the service was short. On that day of grief, she could not have stayed long in that place.

When the minister had finished speaking and a mound of fresh dirt covered the grave, the family slowly walked back to the carriage. As the others climbed in, Louisa shrank back. "I must walk," she insisted. "It's the only thing that will do me any good. I'll feel stifled if I ride, even in an open carriage."

"Very well," said *Papi* wearily. "But I will not let you go alone, not when you are so grieved." *Papi* looked toward Henry, and he in turn focused his gaze on Matthew, who still stood on the street next to Louisa. *Papi* eyed Matthew thoughtfully and then nodded his head. "Will you accompany her, Matthew?"

Smiling at this development, Matthew turned toward Louisa. "I promise to be a pleasant companion. I will remain silent and will walk two steps behind you the entire trip if that will help give you the solitude you want."

"No," Louisa reflected, "that would look a bit odd. I will not mind your company." Even in her grief, this unexpected companionship thrilled Louisa, and she recognized the gross understatement in her final comment.

As they traversed the cobblestone streets, tears rose in Louisa's eyes. Matthew quietly took her arm and guided her to a bench in the same park *Papi* had led her to on an earlier day of grief. Louisa tried to speak, to apologize for her emotion, but she could not. At last she turned toward Matthew and marveled to find his eyes filled with tears that mirrored her own.

Apparently Matthew noted her surprise, for he said, "I also loved Maddie. I know that my loss is nothing compared to yours, but I will miss her terribly."

"She loved you too, Matthew. . . . She adored you. You cared for her like an older brother."

Suddenly Louisa realized that her tears were not only for Maddie, but also for another loss that she selfishly mourned. She finally voiced her thoughts, though she later trembled at her boldness. "I guess this is the last time I'll see you. Unless the carriage overturns on the way home, no one in my family will be needing your care."

Matthew grasped her hand and earnestly exclaimed, "Do you really think Maddie was the only reason I spent all those hours with you? Certainly I did care for her, and I grieve for her, but not to see you again would hurt me even more! Louisa, I have gone out of my way to spend time with you. Ask any of my friends. For the past two months I've kept my evenings free so that I might accompany you home. Can it make sense that I would now abandon all hope of being with you? No, Louisa, I would not have this be farewell!" His eyes scanned Louisa's face, and she rewarded his confession with a countenance of glowing joy that for the moment had driven away any sign of grief.

"I have obviously failed as a suitor, for you have apparently not realized my true intent," laughed Matthew.

"No, no," murmured Louisa. "I'm sure it's not your fault. I just never dared hope that you would hold even the slightest regard for me." Her soft words were nearly inaudible, for at that moment a loud rumble of thunder taunted the city. This surprise interruption brought a quick change in conversation.

"We must make a run for it, I'm afraid," Matthew exclaimed. "Perhaps we can reach your home before the downpour!"

The next evening following supper, Louisa's family gathered in their simple parlor as they did each Sunday. After an hour of quiet conversation, an unexpected knock at the door interrupted them. "I think I can guess who that might be," Henry observed with a chuckle. "*Onkel* August, *Tante* Joanna, and Rudi are out for the evening."

"Yes," *Papi* agreed. "I think we had better let Louisa answer the door this time."

"Who is it?" Anna piped up. "Can I go too?"

"No," *Papi* replied. "Louisa won't need help; although if she does not hurry, her visitor may assume we're away!"

"I'm going now, *Papi*!" Louisa exclaimed, jumping to her feet. She hoped to escape before Henry noticed the blush she knew must be accompanying the tingling warmth she felt on her cheeks.

A minute later Louisa opened the door and discovered that Henry and *Papi* had correctly guessed the identity of their visitor. "Hello, Matthew!" she exclaimed.

Matthew whipped off his hat in greeting. "Good evening, Louisa! I've brought you a bit of cheer," he declared, hoisting a scarlet geranium high in the air as he stepped inside. Its blossoms brightened the drab kitchen the moment he entered.

"What a perfect gift!" Louisa exclaimed as she accepted the flower and carried it to the table. "How did you know of my love for plants?"

"Several weeks ago you told me of a very special *Oma* who gave you a passion for flowers."

"And you remembered?" Louisa responded in amazement.

"I make a practice of tucking away information that might be useful someday," Matthew admitted with a smile. "See how it's paid off!"

"You could not have picked a more perfect gift," Louisa acknowledged. "Thank you."

"But your love for gardening is not the only reason I chose to bring you a plant," Matthew confessed. Louisa obligingly raised her eyebrows with interest. "And there is a reason I picked this particular flower. There were others at the greenhouse that were more bright and fancy. I could have gotten you an entire bouquet of those, but I did not."

"And why not?" laughed Louisa.

"Bright and fancy just isn't your style!" Matthew replied with sparkling eyes and an amused grin. Then, forcing seriousness into his countenance, he continued, "I did not come here to tease you. The truth is, I respect you, Louisa. I admire your resemblance to that geranium."

"You are still teasing," Louisa observed wryly, wondering what meaning there could possibly be in his words.

"I'm not. Hear me out, Louisa. I may not be a great orator, but I will eventually stumble upon my point. This geranium will not die within the next week like a bouquet of hothouse flowers would have. Its strong roots will allow it to endure and hopefully bring you much joy."

"So you chose it because it would bring me long-lasting joy?" Louisa questioned.

"No!" Matthew answered with obvious frustration. "I chose it because *you* bring *me* joy." He stopped, apparently startled by his own boldness. Soon, however, his bewilderment became courage. "The truth is, there is no one I'd rather be with, Louisa. My admiration for you is beyond what I can put into words. Since leaving Germany, you have endured untold hardships, yet you remain steadfast. You're committed to God and to your family. Few sisters exhibit the devotion you showed to Maddie as you visited her day after day."

"Such praise is too great," Louisa demurred. "I'm not so strong. As *Mütti* told me many times before she died, it is God who is our stronghold. Knowing that He will never forsake me has given me strength even on the most painful days."

"I might have guessed that would be your response. How different you are from the winsome yet frivolous women who so often take up space in my parents' parlor. In spite of all their fineness, they pale before you, Louisa."

"I am sure there are many among the ranks of your friends who do not share your sentiments," Louisa replied. "You are not here with their approval; of this I am certain."

"That does not matter to me," Matthew insisted. "I trust I am here with *your* approval, and that is enough." Unrestrained joy glowed on Louisa's face as he continued, "With your permission and that of your father, I too will enjoy the cheer of this geranium day after day, as I come to court the one I love."

Matthew gently clasped Louisa's hands in his own, thrilling her with the same gentle warmth that had soothed and doctored Maddie. In that moment Louisa accepted her heart's insistence that her respect for Matthew had grown into love. A tear spilled over her eyelashes, a single drop born of joy because the one she loved had spoken words of devotion and born of sadness because *Mütti* could not meet the young man her daughter adored.

Matthew reached up to brush the dampness from Louisa's cheek, his eyes silently questioning.

"Despite your words in the park, I hardly dared hope you would visit again," Louisa whispered.

"I will always come back to you," Matthew replied. "Although in due time I hope that I will no longer need to travel beyond my own doorstep to be with you, dearest Louisa."

Historical Glimpses

From the time my grandparents began telling me stories of their childhood, I have been fascinated by the daily life experiences of previous generations. Although all the names and characters in this book are fictional, the details of the Shumakers' lives reflect the reality that many Americans experienced during the 1890s.

Actual immigrants to America during the late nineteenth century endured hardships similar to those the Schuhmachers experienced during their journey. Many fathers traveled alone and sent back for their families, crooks often preyed upon emigrants in ports of departure, and steerage conditions on board the ocean liners were generally deplorable. Millions of immigrants passed through Ellis Island, enduring inspections similar to those described in this book. A small percentage were deported under circumstances resembling those Rudi's family experienced.

Many of those who did enter America found that life in their new country presented challenges they had not anticipated. Living conditions were often wretched, and poor families had to work most of their waking hours to make enough money to provide for their basic needs. Despite child labor laws, some children worked illegally and often did not complete more than a few years of school. In order to save money, it was common for a woman to do all the family sewing and to take on additional work to bolster her family's income. Even household chores, such as washing clothes, required a formidable amount of work. The meager income of many families affected their dinner tables, and thrifty housewives found ways to utilize whatever they could afford. Clabbered milk and headcheese are only two examples.

Horse-drawn carriages, streetcars, boats, and trains were the predominant means of transportation at the turn of the century. "Bumming" a ride beneath a train was unsafe, but that did not stop the practice by those seeking to steal a free ride.

During the nineteenth century, medical knowledge was considerably less sophisticated than it is today. Doctors did not usually receive the extensive training they do now, and much less was known about many ailments and diseases. Childbirth complications and childhood diseases such as rheumatic fever claimed many lives during the 1800s (and earlier centuries). When a person died, family members customarily spent the night beside the corpse, and friends came to visit. A variety of strange (and often dangerous) drugs was available, including some that were used to attempt the abortion of unborn children.

A devastating tornado did hit St. Louis on May 27, 1896, and a violent streetcar strike did erupt during May of 1900 and continued into the summer. Several of the places mentioned in the book are still in existence—Shaw's Garden (The Missouri Botanical Gardens), Tower Grove Park, Eads Bridge, the Old Courthouse, Forest Park, and the West End.

German Glossary

Note: German nouns are always capitalized.

Ach!: Oh!

Amerika: America

Auf Wiedersehen: Good-bye

Biergarten: Beer garden. These parklike gathering spots provided entertainment (i.e., music, rides, food) for the entire family and were popular with German immigrants.

bitte: please

Deine: Yours (a closing for a letter)

den 17. Februar: February 17

den 22. April: April 22

den 27. Mai: May 27

den 31. Mai: May 31

den 10. Juni: June 10

den 15. Juni: June 15

Deuteronomium: Deuteronomy

Deutschland: Germany

die Niederlande: the Netherlands

Ein' Feste Burg: "A Mighty Fortress (Is Our God)." This hymn was written by Martin Luther

Es tut mir leid: I am sorry.

Frau: Mrs.

Guten Abend: Good evening

Guten Morgen: Good morning

Guten Nacht: Good night

Guten Tag: Good day

Ja: yes

Jawohl: yes (of course)

Kirch: church

Land: land

Liebe August, lieber Jakob!: Dear August, dear Jacob (a salutation for a letter)

Liebe Oma!: Dear Grandma (a salutation for a letter)
Mach schnell!: Hurry!
mein Kind: my child
mein Kindlein: my little child
Mütti: Mommy
Oma: Grandma
Onkel: Uncle
Opa: Grandpa
Papi: Papa
Russische Auswanderer: Russian emigrants
Siebzehn: seventeen
Tante: Aunt
Tränen Insel: Island of Tears
und vielen Dank: and many thanks
Unser Vater im Himmel!: Our Father in heaven.
Was haben der Doktor gesagt?: What has the doctor said?
Was ist das?: What is that?
Was ist deine Name?: What is your name?
Wie alt bist du?: How old are you?
Wie schade!: What a pity!
Wilkommen: welcome

In Appreciation

Throughout the writing of this book, I enjoyed the dedicated support of several people. My husband, Garrett, provided steadfast encouragement and involvement. Dianne Chinery prayed consistently for this book for several years. Meg Spear convinced me that a small beginning had the potential to be a novel. And Jennifer Coleman, Edith Struik, Katie Dickson, and my sister, Carolyn Leutwiler, willingly encountered the Shumaker family in rough draft form.

Several other special individuals provided input years before pen was put to paper: My dad shared with me his love of literature and nurtured me as a young reader. Mom and Dad, through their devotion and love, created a home that pointed me to Christ. And finally, my grandparents shared many stories about life at the turn of the century.